AN UNEXPECTED GUEST

THE ISLES OF SCILLY SERIES: BOOK FIVE

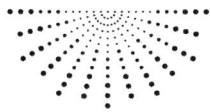

HANNAH ELLIS

Published by Hannah Ellis
www.authorhannahellis.com
Postfach 900309, 81503 München
Germany

Cover design by Mario Ellis

Copyright © 2023 Hannah Ellis
All rights reserved.
No part of this book may be reproduced in any form or by any electronic or mechanical means, including information storage and retrieval systems, without written permission from the author, except for the use of brief quotations in a book review.

AN UNEXPECTED GUEST

CHAPTER ONE

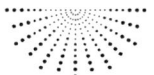

The guy in the aisle seat didn't react to Sylvie standing over him. Not even when she uttered a friendly "hello". With only nineteen seats on the small aircraft the plane felt cramped to say the least. There was no way he could have missed her looming there.

She smiled politely when he finally looked up at her. "That's my seat," she said, pointing.

He twisted, grimacing as his knees scraped along the back of the seat in front before they were dislodged into the aisle.

Sylvie tilted her head as she took in the space he'd created. Depending on which way she manoeuvred herself, she'd either have her boobs in his face or her bum against his chest. Maybe that was his plan but given his scowl she didn't think so.

"I'm fairly petite," she said cheerfully, "but we're still going to know each other pretty intimately if I try and squeeze in there."

His features didn't change as he released his seatbelt and unfolded himself from the chair. For a moment his broad chest blocked her view entirely, then he took a step back along the aisle.

"Thanks," Sylvie said as she shuffled to her seat, noting as she glanced back that he'd not yet said a word.

His silence continued when he returned to his seat and immediately buckled his belt again.

With some difficulty, Sylvie managed to wedge her handbag under the seat in front of her before turning her attention to her seatbelt. She found one end easily enough, but the other disappeared beneath her neighbour.

"Sorry," she said, tugging on the strap. With a sigh, he shifted his weight so she could free the seatbelt. "Thanks!"

He cast her a sidelong glance just as the plane jolted and set off at a crawl along the tarmac. Intrigued as to whether he was mute, Sylvie was about to attempt to draw him into conversation when the captain's voice drifted through the cabin. By the time he'd given his spiel about flight times, weather conditions and safety instructions, they were poised at the end of the runway.

Sylvie gazed through the window while the plane hurtled along. A fizz of excitement stirred in her stomach as they ascended shakily into the air.

"Have you ever been to Scilly before?" she asked as her gaze returned to the cabin. Her silent friend was fixated on the floor, and Sylvie couldn't tell if he was purposely ignoring her or if he hadn't heard over the noise of the plane's engines. Instinctively, she leaned a little closer, getting a whiff of his aftershave, which made her want to inhale deeply.

"Have you been to Scilly before?" she asked again, louder this time.

His gaze snapped up to her and he blinked as though bringing her into focus.

"Once or twice," he said, the softness of his voice taking her by surprise.

"What's it like? I've never been but I've always wanted to. In photos it looks stunning."

He curled his upper lip. "It's quiet."

"I'm not sure quiet is really my thing," she said with a laugh. "Sorry. I talk a lot when I'm excited … or nervous. Actually, I think I always talk a lot. But I'm excited now so I'm kind of in overdrive. I might be a bit nervous too." She was wittering, that was for sure. "Sorry, I'll just …" Pinching her index finger and thumb together she ran them across her lips in a zipping motion.

"I have family on St Mary's," he said unbidden.

Sylvie took it as an invitation to continue the conversation. "Do you visit often?"

It took him a moment to reply. "It's been a few years."

"I'm visiting family too," Sylvie said wistfully. "My cousin. We haven't seen each other for years. We were really close as kids, but we drifted apart as adults." Her eyes slid over to check if he was even listening. The slight hitch at the corner of his mouth was enough of an acknowledgement that she continued. "He doesn't know I'm coming. I thought I'd surprise him."

Her stomach twisted and her previous excitement fizzled away. She'd tried to call Lowen a couple of times. When she couldn't reach him, she decided it was a sign she should track him down in person, but now she wondered if she should have left him a message or tried to contact him through another channel.

"Surprises are fun," she said, not sure why she was seeking reassurance from the stranger beside her.

"Maybe," he murmured.

"I think it'll be good." She had an image of tracking Lowen down in his pottery studio. He'd stop the pottery wheel when he caught sight of her, and his face would break into a wide smile as he wiped his hands on a rag before crossing the room to embrace her. She'd seen videos of him working the pottery wheel on his social media accounts, so she could clearly envision the scene.

"There's a chance he won't even recognise me," she said, almost to herself. She shook the thought away and told herself not to be pessimistic. "It'll be fine," she said determinedly. "Better than fine. It'll be great. I'm excited."

It turned out she was talking to herself. The guy had closed his eyes, either sleeping or just letting her know he had no interest in listening to her droning on for the next hour.

After checking his eyes were definitely closed, Sylvie let her gaze travel over him, taking in his dark blue T-shirt which stretched over his firm chest. His jaw sported a few days' worth of golden stubble, a shade darker than the thick, glossy hair which framed his face.

Slowly, Sylvie leaned towards him, feeling the warmth radiating from him while she inhaled a hefty lungful of his scent. The distinctive notes of sandalwood were a treat for her nostrils, and she braved another deep inhale before shifting to look out of the window with a satisfied smile.

It had been a long time since Jago had been back to Scilly. The closer he got, the more anxious he felt about facing his family, and the rickety plane caused him further stress. As the woman beside him chatted away about her cousin, it all felt too much. He closed his eyes as the plane juddered, then didn't bother opening them again when the woman went quiet.

The last time he'd been back to St Mary's was for his dad's funeral, a little over three years ago. He'd only stayed for a couple of days and only had snippets of memories from that time. Jet lag and grief hadn't been a good combination. He'd also been guilt-ridden about not having seen his dad for a good couple of years before he'd died.

At sixteen, Jago had left the island to go to secondary school on the mainland and had only been back for short visits since then. Having spent longer living away from his childhood home than in it, he shouldn't have been surprised by how removed he'd felt from his family, but it had unsettled him enough that he left again as quickly as possible.

Now he was returning, but this time he was determined not to flee so fast. The wedding invitation from his brother had come around the same time that Jago had found out his American work visa wouldn't be renewed. He wasn't overly upset at the thought of moving on from his life in New York, especially since his job in software development had lost its sheen. The only real problem was that he had no idea what he'd do next.

One step at a time, he told himself. He'd go to Trystan's wedding and set aside enough time with his family that he could start to build some bridges. At the very least he needed to spend some quality time with his mum.

"Oh my god!"

He startled at the screech from the woman beside him, then felt the warmth of her hand on his forearm.

"Sorry," she said. "Did I wake you?"

"I don't know," he said honestly.

"You have to look at this." She squeezed his arm and tipped her chin towards the window. "I know you've been before, but I'm sure this view could never disappoint no matter how many times you've seen it."

His skin tingled where her hand touched it, and his eyes were drawn to her rich auburn hair instead of the view. The look of wonder on her face was mesmerising.

"It's beautiful, isn't it?" she whispered.

"Yes." He smiled to himself, then leaned close to join her in peering out of the window.

Really, he should have anticipated the effect seeing the islands again would have on him, but the tightening of his ribs took him by surprise. The cluster of green islands, edged by pale sandy beaches and surrounded by crisp azure water, was so familiar it took his breath away. When his gaze locked on his childhood home sitting proudly up on the headland on the south coast of St Mary's, he forgot to breathe altogether.

Distracted by the sights outside, Jago didn't take much notice of the captain's announcement, but the word turbulence cut right through him, making every muscle in his body tighten.

"Exciting!" the woman said. "I love a bit of turbulence. It's like a free rollercoaster ride."

The muscles in Jago's jaw loosened enough for his mouth to hang open. Was she serious? How could someone be happy about—

The plane dropped, and it was exactly like a rollercoaster; that horrible weightless feeling in his stomach and the fear that snaked around his every nerve.

"Are you okay?" the woman asked.

"Yeah." He realised he'd grabbed hold of her hand. Sheepishly, he loosened his fingers, but the plane lurched again, causing him to grip her tightly. His eyelids snapped shut and he focused on breathing evenly.

A moment passed before his muscles began to relax again.

The woman's voice came soft in his ear. "I didn't realise you were scared of flying. I thought you were just the strong silent type."

"I'm not scared of flying," he replied, opening his eyes.

A hint of a smile pulled at her lips. "Any chance I can have my hand back then?"

"I'm not scared of flying," he said again as he reluctantly pulled his hand away. "I just don't like it when the plane feels as though it's about to drop out of the sky."

"Are you also scared of rollercoasters? Is it the stomach dropping sensation that bothers you?"

He turned to look right at her, registering how glossy her hair was and the twinkle of amusement in her eyes. "I don't care about my stomach dropping," he told her. "I'm worried about the entire plane dropping out of the sky. I don't see how any normal person would be okay with the plane lurching around so much."

Her lips twitched. "Since you're clearly very stressed, I'm going to ignore the inference that I'm not normal."

"I'm not stressed." He clutched at the armrest when the plane chose that moment to shudder.

"Would you like to hold my hand again?" the silky voice asked in his ear.

"I'm fine," he grumbled, then closed his eyes and pushed his head into the headrest.

CHAPTER TWO

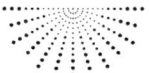

Relief washed over Jago as soon as his feet hit solid ground. Generally, he wasn't scared of flying. Three days ago he'd taken a flight from New York to London with no problem at all. It was the ridiculously small planes that flew to the Isles of Scilly that caused him a problem. But then who wouldn't find it unsettling when the planes wobbled and shuddered so much?

With a sinking feeling he recalled saying the same to the woman seated beside him. He was fairly certain it had come out offensively. Had he said she wasn't normal? Or just implied it? Inwardly, he groaned. The woman might have been overly chatty, but there'd been no reason for him to be rude.

Glancing around as he walked towards the airport building, he caught sight of her a few strides behind him. He tried to catch her eye but she had her head bowed over her phone.

When he reached the building, he held the door and waited for her to reach him. The smile she flashed him when she glanced up made him feel even worse. He'd been rude, yet she still smiled at him.

"Thank you," she said brightly as she passed.

Quickly, he walked after her and had just opened his mouth

to call out to her when he caught sight of his mother across the room. Her beaming smile made him lose focus on anything else. He paused for a moment before launching into quick strides. It had been three years since he'd seen his mum in person, and it struck him just how much he'd missed her.

Guilt niggled, deep in his gut. He'd stayed away for far too long. All because of his own stupid insecurities.

His throat tightened, making it impossible for him to form words as he wrapped his arms around his mum. She was slightly less effective than he was at keeping her emotions in check. Her body shook against his, and when they finally drew apart the tears that streamed down her face were no surprise at all. Not bothering to wipe them away she grinned and kissed his cheek. Then kissed the exact same spot again, making them both laugh.

"I've missed you," she said. "It's so great to have you home."

Jago's smile wavered at the mention of home, the word causing him nothing but confusion. Pushing the thought aside, he focused on his mum.

"If it's so good to have me home, why the heck are you crying?"

She gave his arm a playful tap. "You know there was no chance of me not crying when I haven't seen you for so long."

It wasn't meant as a dig, but Jago's stomach twisted nonetheless as another wave of guilt hit him.

"Come on," Mirren said. "Let's find your bag, then we can get you home and settled in. You might have an hour or so of peace before the rest of them descend."

It wasn't as though Jago had expected a welcome committee, but he couldn't say it didn't sting that there was only his mum to meet him.

"What's everyone up to?" he asked once they were heading out of the building.

"Mostly working, I think. I lose track, but they'll all be over for dinner this evening." She tilted her head and looked as though she was fighting more tears. "I can't believe I'll have all my boys in one room together." She held the door and he pulled his case outside to be hit by a gust of salty air. "I can't wait for you to meet Beth. And Keira and Pippa as well."

Jago twisted to look back over his shoulder, distracted by thoughts of the woman from the plane. When there was no sign of her, he shifted his attention back to his mum.

"Pippa?"

"Yes. She'll be there for dinner too. She's lovely. You'll like her."

His brow crinkled in confusion. "She is ...?"

"Sorry," his mum said. "It must be confusing for you to keep track of everyone. Pippa has the café that sells Lowen's pottery."

"Right. Okay." He shook his head. "Why is she coming to dinner?" He had a brief panic that his mum might be on some sort of matchmaking scheme. Considering how often she asked about his love life, he wouldn't put it past her.

His mum looked up in surprise as they stopped in front of her white golf buggy. "She's Lowen's girlfriend," she said, as though he should know. "I told you about her on the phone."

"Did you?" He wedged his case into the footwell of the backseat. "Maybe. It rings a vague bell." Honestly it was difficult to keep track of his family. His mum's phone calls were often so rambling that he sometimes switched off.

"She's great for Lowen," his mum said. "He's really come out of himself recently. It's lovely to see him happy again." She slipped into the driver's seat as he squeezed himself into the passenger seat. Her eyes lit up. "Oh, and you'll meet Ellie too. You're going to love her. She's the sweetest little thing."

"Beth's kid, right?" He was fairly sure he at least had that one right. He'd been surprised when he heard of Trystan's break-up from his long-term girlfriend and his new relationship with a single mother. The Trystan he knew had clung to his independence so fiercely that he'd never really imagined him settling down and having a family. Apparently he'd been wrong.

"She's adorable," his mum was saying. "She can't wait to meet you. No doubt she'll be up at the house before the rest of them." She glanced at him as she pulled out of her parking spot. "You don't mind staying with me, do you? I'd have put you in one of the cottages, but with all these birdwatchers around we're booked up for the next couple of weeks. You can move into a cottage then, if you want?"

"It sounds as though you don't want me cramping your style," he said, while the familiar landscape passed by. The nostalgia could overwhelm him if he let it, so instead he focused on winding his mum up.

"Of course I want you at my place," she said hastily. "I only thought you might like your own space since you're staying for longer this time. Whenever Trystan used to come over from London he'd complain about staying with me."

"That's probably because he owns one of the cottages," Jago remarked. "Of course he wanted to stay in it when he owns it." His jaw clenched as he was reminded of the money that Lowen had given to him and his brothers. It seemed that everyone had made good use of the inheritance except for him.

The money had come at the perfect time and got him out of a bind, but it also left him cloaked with embarrassment that he didn't have much to show for it.

"Maybe," his mum conceded. "But I think even Trystan would admit it was also because he got sick of spending too much time around his mother."

"Unless Trystan has changed a lot since the last time I saw him," Jago said, "he's too much of a charmer to say that to your face."

"He's definitely a charmer," his mum agreed. "But he's never minded teasing his poor mum." Reaching over, she put a hand on his arm as though proving to herself that he was really there. "How does it feel to be back?"

"I'm not sure." Rounding the bend, they trundled towards

AN UNEXPECTED GUEST

Old Town Bay, where tips of gentle waves sparkled under golden rays of sunlight.

"It must be strange. It's been so long since you were back for more than a few days."

Again, he felt the tug of guilt and shifted in his seat, concerned that his mum would see it in his features.

"I'm looking forward to catching up with everyone," he murmured.

"It will be especially good for you to spend some proper time with Kit," his mum remarked. "The two of you barely know each other."

It was true. Their fourteen-year age gap felt like a chasm between them. His baby brother had been two years old when Jago had left to go to school on the mainland. Their childhoods, while so similar, had played out on completely different timelines. The last time Jago had visited he'd been shocked to find Kit all grown up, and so mature for his age. There hadn't been time for them to become reacquainted, so when he'd returned to the States they still felt like strangers.

"It'll be good to spend time with him," he said as they turned onto the lane which led to his mum's house. His emotions were all over the place and he kept quiet as his mum rambled away, telling him something about Ellie. When she parked and turned to him with a questioning look, he wondered what he'd missed while his mind was elsewhere.

"What did you say?" he asked

"I said it's sweet how she's been telling everybody about her new uncle."

"I'm not really her uncle though," he said with a frown.

"She's family," his mum said, a hint of puzzlement to her voice. "Once Trystan adopts her it will be official. He told you he's adopting her?"

"Yes." If Trystan's hasty engagement and quick wedding hadn't surprised him enough, that had really been a shock.

"Ellie's been beside herself with excitement these last few

weeks," his mum said as she stepped out of the cart. She opened her mouth then closed it again quickly, a look flashing across her face as though she'd stopped herself from saying something she shouldn't. "What with the wedding and your arrival, she's been absolutely hyper."

Jago didn't respond as he heaved his bag out and stared up at the house. It felt as though nothing had changed since he was a teenager. He could have been arriving home from school or football training.

"What time is everyone coming over for dinner?" he asked, dragging his suitcase behind him as they ambled towards the house.

"I'm not entirely sure. They'll no doubt turn up in dribs and drabs over the next few hours."

He nodded, glad he had a bit of time to chill out before having to be sociable.

CHAPTER THREE

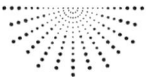

The moment Sylvie took her phone off flight mode a slew of messages came through from her mum. While disembarking the plane she hastily replied with an update on her travel progress, then focused on her excitement at reuniting with her cousin after so long.

At the terminal building the guy from the plane held the door for her. He'd been pretty oafish during the flight, but she smiled up at him nonetheless and brushed aside thoughts of how good it had felt when he'd clutched her hand during the turbulence. The thrill of it had been a sad reminder of the lack of physical contact in her life in recent times.

She made her way to the bathrooms and had just finished washing her hands when a call came through from her mum.

"I just messaged you," Sylvie said into the phone.

"I know but I'm too excited. I can't stop pacing. Now I wish I'd come with you." They'd both found it difficult when they'd drifted out of touch with Lowen, so the email from his mum a few weeks before had been a pleasant surprise for the pair of them.

"Well *you* have a job," Sylvie reminded her mum. "Unlike some people." That had been a determining factor in Sylvie's decision to track Lowen down in person. She'd recently quit her accounting job and was at a bit of a loose end while she figured out what to do next.

"You'll find another job easily," her mum said. "You always land on your feet."

Previously, Sylvie would have agreed – she'd definitely been one of those people who everything seemed to go right for. Except, of course, until it didn't. The past few years had been a struggle, and her usual optimism had waned as a result.

"Anyway," her mum went on, "don't worry about work now. You agreed you were going to forget about everything for a while and go off on an adventure."

"Do you think I might be getting a bit too old for adventures?" Sylvie asked, examining her reflection in the mirror above the sink and hooking an unruly lock of hair behind her ear.

"Never," her mum replied. "Now promise me when you find Lowen you'll give him a big kiss from me."

"I will," Sylvie told her, her smile returning at the thought of it. "Are you going to let me get on with my search?"

"Keep me updated," her mum said before ending the call.

The tiny airport building was almost deserted by the time Sylvie exited the toilets. Dragging her small suitcase out of the main doors, she glanced around, surprised by the lack of taxis. A couple of cars were parked and what appeared to be a golf cart was receding down the narrow lane which led away from the airport.

As she contemplated what to do next, she spotted a bus stop. Reading the schedule, she found she'd have a long wait and was about to return to the airport building when the logo at the top of the bus stop caught her eye. Smiling, she held up her phone and took a quick picture, then sent it to her mum asking whether she thought Lowen might have used his inheritance to buy a bus company. The name on the logo read "Treneary Transport Company" – Treneary being Lowen's surname.

The string of emojis her mum sent in reply made Sylvie chuckle.

Since she had her phone in hand, she brought up a map and found it wasn't much of a walk into Hugh Town. From there, she'd need to get a boat to the smaller island of Bryher, where Lowen lived.

The air was fresh and blustery as she set off down the lane, and the sky was lined by streaks of cirrus cloud. After a couple of minutes she stopped to look out over the fields bordered by stone walls. Down at the coast, the sweeping sandy beaches and rocky coves gave way to turquoise water that turned dark blue further from the shore.

Taking a lungful of briny air, she continued in the direction of Hugh Town, which sat on a thin stretch of land on the southwest of the island. After spending her entire life living in cities, the peace and tranquillity was a stark contrast. It was a shock to walk without encountering anyone. When she did finally pass a couple of cyclists, then a group of hikers, they exchanged friendly greetings.

Nearing the town, a couple of cars passed her, then she panicked slightly when a quaint tourist train rounded the bend on a direct course with her. The driver slowed while she scrambled onto the grass verge and battled to get her case out of the way too.

"Don't worry!" the young guy in the driver's seat called. "There's plenty of room."

He was right; as the train got closer, she saw there was more space than she'd initially thought.

"I'd have given you a lift if I was going the other way," the driver told her, smiling widely.

"Am I almost at Hugh Town?" she asked.

He nodded encouragingly. "Keep going on this road. You'll be there in no time."

"Thank you!"

He told her to have a good holiday, then delighted the children on board when he rang the bell and picked up speed again. She waved at the passengers before stepping out of the grass verge and continuing on her way.

Hugh Town was sleepier than she expected. With its quiet roads and smattering of shops and businesses among the cluster of stone houses and cottages, it almost felt like stepping back in time. There was a bit of bustle at the harbour with people milling around, getting on and off various small boats.

Reading the timetable, she checked her watch. A boat was about to leave for Bryher, but, surveying the boats, it was difficult to figure out which was going where.

"Are you going to the off islands?" a man asked, startling her with his deep baritone.

"The what?" she asked, swinging around to him.

"The off islands," he said again, a smile breaking through his bushy beard. "That's what we call the smaller islands. You'll find boats going to each of them."

"I need to get to Bryher," she told him. "I'm not sure which boat I need."

"That blue one, there." He pointed to the boat making its way out of the harbour. "I'm afraid you've just missed it. It'll be a few hours until the next one. Are you staying in the hotel on Bryher?"

"No, I'm visiting an old friend."

"You should give them a call. If they're local, they'll likely have a boat themselves and can nip over and pick you up."

"I might do that," she said, thanking him and moving away to stare out over the water and the collection of boats bobbing on the gentle waves.

Maybe the surprise approach hadn't been the best idea after all. Prior to her trip she'd looked into booking a hotel but hadn't had any luck finding any with availability. She'd assumed she'd be able to stay with Lowen, so hadn't been worried. Now that felt presumptuous. She should have tried harder to find a hotel. Or she could have arranged the visit with

Lowen's mum. Mirren had always seemed very friendly in her emails.

With a few hours to kill before the next boat, she set off to the tourist information office she'd passed earlier to enquire about a place to stay. Lugging her suitcase around made her thankful that the town was so compact. Nevertheless, she was beginning to get fed up with it as she dragged it through the open doorway of the tourist information.

An older man looked up from his computer screen behind the counter. "What can I help you with?"

"I need a place to stay. I didn't have any luck finding anywhere online. I wondered if you could help me out?"

He pushed his glasses up his nose. "You don't mean immediately, do you?"

"Yes." She parked her suitcase beside her leg, then rolled her shoulders. "I'd intended to stay with family, but now I think it might be better to have my own space."

"Well, it's a good job you've got family to stay with. You'll have trouble finding other accommodation for the next week or two."

"Really?" She hadn't expected the islands would be busy in October. Surely the holidaymakers were long gone at this time of year.

"Birdwatchers," the man said. "The islands are full of them. Always the same at this time of year. We get lots of migrating birds, you see."

Sylvie blinked a couple of times. "Surely there must be some accommodation available?"

"There may well be," he replied. "But good luck finding it. If I was you, I'd go and talk nicely to that family of yours." He motioned to a wall of flyers advertising local attractions. "Now, if you'd like some information about what to do while you're visiting I'd be happy to help."

"Thanks," she said, backing away. "I'll get back to you on that."

"Good luck," he called as she schlepped her case back out onto the street. With the sun momentarily blinding her, she almost crashed straight into a woman with striking blonde curls.

"Sorry," they both said at once.

"Did you find what you were looking for?" the woman asked.

"Excuse me?"

"At the tourist information." The woman smiled sheepishly. "I work there. I'm not just being a weirdo."

"Oh, right. I see. I was looking for somewhere to stay, but apparently I've arrived at the wrong time."

"You have," the woman said. "The islands are crawling with birdwatchers."

"My cousin lives on Bryher." Sylvie sighed. "I'm hoping I can track him down and stay with him. I haven't been able to reach him by phone though." She was sharing too much, as she tended to do, but the woman's welcoming smile invited conversation.

"The phone signal can be tricky," she said. "I'm sure you'll have more luck tracking him down in person."

"Fingers crossed," Sylvie replied.

The woman rooted in her handbag, then produced a business card. "If you find you're really stuck for a place to stay, give me a call. I'll probably be able to help in a pinch."

"Thank you …" She read the name on the card. "Holly. That's really kind of you."

"Good luck with finding your cousin. You'll have a bit of a wait for the boat to Bryher, but if you're hungry I can recommend the food at the Mermaid Inn. It's down at the harbour. You can't miss it."

Sylvie thanked her again, then took her advice and headed for the pub.

∼

As it turned out, all Jago had time for was to drop his bag in his old childhood bedroom and have a quick shower before the first of his family arrived. Stepping out of the bathroom with a towel around his waist, he caught the voices drifting up from the kitchen and strained to hear them better. It wasn't any of his brothers. A female voice, alongside his mum's, and the high-pitched chatter of a little girl. At the sound of his name he continued to his room and had only just managed to pull on some clothes when the door was pushed open.

"Hello," the dainty little girl said, looking up at him with bright blue eyes.

"Hi," he replied, straightening his T-shirt, then picking up the towel to rub his hair.

"You're Jago," she stated without moving from the doorway.

"Yeah. I suspect you're Ellie."

"You live in America."

He paused in rubbing his hair. "And you live on St Mary's. This is kind of a weird game."

Her eyebrows twitched together. "You're Trystan's brother."

He nodded.

"I'm going to have a brother soon," she said. "Or maybe a sister. We're not sure yet. The baby is growing in Mummy's tummy, and that takes a long time."

"I didn't know that" he mused.

Ellie nodded. "It takes nine months."

Jago rolled his eyes. "I knew *that*. I just didn't know your mum and Trystan were having a baby."

"Yes. Trystan is the daddy. He'll be my daddy too. You'll be my uncle."

"So I heard."

"Kit is my uncle as well. So is Noah, and Lowen."

"That's quite a collection," he told her. "Who's your favourite?"

"Kit," she said without missing a beat. "He has a train and he's lots of fun. But I also like Noah because sometimes he swings me around until I'm dizzy. Or until Keira shouts at him to stop." She barely paused for breath. "Lowen is very nice too because he makes me pretty things with my name on. Like a mug and an egg cup. And he lets me play on the pottery wheel. He's a very nice man. But Kit is my favourite person in the whole world."

Finally, there was a break in her chatter. "You really like to talk, don't you?" Jago asked while thinking of the woman from the plane. Was his entire trip going to be filled with females who couldn't stop talking?

Ellie beamed as though he'd paid her a compliment. "Mummy told me not to come upstairs. I was supposed to leave you in peace and wait for you to come down."

"And yet," he said, "here you are."

"Are you ready to come downstairs now?"

He dragged his fingers through his damp hair. "I suppose I'm as ready as I'll ever be."

Taking a couple of steps into the room, Ellie reached for his hand, her dainty fingers only managing to hook around his pinkie and ring finger. "I can show you the way."

"I think I know the way."

She pulled on his hand and led him onto the landing. "You used to live here, didn't you?"

"Yes," he replied.

"When you were a little boy?"

"Yes."

"Was that a very long time ago?"

"Quite a while," he admitted, a smile tugging at his lips.

"Are you as old as my mummy?"

"How old is your mum?"

"Forty-one."

"In that case, no, I'm not as old as your mum." He hadn't realised there was such an age gap between Trystan and Beth. It seemed as though he was constantly surprised by his family at the moment.

"How old are you?" she asked.

"I always thought it was rude to ask people their age."

"It is for adults," she said matter-of-factly. "But it's okay for kids to ask."

He rolled his eyes at her precociousness. "I'm thirty-six."

"That's older than Trystan," she stated.

He eased his fingers from her hand. "You should hold the banister." He pointed. "So you don't fall down the stairs."

"I'm not a baby," she told him with a pout.

"Obviously." He quirked an eyebrow. "Babies don't talk so much."

She giggled as they descended the stairs.

The conversation between his mum and Beth stopped when they entered the kitchen.

"It's great to finally meet you," Beth said once his mum had made the introductions. "We're so happy you could make it over for the wedding."

"I wouldn't miss it," he said, forcing brightness to his voice. "I hear more congratulations are in order. Ellie's been telling me she has a brother or sister on the way." It shouldn't matter who he'd heard the news from, but it annoyed him nonetheless.

Beth's eyes slid to Ellie, then back to him. "Trystan wanted to tell you himself, but this little minx is terrible at keeping secrets."

"It's brilliant news anyway," he said, then turned at the sound of the door.

Trystan walked in and wrapped him in a tight hug. They only managed a brief greeting and more congratulations before the door opened again and Noah and Keira bundled in.

After more hugs and greetings, Jago asked Keira a few questions while trying to keep up with the chatter around the room at the same time. He took a beer when Noah offered one and gulped at it, grateful for the momentary respite as Keira went to get herself a drink.

Through the window he watched a red Mini pull up at the

end of the lane. Seren's ginger hair drew his eye as she stepped out of the driver's seat. Laughing, she looked across the roof of the car, clearly mid-conversation with Kit, who beamed at her. Lowen got out of the back with a woman he presumed was Pippa, but Jago's gaze was fixed on Kit and Seren as they ambled up the path hand in hand.

"That's so weird," he murmured.

"What?" Noah asked, startling him.

"Those two." He tipped his head to indicate. "I always thought *you'd* end up with Seren." Grimacing, he glanced around, relieved to find Keira deep in conversation with Beth. "Sorry."

"It's fine. I think Keira's used to hearing that by now."

"Is it weird for you seeing Seren with Kit?" he asked quietly.

"Not in the way you're suggesting. I honestly never saw Seren that way." Noah smiled. "I was surprised when they got together, but they're good for each other."

"They just bought a house, right?"

"Yep." He looked pointedly out across the water. "You can see it if you know where to look. Round the other side of the bay."

They were interrupted by the door opening and a bustle of more greetings. The noise level increased dramatically, and the thrum of different conversations was interrupted occasionally by someone shouting across the din about drinks and food.

Considering Jago had spent so long living in New York, he should be used to crowds of people in small spaces but being surrounded by his family felt overwhelming. He rubbed discreetly at his temple as he made small talk with Pippa, asking her about her cafe.

It was probably the jet lag which made the conversation feel like such hard work. At least that's what he kept telling himself. All he had to do was get through the next couple of hours and then he could retreat to the quiet of his bedroom.

Smiling, he zoned back into what Pippa was saying, hoping

she didn't notice that he was barely registering her words. Snippets of all the other conversations in the room attacked his ears, and he found the whole situation dizzying.

It probably wasn't a great sign that he'd only just arrived back and already felt the compulsion to flee.

CHAPTER FOUR

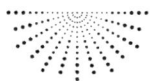

The inside of the Mermaid Inn was a feast for the eyes, with every inch of wall space adorned with nautical memorabilia. Sylvie's gaze roamed over it all as she crossed the room to the bar. A group of men sat at a table by the window and a young couple were perched on barstools at the far end of the bar, but otherwise the place was empty. After a moment, a middle-aged man walked out from the back room and greeted her with a welcoming smile.

"Looks as though you've just arrived in town," he said with a subtle nod to her suitcase. "Did you fly over or get the ferry?"

"I flew."

"You get some good scenery on that little trip," he remarked, then tapped the bar. "Now, what can I get you to drink?"

She debated for a moment before ordering a glass of wine. Coffee was probably the wiser choice, but she was on holiday. Also, the wine might help to calm her nerves.

"Are you over here on a bird hunt as well?" the barman asked as he set a glass of white in front of her.

"No. I didn't even realise this was a popular bird-spotting area until today."

He leaned in and whispered, "I didn't think you looked the

type, but I didn't want to put my foot in it." His eyes sparkled with mischief. "They're quite a fanatical lot, those twitchers."

"I'm sure they are," she said, giving him a knowing smile before taking a sip of her drink.

"I assume you're waiting for a boat," he remarked. "Which island are you staying on?"

"Bryher, hopefully." She shook her head. The sip of wine must've done the trick, because she suddenly found her predicament amusing. "My cousin lives on Bryher. If I can track him down, I'm hoping I can stay with him. It seems all the accommodation on the islands has been taken by the birdwatchers."

"A cousin on Bryher," he repeated. "Who is it? I'd say it's a fair bet that I know them."

"Lowen Treneary. He has a pottery studio."

The barman let out a burst of laughter. "I've known Lowen since he was a little boy. I know all the Trenearys. Noah works for me, and my niece is just about to move in with Kit. I can't believe you're a cousin of the Treneary boys. Is that Mirren's side of the family or Terry's?"

Sylvie shifted on the barstool. "Neither actually. It's only Lowen who's my cousin. My dad is the brother of his birth mother."

He scratched his beard. "I always forget that Mirren isn't Lowen's biological mother."

"I've never met the rest of the family." She twisted the stem of the wine glass. "I spent a lot of time on holiday with Lowen when we were kids – with our grandparents. We often talked about me coming over to Scilly to meet his family, but it never happened. Though I always heard so much about Lowen's brothers that I felt as though I knew them."

"Lovely family," the barman said fondly. "I'm sure you'll enjoy meeting them all." Straightening up, he looked thoughtful, then wrinkled his brow. "Did you say you were getting the boat to Bryher today?"

"Yes." She checked her watch. "I still have a couple of hours to wait."

"Is Lowen expecting you?"

"No. I tried calling him a few times over the last couple of weeks, but I couldn't get hold of him, so I thought I'd go for the surprise approach."

"That's typical of Lowen. He's notorious for not answering his phone. If you leave a message he's pretty good at calling back. And he's not bad with texting either."

"I've come this far," she said. "I think I'll just surprise him now."

"If you'd been here a couple of hours earlier, you would've caught him. He came in for a drink at lunchtime."

"That would've been funny."

"He's having dinner at his mum's place this evening, so you won't find him on Bryher. Plus, he's currently renovating his house, so he's staying with his girlfriend on St Mary's. I'm not sure how long for, but at least the next couple of nights."

Sylvie's eyes widened. "Are you serious?"

He nodded gravely. "There's no use getting the boat over to Bryher this afternoon. You won't find him there."

"I've got nowhere to stay," she said in a panic, then remembered the woman from the tourist information and wondered about taking her up on her offer of help.

"Don't be daft," the barman said. "I'll give you directions to Mirren's place. You can catch up with Lowen there."

"But if he's staying with his girlfriend …"

"They'll fit you in somewhere. Don't worry."

Sylvie slapped a hand across her forehead. "Why on earth did I think surprising him was a good idea? This is a disaster."

The barman laughed heartily. "Don't be so dramatic. It's not far to Mirren's place. You can walk there easily enough. I bet Lowen will be delighted to see you." He glanced around the room. "You know what? I'll get the chef to come out and watch the bar for five minutes and I can drive you up there."

"That would be amazing," Sylvie said, not keen on the thought of lugging her case any further.

Picking up her glass, she took a few gulps of her wine, wondering again what she'd got herself into.

∽

With so many of them crammed into Mirren's kitchen, dinner was somewhat of a free-for-all. There was a fair bit of tussling over the boxes of takeaway pizzas, and only enough seats for those quick enough to grab one. Noah, Trystan and Seren ate standing by the counter, while the rest of them occupied mismatched chairs around the solid oak table. The exact same table that they'd sat around as kids.

As he worked his way through the pizza slices on his plate, Jago was aware of Ellie's gaze on him. Her earlier friendly disposition had morphed into something closer to suspicion.

Ignoring her, he swallowed his mouthful and looked across the table at Kit, who'd been telling him about getting the keys to their new house a couple of days before.

"How much work does it need?" Jago asked.

"A lot." He grinned through a mouthful of pizza. "If you'd like to volunteer to help while you're here, we wouldn't say no."

"Sure," he said.

Lowen raised his eyebrows at Kit. "No one's going near your place until my house is finished."

"What's happening with your place?" Jago asked.

"It needs some renovating. We're painting this weekend."

"His place has been in need of renovation forever," Kit said, leaning back in his chair. "He waited until I bought a house, then conveniently decided he needs everyone to help with *his* place."

Lowen rested his arm along the back of Pippa's chair and beamed at Kit. "As I recall, you were the one to suggest we do my house first. Something about owing me!"

The look his brothers exchanged gave Jago the impression

he'd missed something, but he didn't have a chance to ask before Kit spoke.

"That was before I knew how quickly things would move with our house."

Trystan caught Jago's eye as he lifted a slice of pizza from the box beside him. "You should come and help us with Lowen's place tomorrow."

"It will involve a boat ride though," Seren said with a barely suppressed grin. His mum's lips lifted while a ripple of laughter emerged from his brothers.

"I feel as though I've missed a joke," Beth said while Keira and Pippa looked equally puzzled.

"Jago gets seasick," Noah said with a wicked grin.

"Seriously?" Keira's eyebrows shot up. "You grew up *here* and you get seasick?"

"Yep." Jago's appetite vanished and he dropped the crust of pizza onto his plate, waiting for the inevitable jokes at his expense.

"Wow." Beth's delicate features brimmed with kindness. "That must've been a nightmare growing up."

"Yep," he said again. "You could say that."

"You don't really think of kids getting seasick," Keira said. "Like the way kids can spin around and around without getting dizzy. But as an adult it makes you immediately nauseous."

Noah lifted an eyebrow. "You feel ill even watching Ellie spin around."

"True," she said, putting her hand in front of her mouth as she spoke with her mouth full.

"Spinning around is fun," Ellie put in, then leaned closer to Jago. "Why don't you like boats?"

"When I was a kid they always made me feel sick."

"Why?" she asked, squinting at him with even more suspicion in her eyes.

"I don't know."

His mum chuckled. "When he was seven, he was in a lug

dinghy race in the harbour. He vomited all over the side of the boat." She chuckled some more. "The two kids in the boats beside him were so distracted that they capsized and ended up swimming in Jago's vomit. They're probably traumatised to this day."

"*I'm* traumatised to this day," Jago said. "But thanks for telling that story *again*." He hadn't meant to sound so brusque, but it wasn't exactly a pleasant memory. He shifted in his seat as a stony silence settled around the kitchen.

"Did you grow out of it?" Beth asked, gently easing the tension in the room. "Or do you still get seasick?"

"I'm not entirely sure. It's a while since I've been on a boat." Considering the mere thought of getting on a boat made his stomach roll, he suspected he hadn't outgrown it.

"How was the flight over here, by the way?" Lowen asked with a smirk.

"Don't say you get sick on planes as well," Pippa said with wide eyes.

"It's only the flight *here* that I have a problem with," he said defensively. "And it's not that I get sick. I just don't like the way the plane rattles around."

"I can understand that," Beth said. "It's not exactly a smooth ride."

Jago caught Lowen and Trystan exchanging a look of amusement and was transported back to mealtimes when they were teenagers. Apparently the teasing would never change.

"Thankfully Jago was always big for his age," Trystan remarked. "None of the kids at school dared to tease him about his seasickness."

That was at least true. If he'd have had a different build in his school days, he'd no doubt have been bullied mercilessly.

Trystan switched to asking Lowen about the renovation plans for the following day and Jago let the chatter and banter whirl around him until a knocking sound got his attention.

"Is that the door?" he asked no one in particular.

"Come in," Kit shouted.

Jago did a double take when the woman from the plane walked in. Her wavy brown hair looked dishevelled now, and her cheeks were flushed as she glanced nervously around the room.

Presumably she was a guest in one of the cottages his mum rented out. It should have occurred to Jago that their paths would cross again. He'd definitely left the anonymity of New York behind.

Sinking down in his seat, he hoped she wouldn't spot him. His mum would check her into whichever cottage she was staying in and she'd be on her way. Sometime in the next couple of days he could strategically bump into her and apologise for being so grouchy on the plane without his family gawking.

"Sorry to disturb you," she said, her eyes darting, clearly trying to figure out who to aim her words at. "I'm looking for Lowen."

At that, Jago sat bolt upright. Her head shot to him, recognition clear in her gaze as their eyes locked.

So much for his plan to go unnoticed.

CHAPTER FIVE

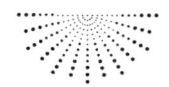

"Hi," Lowen said, breaking the silence and dragging the woman's gaze from Jago.

"Hi," she replied, a nervous smile playing at her lips.

"You're looking for me?" Lowen asked.

She shifted her weight. "God, this is awkward. You don't even know who I am, do you?" She didn't wait for him to respond but babbled away. "I did try to call, but you never answered your phone. I should have left a message, but somehow I got it in my head that turning up to surprise you might be fun."

Lowen's eyebrows rose sharply towards his hairline. "Sylvie?"

"Yes!" She made an awkward "jazz hands" type gesture. "Surprise!"

Lowen froze for a moment before his brain seemed to jump into gear and he stood abruptly to wrap her in a fierce hug.

"You got so old," the woman remarked.

"Same to you!" He stepped back to hold her at arm's length. "This is crazy! I can't believe you're here."

She gave him a playful jab to his stomach. "If you'd have answered your phone, you wouldn't have been so surprised."

"Don't take it personally," their mum said with a bemused smile. "He's the same with all of us when it comes to answering his phone."

"Sorry," Lowen murmured, his gaze fixed on the woman beside him with a look of complete disbelief. He shook his head and apologised again, louder this time as he turned to the rest of them. "This is my cousin, Sylvie." He grinned at her. "This is … my family."

Her gaze flicked back to Jago. "What are you doing here?"

"I'm Lowen's brother." He recalled her talking on the plane about surprising her cousin. "You're his cousin?"

Her brow wrinkled. "Jago?"

"Do you guys know each other?" Lowen asked.

"We sat together on the plane," Sylvie explained. "I had no idea who he was. I rabbited away as usual, and Jago pretended to be asleep so he didn't have to speak to me."

"That sounds about right," Kit remarked happily.

Sylvie's eyes widened. "Wait … I know you as well."

There was a pause before Kit's eyes lit with recognition. "Did I almost run you off the road with my train earlier?"

"Not quite," she said, seeming to relax. "But I was a little worried when I saw the train driving towards me."

Kit beamed. "If I'd have known you were heading here, I'd definitely have given you a lift."

"I was actually headed for Bryher," she said, glancing at Lowen. "But the barman in the pub told me that would be a wasted trip. He gave me a lift here." Her smile faltered. "But I seem to have interrupted dinner."

"It's fine," Mirren reassured her while Kit jumped up and gave her his chair.

"I didn't mean to interrupt your family dinner," Sylvie said apologetically as she took a seat.

Mirren smiled warmly. "It's lovely to have you here. I've exchanged a few emails with your mum recently."

"That's why I came."

"Where are you staying?" Lowen asked, sitting back beside Pippa.

"That's a bit of a conundrum." She looked sheepishly at Lowen. "I tried to find a hotel, but apparently everything is booked up with birdwatchers. I thought maybe I could stay with you ..."

"Yeah, of course," Lowen replied.

"But the barman told me you're staying with ..."

"Me," Pippa said and introduced herself.

Lowen grimaced. "I forgot. We're doing a bit of work on my place over the next few days, it'll be full of paint fumes."

"A woman at the tourist information said she might be able to help me out with a place," Sylvie said, her cheeks pinking once again.

"You can stay here," Mirren said.

Sylvie shook her head. "I don't want to put you out."

"You're not. I've got plenty of space."

"Are you sure? I feel terrible for imposing."

"I like having people around," Mirren said. "It's really not a problem."

"Thank you."

"How long are you staying for?" Lowen asked.

"I'm not entirely sure. To be honest, I don't have much of a plan." The smile crept back over her face. "I just had the urge to catch up with my cousin." She looked to Mirren. "After Mum got your email, we were excited to get back in touch with Lowen."

"It's lovely that you're here," Mirren said kindly. "It will be good for you and Lowen to catch up and reminisce."

Sylvie's gaze swept around the table, the corners of her mouth twitching in amusement. "It's so strange to be here after I heard so much about you all. In my head Kitto is still a baby, so that's a bit of a shock."

"He *is* still a baby." Noah ruffled Kit's hair. "Our baby Kitto."

"Most people call me Kit," he told Sylvie while swatting Noah away.

"Kitto is such a lovely name," Sylvie remarked, her eyes sparkling with mischief. "I always loved the Cornish names, but our grandmother had quite an issue with them. Didn't she, Lowen?"

The smile slipped from Lowen's face. "She wasn't the biggest fan," he said tightly.

"I will never forget that day you squared up to her over it," Sylvie continued happily. "I was convinced either you were going to hit her or she was going to hit you." Her eyes shifted to Lowen, then Mirren as an uncomfortable silence descended around the table. "No one hit anyone," she said with a nervous laugh. "And she might have been awful, but at least we got a million out of it." That nervous laugh again. "Although, a million can vanish surprisingly quickly once you factor in tax, and a husband who conveniently decides he'd like to divorce you and take half of your money." She swallowed hard when she finally stopped talking.

When her incessant chatter wasn't directed solely at him, Jago found her quite amusing. A smile tugged at his lips but fell away as he registered Sylvie's words. "Were your grandparents really sexist?" he asked, straightening his spine.

She gave a small shake of the head.

"How come they left Lowen more money than you?" he asked.

"They didn't. We both got a million."

"Lowen got more than a million," he told her, then glanced at Lowen, wondering if she wasn't supposed to know.

"I saw their will," Sylvie said blithely. "We both got a million. My dad got the rest, mostly their various properties."

"That doesn't make sense." Jago leaned on the table. "Lowen gave me a hundred and fifty thousand. And the same to Trystan, Noah and Kit. If you take into account tax, that would mean that Lowen was left with nothing." He looked to his older brother, who'd sunk down into his seat, chin tucked against his chest.

A gasp erupted from Sylvie, and she slapped her hand across her mouth. "No?" she said her voice barely above a whisper as she stared at Lowen. "You didn't? Oh my goodness, you did, didn't you? You gave it all away."

"Why the heck would he give his entire inheritance away?" Jago asked, sure there must be some confusion.

"It's like the final revenge," Sylvie said, a glimmer of something like awe in her eyes. "What's the one thing Grandma would never have wanted you to do with her money?" She grinned at Lowen. "Did you seriously give all of the money to your brothers?"

"Every last penny," he said.

Jago checked around the table, but no one else seemed surprised by the information. "You gave us all of your money?" he asked Lowen and got a shrug in response.

Sylvie beamed. "Grandma would turn in her grave."

"How come I never knew this?" Jago asked.

"I didn't want you to feel weird about it," Lowen said.

Jago could kind of see his point. What he took issue with was the fact that he was apparently the only one who didn't know.

"Your grandmother sounds awful," Kit said.

"She was pretty unpleasant," Sylvie agreed. "If you imagine Cruella de Vil, but worse, you'd be on the right track."

The whole conversation had Jago confused. As far as he was aware, Lowen had always had a great time spending the school holidays with his grandparents. But he supposed first-class travel to exotic places and being showered with gifts probably overshadowed the fact that his grandmother might not have been the warmest of characters.

"I feel as though I've just waltzed in and disrupted your family dinner," Sylvie said with a frown. "Were you celebrating something? Is it someone's birthday?"

"Jago just arrived back from America," Mirren told her. "It's the first time we've had the whole family together for a few years."

She slid her eyes to him. "No wonder you were crabby on the plane if you'd come all the way from America. You must be horribly jet-lagged."

"I stopped off in London for a couple of nights," he told her before realising it might have been better not to mention that and let her believe there was a good reason for him being grumpy on the plane. "I'm still feeling a bit groggy though."

She smiled at him, apparently willing to overlook his previous bad mood.

At least now he'd get a chance to apologise. Later, anyway. Once his family had finished quizzing her and foisting lukewarm pizza on her.

CHAPTER SIX

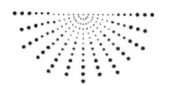

When the various family members began to disperse, Mirren gave Sylvie a quick tour of the house, then showed her up to a gorgeous guest room and insisted she was welcome to stay as long as she liked. Embarrassed by the imposition, Sylvie told her it would only be a day or two. Just enough time for her to catch up with her cousin.

She'd found it slightly odd when Lowen had left with Pippa shortly after dinner. Maybe Sylvie was being overly sensitive, but she'd expected him to hang around for the evening, especially since he hadn't mentioned any particular reason why he had to leave so early.

There was probably nothing to it – and he *had* promised they'd catch up the following day. Hopefully they'd get some time alone to properly reacquaint themselves.

Sylvie's phone rang as Mirren was talking about finding clean towels, and she left Sylvie alone in the bedroom so she could answer it in private.

"Hi," she said to her mum, perching on the foot of the bed.

"Well?" she said in a rush. "What's going on? Did you find him?"

"Yes," she said with a lack of enthusiasm.

"And? How was it seeing him again? Has he changed much?"

"Of course he's changed," Sylvie said impatiently. "He's a forty-year-old man." It hit her then how sad it was that they'd gone for so long without seeing him. In her head he was still a playful teenager, but that obviously wasn't reality. He'd grown up and moved on, and she had no idea who he was any more.

"What's wrong?" her mum asked. "Wasn't he happy to see you?"

"He seemed happy enough." She sighed, then explained how she'd tracked him down at Mirren's house and how she'd interrupted the family dinner, then the situation with Mirren offering her a place to stay.

"Mirren sounds lovely," her mum remarked. "If Lowen was subdued it's probably because you caught him off guard. It must have been a shock for him to see you again."

"It was more than that," Sylvie said sadly. "There was something weird …"

"How do you mean?"

"I made a few jokes about Grandma and how awful she was. But it almost felt as though none of his family knew what she was like."

"Your grandparents were particularly awful to Lowen. Maybe he prefers not to talk about them."

"I guess." She hung her head. "He also gave his entire inheritance away to his brothers. Didn't keep any of it for himself."

"Why?" The surprise was evident in her mum's tone.

"I'm not sure. But at least one of his brothers didn't seem to have a clue that Lowen hadn't kept any money for himself, so I felt a bit of a twit for putting my foot in it."

"That does sound a bit odd, but it must have been a strange situation with the whole family there. I'll bet everything will be better once you've had a chance to catch up with Lowen without everyone else around."

"I hope so." At the sound of footsteps in the hall, Sylvie

wound up the conversation and had just ended the call when a light knock came at the door. Jago eased it open, then walked in with a stack of fluffy white towels.

"Either Mum thinks you like to shower a lot, or she reckons you're staying for six months." He smiled as he set the towels on the dresser.

"Thank you."

"Are you okay?" he asked, looking at her properly.

"Yes."

"Are you sure? You look like you …"

"Gate-crashed a family gathering and put my foot in my mouth every time I opened it?"

"I was going to say you look like you just got bad news."

"I made a complete idiot of myself, didn't I?"

"No. I don't think so."

"I feel like I did. There were a lot of people and I got nervous and forgot to filter my thoughts …"

"It was fine."

She rested her elbows on her knees and dropped her head to her hands. "Remind me never to surprise a long-lost family member again."

He laughed lightly. "It really wasn't that bad." After taking a step towards the door, he stopped again. "Mum said to tell you to make yourself at home."

"Your family are all so lovely," she remarked, looking up at him.

He had his hand on the door and looked suddenly unsure of himself. "I'm sorry about the plane, by the way. I was kind of rude."

"A little," she said with a hint of a smile. "But it's okay."

"I'm blaming it on jet lag."

"And the fact that I drove you crazy with my inability to stop talking?"

His eyes twinkled. "Maybe a bit of that." He wished her goodnight and slipped out of the room.

Feeling suddenly exhausted, she rummaged in her case for her pyjamas and got ready for bed. As she snuggled into the fresh bedding, she decided all she could do was put the less-than-spectacular reunion behind her and hope tomorrow was a better day.

~

After sleeping for almost twelve hours straight, Jago still woke feeling groggy. He was mid-yawn when he entered the kitchen to find his mum and Sylvie drinking coffee at the table.

"We're all a bit slow this morning," his mum remarked. "You two can blame it on your travelling yesterday, but I've got no excuse."

"Have you got plans for today?" he asked, making a beeline for the coffee pot.

"I've got a changeover at Kensa, so I need to go and give it a clean before the new guests arrive."

"Kensa?" Sylvie asked.

"One of the holiday cottages I rent out," Mirren explained.

"Kensa is the Cornish word for first," Jago added, taking his coffee and leaning against the counter. "The cottages are imaginatively named first, second, third and fourth, but in Cornish."

"How do you say the rest of them?" she asked, a sparkle of delight in her eyes.

"Kensa, Nessa, Tressa, Peswera."

She beamed. "Your accent just changed."

"Did it?"

"You have an American lilt, but it disappeared then entirely." The warmth of her smile stirred something in the depths of his stomach. Feeling self-conscious under the weight of her gaze, Jago turned to look out of the window. A couple of gulls wheeled on the wind beyond the rocky shore. The sight stirred something else in him – a pang of peacefulness and home.

"So you have four holiday cottages that you rent out?" Sylvie asked his mum.

She shook her head as she swallowed a mouthful of coffee. "I rent out two cottages. The other two belong to Noah and Trystan. They live in them."

Sylvie cradled her mug at her chest. "You've got your family nice and close."

"Except for this one." Mirren tilted her head in Jago's direction.

"How long have you lived in America?" Sylvie asked.

"Six years now," he said, then remembered that technically he didn't live there any more. He needed to break that news to his family at some point but would like to have some firm plans in place first, so he didn't have to listen to his mum trying to convince him to move back to St Mary's.

"Do you like America?" Sylvie asked.

"Yeah." He shrugged, not entirely sure that was the truth. "I'm used to it."

She paused for a moment before changing the subject. "I thought I might go over to Bryher today. I had a message from Lowen asking if I wanted to grab breakfast with him in Hugh Town before he went to work, but I was still asleep when it came. I'd like to see Bryher and his studio anyway. It's not far, is it?"

"No," his mum said. "Twenty minutes on the boat and then a short walk across the island. It's beautiful over there. You should definitely make the trip." She turned in her chair to look at Jago. "Are you going over to help Lowen with the painting?"

"I hadn't planned on it." Lowen hadn't specifically asked him to, so he didn't feel obliged. Plus, he wasn't sure he wanted to brave the boat trip.

"You should," his mum said firmly. "That way you can show Sylvie how to get there."

"I'm not even sure I know how to get there myself," he said, only half joking.

"It will all come back to you."

"I'm sure I'll manage without a tour guide," Sylvie said. "Don't feel you have to come on my account."

Suddenly, it didn't seem like a bad idea. "I actually wouldn't mind going over there." It wasn't as though he had any other plans for the day, and visiting Lowen felt more manageable with Sylvie along as a buffer.

"You've missed the morning boat," his mum told them. "You'll either need to wait a few hours or take our boat. Depends if you think you can manage it …"

"We can take your boat," Jago said with a sudden desire to prove a point – to who he wasn't quite sure. Maybe himself. He was Scillonian and ought to be able to pilot a boat between the islands.

His mum smirked. "Try not to embarrass yourself in front of Sylvie."

"Mum!" He gritted his teeth as he crossed the kitchen. "I was seven years old. Can we please let it go!"

"Sorry," she said, sounding entirely insincere.

Sylvie had missed that conversation the previous evening and looked confused now, but he wasn't inclined to fill her in.

"I'll jump in the shower," he told her. "After that, I'm ready when you are."

CHAPTER SEVEN

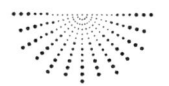

Fifteen minutes later, they walked down to the garage at the end of the lane. It was in pretty much the exact same state as it had been when Jago was a kid, filled with an assortment of bikes and boats, old fishing tackle and a bunch of sand toys and extra garden furniture.

"Motorboat or sailboat?" Sylvie asked, as she surveyed the chaos with him.

"Motor," he said.

"I always like the idea of proper sailing. With the wind filling the sail and everything quiet and peaceful."

"The sailboat was my dad's," he told her, only letting his gaze linger on it for a moment.

"What happened to him?" she asked gently.

"He died," Jago said, confused by the question, since he assumed she'd know that.

She sank her teeth into her bottom lip. "I'm sorry."

"Didn't you know?"

"No. I kind of guessed when he wasn't there last night, but it didn't feel appropriate to ask. What happened to him?"

Jago inhaled deeply before tilting his chin in the direction of the sailboat in the corner. "He went out sailing one day and didn't come back." He twisted his lips to one side. "He was always out sailing. Knew what he was doing. So you'd think he would've been safe." He shrugged. "At least he died doing what he loved."

Sylvie's eyes widened but she didn't say anything.

"Are you sure you still want to get in a boat with me?" he joked, attempting to bring the light back to her eyes but failing miserably.

Her features were filled with sympathy. "How long ago did he die?"

"Three years," he said quietly, then corrected himself: "Three and a half."

"I'm sorry," she said again.

His shoulders hitched in another shrug. "Shit happens."

He stepped towards the boat, desperate to steer the conversation away from his dad. Taking hold of the front of the trailer, he tipped it onto the wheels and began to manoeuvre it out of the garage.

"Should I do something?" Sylvie asked when she finally snapped out of her trance.

"Sure. Put a hand on the back of the boat and help me steer it."

They'd just made it to the sand when Sylvie shot him a puzzled look. "I don't feel as though I'm helping."

He failed to rein in his smile. "You're not. I was just trying to make you feel useful."

Removing her hand from the boat, she propped it on her hip and glared at him.

"What?" He laughed as he continued towards the shore. "Come on. Take your shoes off. I'll definitely need your help getting it into the water."

"Well now I don't believe anything you say," she told him, following reluctantly.

He laughed again. "You think I'm lying about having to take your shoes and socks off to get the boat into the water?"

"I don't know, because I don't trust you any more."

"In that case you're welcome to keep your shoes and socks on. I just hope you don't mind them getting wet." Stopping at the waterline, he removed his shoes and socks and dropped them into the boat then rolled up the legs of his jeans before continuing to push the trailer out into the water. Only when he'd floated the boat off the trailer did Sylvie finally remove her shoes and socks.

"Hang on to the boat," he instructed when she waded out to him, gasping at the cold as she went. As he took the trailer back up the beach, the wet sand under his feet felt therapeutic, and the fine sea spray on his face rejuvenating. "Get in," he told Sylvie, splashing back out through the small waves.

She stared down at the boat. "How?"

A smile tugged at his lips as he realised he'd managed to find someone who was even less adept at boating than he was. "Step, hop, jump … However you like, really."

With a look of scepticism, she pushed down on the taut, inflated rubber that made up the edge of the boat. "I feel as though it might flip over."

"It won't." He placed a hand beside hers and held the boat steady against the motion of the water. "I promise."

"I'm not sure what your promises are worth," she stated, her nose wrinkling as she frowned.

He waited a moment, but when she didn't move he slipped an arm around her waist and lifted her easily from the water and into the boat.

She grinned as she settled herself on the bench seat. "It seems as though there's a gentleman under that buff exterior."

"Don't tell anyone," he said conspiratorially as he walked the boat out a little deeper. Once he'd hopped in and sat beside the tiller, his eyes locked with hers. "Did you just call me *buff*?"

Her cheeks heated adorably. "I think I said gruff."

"I'm fairly sure you said buff." He pulled his shoulders back to push his chest out.

She rolled her eyes. "*Gruff,*" she insisted. "Definitely gruff."

His smile stretched wide as he handed her a life jacket, then he slipped his arms into his own. He pulled sharply on the cord to start the engine. He'd probably been about fifteen years old the last time he'd succumbed to peer pressure and been out on a boat, but it all came back to him as he manoeuvred out of the bay.

After a few minutes, Sylvie's silence began to unsettle him. "Have I embarrassed you?" he asked. "I've never known you go this long without speaking before." Admittedly he'd only met her the previous day, but he got the impression it was out of character for her to stay quiet for so long.

A subtle smile pulled at her lips. "I was taking in the scenery."

He couldn't help himself – he puffed his chest up once again. "I suppose no one can blame you for that. Just don't stare too much or things might get awkward."

She extended her leg and kicked his foot. "I said *gruff,* not buff!"

"I think we both know you're lying."

Her eyes flashed with mock irritation. "I was looking at the view. It's beautiful."

He looked down at himself with a smirk. "Thank you."

She laughed loudly. "Stop it! I mean the beach and the waves and the boats and the rocks."

"Your face is all flushed. I wouldn't have pegged you as someone who'd be so easily embarrassed."

"I'm not embarrassed." She tilted her head. "Speaking of embarrassment, what happened when you were seven?"

He shifted his gaze to the horizon and pulled the tiller towards his body, hoping to look as though he was concentrating on what he was doing.

She kicked his foot again. "Now who's looking flushed? It seems as though I've touched a nerve."

Ignoring her, he kept his focus on the horizon.

"Tell me," she said in a silly singsong voice that should have been like nails down a blackboard but somehow had his mouth curling to a smile.

"I am somewhat prone to seasickness," he finally told her. "Which isn't exactly fun when you grow up on an archipelago. When I was a kid, most of the social events revolved around boating."

Her brows drew together, but amusement danced in her eyes. "I'm assuming there was a particular incident when you were seven?"

He sighed. "I was in a boat race in the harbour, and I vomited over the side of the boat."

"Okay," she said slowly. "Your family has a very low bar for embarrassing stories."

He stretched his neck before he continued. "Some other kids fell in the water and ended up swimming in my vomit."

Her lips pressed together and a small snort erupted from her nose.

"I appreciate your attempt not to laugh, but you realise you just made a noise like a pig?"

"I know," she said, then laughed properly. "It's funny! *You,* I mean, not my pig impression."

"My mum thinks so too. I reckon it's her favourite story."

The wind snatched at Sylvie's hair and she captured it to tie it in a messy bun. "Do you know what's disturbing about that story?"

"Kids swimming in vomit?"

"Well *that* obviously, but also that your mum put you in a boat race when she knew you got seasick."

"It was my dad," he admitted, feeling almost treacherous for saying it. "He was the one who was into boating. It wasn't that he pushed me into it, but I always wanted to make him proud. I wanted to love the thing that he loved." A lump lodged itself in his throat, and he pushed his hair off his face while doggedly avoiding eye contact.

There was only a short lull in the conversation before Sylvie spoke again.

"Do you reckon the kids who swam in your vomit can laugh about it yet? I'm wondering if they ever managed to swim again or if they were scarred for life."

"I may have cost them a fortune in therapy," he joked, grateful to her for lightening the atmosphere. "Especially if their family members insist on raising the subject at every family gathering like mine do."

"Surely you can laugh about it now?" Sylvie asked. "It must've been ... what... thirty years ago?"

"Something like that." He probably should be able to laugh about it by now. He wasn't sure why he always got so wound up when it was mentioned. "I don't think I'll ever be able to laugh about it," he confided. "Even though objectively I can see it's pretty funny."

He only managed to hold eye contact with her for a moment, then looked away. A flash of white caught his eye on a rocky outcrop and he slowed the boat before cutting the engine.

"What's wrong?" Sylvie asked.

He pointed to the rocks. "Seals."

"Is that a baby?" Her eyes widened as she leaned on the edge of the boat.

"Yes."

"It's so fluffy and cute." She took her phone from her pocket. "I read that there are seals around the islands, but somehow I didn't think they'd be that easy to spot."

"Scilly has the largest population of Atlantic seals in the UK. They're everywhere."

She concentrated on taking a bunch of photos while murmuring about how gorgeous they were. For the next ten minutes they rocked on the gentle waves, chatting quietly while watching the mother and pup.

"How are you feeling?" Sylvie asked, as they continued on to the concrete jetty on the eastern side of Bryher.

"Good." He felt his brow wrinkle. "Why?"

"You grew out of the seasickness?"

"I guess I did." He hadn't even thought about it. "It's a long time since I've been on a boat, so I wasn't sure. But I feel fine."

"That's good. At least there are some positives about getting older."

"There's a small chance I was just too distracted by you wittering away."

She beamed. "I'm happy to find someone who views my talkativeness as a positive."

"I'm not sure that's what I said. I think realistically you just found someone who can listen to your endless chatter without wanting to vomit."

"Well, now *you're* being mean." They grinned at each other before he focused on bringing the boat up beside the quay.

The realisation that he no longer suffered from seasickness kept him smiling, along with no small amount of pride at how expertly he managed to bring the boat up beside the jetty. He jumped out and tied up, then offered Sylvie his hand to help her out of the boat. The warmth of her fingers against his made his stomach flutter. He would have put it down to hunger, if it weren't for the fact that when his eyes met hers, he could have sworn she'd felt the same.

Reluctantly, he released her hand. "Welcome to the famous Anneka Quay."

"Famous?" she asked with a sceptical hitch of her eyebrow.

"Anneka Rice built it."

"No way." She gasped. "Are you serious? This was built on Challenge Anneka?"

"Yes. Her and her team of helpers." He'd been very young when the popular TV show was filmed back in the early 90s, but he still remembered the buzz of excitement on the island.

"I'm not sure I believe you."

He barked out a laugh. "And I'm not sure why you have me down as a liar."

"Because you lied earlier about me helping with the boat."

"That wasn't a lie, it was a joke."

"Fine," she huffed. "How do I know you're not joking about Challenge Anneka?"

"Ask anyone," he said, grinning at her. "Or look it up on the internet!"

"Now I really think you're joking because you're laughing so much."

"I'm laughing at how untrusting you are! Go on, look it up. I promise I'm not lying."

With a gentle shake of the head, she pulled her phone from her pocket, then rolled her eyes when she looked at the screen. "I don't have any signal. But I guess you already knew that."

Now he was really laughing. "I swear to you, it's true." He looked along the quay to where an older man in a wax jacket walked along with a fishing rod in his hand. "Let's ask that guy. He'll back me up."

"No." She sighed. "Don't drag some poor passer-by into this."

"We're asking him," Jago insisted, striding along the quay.

"Don't ask him." Sylvie snatched at his arm in a futile attempt to stop him. "He's going to think we're complete nutters."

"Only if I was lying to you. Which I wasn't. Excuse me!" he shouted to the man as they neared him.

"I don't know anything about birds," he called out with a dismissive flick of his hand. "If that's what you're after, I can't help you."

"We're not birdwatchers," Jago replied, amused. "We were wondering if you know why the jetty is called Anneka's Quay?"

"*That* I can help you with." He took steps towards them, his features brightening. "You're old enough to remember Challenge Anneka, aren't you? The TV show?"

"We are," Jago proclaimed, shooting a smug smile in Sylvie's direction.

"The quay was built for a challenge on her TV show," he said, then stabbed the end of his fishing rod into the sand and folded his arms across his chest. "I was here for all of it," he told them proudly. "My dad even lent his tractor to help with unloading the timber. Originally it was made from wood, you see, not concrete like it is now ..."

When Jago caught Sylvie's eye he felt like a schoolchild trying not to laugh in class. Focusing on the man and his story, he nodded politely and decided he should avoid looking at Sylvie entirely.

CHAPTER EIGHT

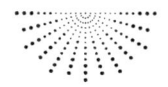

It was twenty minutes before they managed to extricate themselves from the conversation with the fisherman. By then, the effort of holding in laughter was painful. It was Sylvie who cracked first, the laughter bursting out of her in an indelicate snort as soon as they were out of the man's hearing. Jago wanted to comment on her pig-like noise, but it turned out he couldn't speak for laughing.

"I told you not to ask him," Sylvie said. "Why didn't you listen to me?"

"I really wish I had done." He pressed a hand to his side as he struggled to calm himself down. "I thought we were never going to get away."

"How long were we there for?" Sylvie asked.

"A very long time." He dipped his head and ruffled his hair. "Have I gone grey? I feel as though I've probably visibly aged."

"That was hilarious," Sylvie said.

"I knew as soon as I saw the glint in his eye when I asked about the quay that I'd made a mistake. No one should be that excited by a concrete jetty."

"Bless him. He was very sweet, really."

"For the first three minutes, maybe," Jago agreed.

"I'm hungry," Sylvie remarked.

"You read my mind."

"Can we stop off at the fudge place?"

"What fudge place?"

"There's a stand that sells fudge. Outside a farm, I think. I read about it when I was researching Bryher. There's an honesty box that you leave the money in."

I have no idea what you're talking about."

"Do you even know the way to Lowen's place?" Sylvie asked.

"Yes." He inhaled deeply as the wind picked up, rustling the hedges beside the lane. "Although I've not been here while Lowen's had the pottery studio."

"How long has he had it?"

"Since he got the inheritance from your grandparents. How long is that?"

"Five years?" She shrugged. "Six?"

"He used the inheritance to buy the studio and the house beside it." The previous evening's conversation came back to him and he shook his head. "At least that's what I always thought."

"If he didn't buy it with the inheritance money, how did he afford it?"

"I guess he had money saved." Jago considered it. "He always kept his cards close to his chest when it came to money. He had a good job though – investment banking – and I think he made some good investments on the stock market."

"That makes sense. He was always pretty interested in Grandpa's businesses when he was a teenager. He taught him about the stock market. It was their only common ground."

"I didn't know that," Jago said. "Although it seems there's a lot I didn't know about my big brother."

"Did you really not know he hadn't kept any of the inheritance for himself?"

"I had no idea until yesterday." He pushed his hands into his pockets and kicked a small stone, sending it tumbling along the lane ahead of them.

"Maybe he was worried you wouldn't take it if you knew."

"If that's the case, he sorely misjudged me."

"You were lucky to have benefited from their wealth without ever having to meet them."

"You make them sound awful," Jago said. "But Lowen had a great time going on all those fancy holidays. I was always a bit jealous."

Sylvie stared at him, her expression unreadable.

"What?" he asked when she continued to silently search his features.

"I just ... It wasn't ... I mean ..." She looked away. "Never mind."

"What?" he asked again, the serious set of her features unnerving him.

"Nothing," she said firmly. The smile returned to her face when she pulled her phone from her pocket. "I have a signal now. I'll look up the fudge place."

"What are you going to search for?" he teased. "I'm not sure searching for 'fudge' on the map is going to be overly helpful."

"Then you'd be wrong." She tilted the phone in his direction, a smug glint in her eyes. "We're on the right path. It's just up ahead."

A few minutes later, they were chewing on delicious homemade fudge by a stand outside a flower farm.

Jago popped a second piece in his mouth. "I learnt something new today."

"It's slightly ironic that I'm teaching *you* things about the islands," Sylvie said.

"I'm happy to let you be my tour guide."

"You can lead the way from here." She took another piece of fudge. "I'm too busy enjoying the fudge to get my phone out again."

"We came over to Bryher a lot as kids," Jago told her as they ambled on at a slow pace. "One of Mum's best friends owns the hotel over here, so we used to visit her regularly. Maddie would always give us Coke and chips." He pointed at the hotel looming in the distance. "There it is. Maybe we can grab food there later. I wouldn't mind having a look around. Apparently Maddie put a lot of work into it in the last few years. Mum's always raving about how lovely it is."

"Coke and chips sound good to me," Sylvie remarked, then pushed the stray strands of hair from her forehead as she stopped to look out at the view.

"The pottery studio is down there between the sand dunes," Jago told her. "You can just about make out the roof of it." He stretched his arm out, pointing a little further along. "That's Lowen's house."

"I remember Lowen used to work in a pottery studio when he was younger," Sylvie said as they set off walking again. "But I was shocked to find out he bought his own studio and was selling his stuff. I always thought it was a hobby. The pieces in his online shop are stunning."

"He bought the studio from the couple he used to work for," Jago explained. "They were retiring and moving to the mainland to be close to their kids. I suspect Lowen got the place for a bargain."

"I can't imagine living somewhere like this." Sylvie looked up at a couple of terns screeching overhead as they glided on the gusty winds. "It's absolutely stunning."

"It is," Jago agreed softly. The views which had been so familiar growing up, looked different now, after so much time surrounded by skyscrapers in New York.

"Have you always lived in London?" he asked, realising he knew very little about her. He wasn't even sure that she *did* live in London but had that in his head for some reason.

"I grew up in Cambridge but I've spent a lot of time living in the north ... Manchester."

"But you live in London now?"

"I've never lived in London. I'm currently living with my mum back in Cambridge."

"Is your dad around?"

"My parents split up when I was at university. I see Dad now and again but we're not close."

They reached the beach and stopped to remove their shoes and socks.

"It's on my bucket list to live by the sea someday," Sylvie said. "But I suspect it's one of those things that will never happen."

"It's probably overrated anyway," he told her. "You'd start to take it for granted pretty quickly."

"I wouldn't," she said adamantly.

"All right," he said with a mocking eye roll. "I was only trying to make you feel better about the fact that you're never going to live beside the sea."

"Hey!" She scowled at him. "I might."

"Nobody actually gets around to their bucket list items."

"What's on your list?" she asked.

He was saved from having to answer by their arrival at the pottery studio. "Oh look," he said with a cheeky grin. "We're here." He pushed open the door, making the bell tinkle.

"Wow," Sylvie whispered as she stepped inside. She drifted towards the nearest shelves and Jago followed. They remained silent as their eyes travelled over his brother's creations.

"Hi," a chirpy voice said. A teenage girl walked out from the back room. "Feel free to browse. Give me a shout if you have any questions." She moved behind the counter and Jago didn't have a chance to say anything before she spoke again. "Have you had any luck spotting any interesting birds?"

Jago beamed. "Just this one next to me that can't stop chirping away." Immediately, Sylvie's hand shot out and lightly connected with his stomach.

"Joking!" he said, chuckling as he took a defensive step away from her. He turned back to the girl. "We're not birdwatchers. Though I may have to reconsider my clothing choices, because you're not the first person to think that today."

She laughed. "You didn't actually look the type. But it seems as though they're the only customers we've had in the past week, so I'm getting quite good at conversations about birds."

"I'm actually looking for my brother – Lowen."

"You're Jago?" She came around the counter towards them. "Now that you say it, it's obvious you're a Treneary. I'm Mia," she said brightly.

"I thought Lowen worked alone," Jago said once Sylvie had introduced herself.

"I just started working here in the summer," Mia said.

"I remember now." Jago recalled a phone conversation with his mum. "You're related to someone, right? Pippa?"

"She's my aunt. I was supposed to be staying with her for the summer, but now I'm staying for a year."

"I can see how that might happen," Sylvie said. "It's beautiful here."

Jago narrowed his eyes. "What's it like working for my brother?"

"I like it," she said with a mischievous smile. "It's good fun to wind him up."

"I guess that would be quite enjoyable," Jago remarked. "Is he around?"

"No." She checked her phone. "But I'm expecting him to turn up any minute now. He's at his place if you want to go up there. Or you can have a nosy in his workshop while you wait for him if you want?"

"I'd like to see his workshop," Sylvie said.

Mia held out an arm, gesturing to the archway at the back of the room, but they'd barely taken a step when the door swung open, the bell twinkling loudly.

"What's the emergency?" Lowen said loudly, before registering the presence of Jago and Sylvie. "Oh hey," he said, adopting a gentler tone. He moved to Sylvie and kissed her cheek. "I wasn't expecting you since you missed the morning boat."

"I brought Mum's boat over," Jago told him.

Lowen's eyebrows shot up. "And you managed without vomiting?"

"Yep," Jago said, his jaw clenching.

"This place is amazing," Sylvie said, seeming to notice Jago's irritation.

"Thank you," Lowen replied.

Beside him, Mia cleared her throat and glared at him.

"*What?*" he asked. "Can't you let me take the credit for my own studio?"

"The place was an absolute state when I got here," she told them. "I have no idea how he managed to keep a business running before I came along."

Lowen rolled his eyes. "It wasn't that bad."

"It was," she said cockily.

Ignoring her, Lowen looked to Jago. "Do you want to come up to the house and help with painting? Trystan and Kit are there."

"I need you here," Mia complained. "That's why I messaged you."

"What do you need me for?"

"I told you first thing that you need to get a batch in the kiln today, and you went off home without doing anything about it."

"I'll do it later."

"When? You need to fire two batches in the next week, which means you need to get one in now. We need more pieces with birds ready for the market next weekend."

"You could have loaded up the kiln yourself," he told her, while Jago watched their back and forth with interest. The pair of them sounded more like an old married couple than employer and employee.

"I *could* have done, but the last time I did that you told me off for loading it wrong."

Lowen let out a low growl as his phone began to buzz in his pocket. "One second," he said to no one in particular. "What's up?" he asked into the phone, then squeezed his eyes shut before pacing away from them. "I just told you which paint." He sighed heavily. "Ask Trystan, he'll know. Mia needs me for something. And Sylvie and Jago are here now too." He shook his head. "Okay. I'll come back up and have a look. Hang on." He ended the call and slipped the phone back into his pocket. "Kit needs me back at the house," he told Mia. "Can you please load the kiln and set it running?"

"Only if you promise not to be grumpy with me if I put a mug in at slightly the wrong angle."

"It wasn't because you put something at the wrong angle ..." He trailed off as though he couldn't be bothered with the conversation. "Please just do it. It'll be fine."

Mia sashayed towards the open archway at the back of the room. "Thank you, Mia," she said mockingly.

Lowen lifted his chin as he shouted after her. "As I recall, it was you who insisted we sign up for the craft fair, which created a load more work for us."

"It will also bring us a load of money," she shouted back before she disappeared.

"Sorry," Lowen said, turning his attention to Sylvie and Jago. "Do you want to come up and have a look around the house?"

"Fine by me," Sylvie said, but Jago caught the longing in her eyes when she glanced at the room that Mia had gone into.

He contemplated suggesting Sylvie might like a tour of the pottery studio first, but given how stressed Lowen seemed he decided to let it go.

Up at the house, Jago was surprised at how rundown it was. The renovations were definitely necessary. Lowen gave them a quick tour, but with the furniture gathered in the centre of each room and covered in drapes, there wasn't much to see. The pungent stench of paint in the air was overwhelming, so they didn't linger inside for long but gravitated out to the patio with its gorgeous view of the beach and the Atlantic.

Trystan and Kit joined them for a coffee break and they settled themselves on weather-beaten wooden chairs around the slatted table.

"It's kind of weird that you're Lowen's cousin and not ours." Kit looked over his mug at Sylvie. "Are there any more long-lost relatives?"

"Just me and my parents I think."

"So you're first cousins?" Kit asked.

"Yes." She looked to Lowen, a nervous smile playing on her lips. "My dad and Lowen's mum were brother and sister."

"Birth mother," Lowen corrected her, an air of irritation to his tone.

"Yes." Sylvie shifted in her chair. "That's what I meant."

Kit took a swig of his coffee, then set his mug down. "Did you get to go on fancy holidays with your grandparents too?"

"Yeah." Swallowing hard, Sylvie looked searchingly at Lowen. "We went on lots of holidays together."

"What time do you need to be at work?" Lowen asked Kit.

"That sounds like a subtle hint for me to stop gassing and finish off the spare room." Standing, Kit checked his watch. "I'll need to leave in half an hour or so."

Trystan stood to follow Kit inside. "I'll head back when you do. I promised Beth I wouldn't be out all day."

"I will never get over this view," Sylvie said, leaning back in her chair. The light caught her hair, highlighting the rich auburn tones.

Lowen stared at her while she closed her eyes into the sun.

"I might wander over and see if Maddie is around," Jago said, suddenly feeling like a third wheel. "I fancy having a look around the hotel at the changes she's made."

"The food is great," Lowen said, shifting his gaze abruptly away from Sylvie and looking slightly dazed, as though he'd been lost in a daydream. Quickly, his features tensed and he pulled his phone from his pocket and began tapping on the screen. "You should have lunch at the hotel. The view from the restaurant is even better than here."

Jago tapped his thumb on the armrest of his chair. "I thought you guys might want some time to catch up."

Glancing up from his phone, Lowen offered Sylvie a tight smile. "Sorry. You arrived at a crazy time. I'd never have started renovating my place this week if I'd realised Mia was going to sign us up for a craft fair next weekend."

"It's fine," she said, but the hurt was evident in her eyes. "If you've got too much on today I can see you tomorrow, or Monday. I'm not in a massive rush to get home. As long as your mum isn't in a hurry to get rid of me," she added.

"How about you guys head up to the hotel and I'll join you once Trystan and Kit leave? I'd feel bad leaving them to get on with all the work here."

Jago felt like pointing out that since he hadn't seen his cousin in years he didn't think Trystan or Kit would mind but held his tongue.

"Fine by me," Sylvie said, with what Jago suspected was fake positivity. He smiled when she looked questioningly at him.

"It's good for me," he said. "I'm starving."

On the short walk to the hotel, Sylvie kept up a steady stream of chatter about the scenery and the wildlife, but for the first time the conversation felt unnatural and forced. Jago suspected Sylvie was feeling slightly rejected by how cool Lowen had been towards her.

It was tempting to say something, but given the way Sylvie didn't pause for breath on the way to the hotel, he was sure she wouldn't thank him for raising the subject. Besides, he was probably reading too much into his brother's behaviour.

CHAPTER NINE

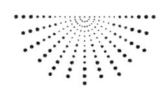

Even with the renovations to the hotel, walking back in there felt like stepping back into Jago's childhood. Especially when he caught sight of Maddie behind the bar. Her face lit up when she spotted him.

"This is a treat," she said, embracing him tightly. "I get a visit on your first day back."

When she didn't let him go, Jago spoke into her shoulder. "You're always top of my list of people to visit."

"Such a charmer," she said, gazing at him fondly as she relaxed her hold on him. "I'm guessing you were visiting Lowen and I was an afterthought."

"Never," he said, giving her arm a squeeze.

Surprise flashed in her eyes when she registered Sylvie. "Your mum didn't mention you were bringing someone back with you."

"Oh," Sylvie said quickly. "We're not together. I mean we're together in that we're both here … but we only met yesterday so we're not *together* together."

"The more emphatic you are about that," Jago said, "the more people will wonder why."

Sylvie shot him a look of mock contempt. "I'm Sylvie," she said, offering her hand to Maddie. "Lowen's cousin."

"Lowen's cousin?" Maddie asked, the slow question radiating confusion.

"Just Lowen's cousin," Jago told her. "Not mine. We're not related."

Sylvie raised an eyebrow. "You know, the more emphatic you are about that, the more people will wonder why."

He shook his head, hoping his cheeks weren't betraying him by flushing bright red. "Sylvie is related to Lowen through his birth mother."

"Ah." Maddie's eyes rolled towards the ceiling. "Of course. Now I understand. We haven't seen you on Scilly before, have we?"

"It's my first visit," Sylvie told Maddie. "I lost touch with Lowen but decided it was about time for a catch-up."

Maddie patted her arm. "I bet you'll love Scilly. How long are you staying?"

"Probably a few days. I don't have a firm plan."

Jago glanced around the almost empty restaurant. "This place is pretty much unrecognisable from the last time I was here."

"You shouldn't have left it so long, should you?" Maddie teased. When she leaned into him, he put an arm around her for a side hug.

"Are you going to show us around first or feed us?"

"I'd love to show you around but the hotel's fully booked. You'll have to come back in a couple of weeks when things are quieter. I can feed you though." She took their drink order, then directed them to a table by the panoramic window to browse the menu.

They gave Lowen half an hour, then gave up and ordered food without him. While they chatted, Sylvie glanced repeatedly out of the window. The view over the bay was breath-taking, but Jago had the feeling she was looking out for Lowen.

He still hadn't arrived by the time they finished eating.

"I guess Lowen got caught up at the house," Jago said gently, when Sylvie checked her watch. "Or work, maybe."

"It seemed as though he was a bit snowed under." Her eyes flicked to the door when it burst open. Lowen smiled at her as he strode across the room.

"Sorry," he said, taking the chair beside her. "Mia insisted I check what she'd put in the kiln before she turned it on. Good that you didn't wait for me to eat."

"It seems as though you've got a lot on your plate at the moment," Sylvie said.

He brushed his hands down the front of his paint-splattered T-shirt. "It's all a bit hectic this week."

"I can help out with the house if you want," Jago offered.

He waved a hand dismissively. "Don't worry. You're probably jet-lagged. The last thing you'll want to do is redecorate my house."

"I don't mind."

"You must have lots to catch up on too. Have you got much planned for while you're here?"

"Not really." Jago had lost touch with most of his old friends, so it was only his family to catch up with. And since they all had their lives to get on with, he supposed he was going to have a lot of free time.

"It'll be nice for you to chill out and have a holiday," Lowen remarked, making Jago adopt a slow nod of agreement, while privately thinking he was on holiday indefinitely until he found a new job. "When was the last time you had a proper break?"

"I can't even remember," Jago said truthfully. He felt as though he'd spent the last few years running on a hamster wheel and getting nowhere.

"Do you know how long you'll stay for?" Lowen asked Sylvie, the question feeling slightly loaded, as though he was forcing himself to sound casual.

"My only plan was to catch up with you," she said with a crooked smile.

"It's really good to see you again." A flash of genuine warmth hit his features but faded quickly when his phone buzzed on the table. He swore lightly as he read a message. "Mia thinks the kiln is broken."

"That doesn't sound good," Sylvie said.

"It can be a bit temperamental. Hopefully it's a user error and not that it's finally packed up."

"Do you need to go and sort it out?" she asked. "If it's easier we can do something tomorrow."

"That would be great," Lowen said, resting a hand on her upper arm. "If you don't mind? I feel bad for ditching you."

"I'm not sure it's possible for you to ditch me considering I turned up unexpectedly."

"I really want to hang out." Standing, he smiled at Sylvie, then patted Jago's shoulder. "We need to catch up properly too."

"Plenty of time," Jago replied.

∼

The trip to Bryher had been perfectly pleasant thanks to Jago. Walking back across the beautiful island, he managed to rival Sylvie with his ability to keep up a stream of inane conversation. She suspected he was doing it on purpose to make up for how aloof Lowen had been with her.

On the boat ride back to St Mary's she contemplated how wrong she'd been with her expectations for the trip to the Scillies. After the recent emails from Mirren, with her insistence that Lowen wanted to be in touch again, she'd genuinely expected a warmer welcome. So far, the person who seemed happiest at her presence was Jago, who wasn't at all how she'd imagined him from Lowen's descriptions. Having said that, the version of him she had in her head was a cocky, obnoxious teenager, so it was more than a little outdated.

The wind whipped wisps of hair around her face and she pulled a strand from the corner of her mouth, taking a moment to sweep her gaze over Jago while he wasn't looking. There was nothing of the teenager left in him. His grey hoodie emphasised his broad shoulders and chest, while the pushed-back sleeves revealed his toned forearms.

"Checking out the scenery again?"

She winced at having been caught out. "Lost in a daydream," she said, blinking a couple of times for effect.

"Daydream or sexual fantasy?" he asked with a hint of a grin.

"Daydream!" she blurted out, shocked by how forward he was. "I was thinking about something else and happened to be looking in your direction. I was staring into space, not …" She caught his smirk and cracked up laughing. "You're such a tease!"

"Just promise not to get mad at me later when you catch me staring at your chest and I claim I'm staring into space and your boobs happen to be in the way."

She tried to look indignant but failed. "Is this as fast as this boat will go?" she said, looking for a distraction.

"I don't think so. I was just taking it slow to give you time to enjoy the scenery." He winked before increasing the speed.

Sylvie turned into the wind, her smile stretching wide as they bounced over the waves. They arrived back at Old Town Bay before she knew it and kept up a steady stream of banter while they put the boat away. Her smile was beginning to make her cheeks ache when they walked into the kitchen. Mirren was sitting at the table with her phone in her hand.

"Did you have a good time?" she asked.

"Yes," Sylvie replied, choosing to think about the trip overall, rather than Lowen's somewhat cool reception. "Bryher is gorgeous. And Lowen's place is amazing."

"It must be good for you and him to reconnect after so long."

Sylvie took a seat at the end of the table. "We didn't get

much time to chat. He's in the thick of it with so much going on at work and with the renovations on his house." Swallowing her emotions, she made a point of not looking in Jago's direction, sure that all she would find was sympathy in his features.

"It's a busy time for him," Mirren said softly. "It's good for him to be busy though. Mia's given things a shake-up with his business. I presume you met her?"

Jago leaned casually against the sideboard. "The girl working in his studio?"

"She's a sweetheart," Mirren remarked.

"They bicker like an old married couple," Jago said.

"They do." Mirren chuckled. "They have a sweet relationship. She's brought him out of himself these last few months. Pippa too." Mirren's phone lit up and she reached for it, then looked guiltily at Sylvie. "I emailed your mum this morning, telling her how lovely it is to have you here. We swapped numbers and have been messaging away. She was saying you're between jobs?" Her eyes widened and she grimaced. "That sounds as though we've been gossiping about you, doesn't it?"

"No," Sylvie said lightly. "It's fine."

"She's being polite," Jago put in. "That's exactly what it sounds like."

"It's good that you don't have anything to rush back for," Mirren said, ignoring him. "You can explore the islands and make a holiday of it. Plenty of time for you and Lowen to get to know each other again too."

Sylvie shook her head. "Lowen said he'd have some time tomorrow. I really only planned on staying for a day or two. I already feel uncomfortable about showing up unexpectedly and putting you out."

"You're family," Mirren said, reaching out and placing a hand on Sylvie's forearm. "You're always welcome to turn up unannounced. It's not putting me out. Make yourself at home and stay as long as you want."

"Thank you. That's very kind." Mirren was exactly as Sylvie

had always imagined her – warm, homely and kind. At least that was one thing about her visit which was as she imagined.

Lowen's lukewarm reaction to her being there niggled at her over the course of the evening, and she was thankful that dinner with Mirren and Jago provided some distraction. Later, when she was all tucked up in bed, she fired off a message, telling Lowen again how good it was to see him and how much she was looking forward to seeing him the following day.

There was no reply before she fell asleep and still nothing when she checked her phone when she woke. Squinting at the time on the screen she was surprised to find it was already mid-morning. The sea air must be working its magic. She hadn't stirred all night.

After a leisurely shower there was still no word from Lowen, and she arrived in the kitchen to find Jago and Mirren having a lively conversation punctuated by bursts of laughter.

"Oh, good," Jago said, beaming at Sylvie. "Come and help me explain the difference between a walk and a hike. Apparently Mum's managed to live more than sixty years without having any clue what the difference is."

"Of course I know!" Mirren tutted as she placed a couple of Tupperware boxes into a backpack. "We're going for a hike and a picnic. Would you like to join us?"

"We're actually going for a walk," Jago said, then took a couple of quick steps backwards when his mum glared at him.

"It's a hike! We're going up on the coastal path around the island. That's a hike. A walk is when you have a particular destination in mind. For example, I would walk into town, not hike there. But since I have no particular purpose when I go off around the island, that's a hike."

"That's absolutely not the difference," Jago said, thoroughly amused. "Apart from anything else, you do have a purpose: hanging out with your son and going for a picnic. A hike is more strenuous. I can guarantee there will be nothing strenuous about our little stroll around the island. Plus, if you're going in those shoes, it can't be considered a hike."

"What's wrong with my shoes?" Mirren asked, sticking out a foot to show off her beige loafers.

"There's nothing wrong with them," Jago said. "You just can't go hiking in them." He caught Sylvie's eye and a dimple puckered his cheek. "We're going for a walk, if you'd like to join us."

"It's a hike," Mirren said under her breath.

"It sounds great," Sylvie said, "but I'm waiting for Lowen to get back to me, then I'll go and meet up with him." On cue, her phone vibrated and she lowered herself to a chair as she read the message. "He's busy with the house," she said, trying not to let her disappointment show. "He wants to take me out to the pub tomorrow evening instead."

"For the quiz?" Jago asked.

She looked up at him in confusion.

"It's the pub quiz on Monday nights," Mirren said. "Keira's always trying to get people to go. She's been messaging on the family group this morning trying to get everyone to go tomorrow."

"Oh, right." Sylvie looked at the message again. There was no mention of it being a group event. Not that it really mattered – it'd just be nice to see him.

"You'll have a great time," Mirren said. "The quiz is always fun."

"Are you going?" Sylvie asked her, trying to focus on the conversation and ignore the niggling feeling that Lowen was avoiding spending time alone with her.

"I'm babysitting Ellie. Everyone else should be there though. You're going, aren't you, Jago?"

"Yeah." He nodded slowly and Sylvie forced herself to smile at him.

Mirren lifted her jacket from the coat rack. "If you're not

doing anything with Lowen today, do you want to come on this hike with us?"

"Walk," Jago muttered.

Sylvie thanked Mirren for the offer but declined, not wanting to impose on their time together. She also needed time to herself to get her thoughts in order.

CHAPTER TEN

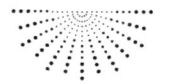

Keira took the quiz night surprisingly seriously. Apparently she'd built up some friendly rivalries with a few locals and was determined to win. On that basis, she picked her team strategically with a mix of ages and interests. It meant Sylvie didn't get to sit with Lowen as she'd hoped. Her team with Jago, Kit and Seren was entertaining nonetheless, especially since Kit was intent on winding Keira up and often gave a wrong answer in a loud whisper for her to overhear.

In the end a group of fishermen at the bar showed them all up, only getting two questions wrong and attaining the highest score in the history of quiz night, earning them some heckling and taunts about cheating.

"Do you want to get going?" Kit asked Seren immediately after the quiz ended.

"Yes." She put a hand over her mouth as she yawned, and her eyes twinkled as she smiled at Jago and Sylvie. "Sorry. I was working a lot over the weekend and was looking forward to an early night tonight until Keira bullied me into coming here again." She raised her voice for the benefit of Keira at the next table.

"I didn't bully you," Keira replied. "I asked you if you

wanted to come. Just admit that you can't stay away from the place."

"It certainly seems that way," Seren admitted, yawning again as she stood and slipped her coat from the back of the chair.

Kit got up too. "You should come on the train sometime while you're here," he said to Jago, looking unsure of himself. "You've never been on it before, have you?"

"No." Jago smiled at him. "I'll definitely come for a ride along one day."

"Great." Kit said a collective goodbye before he and Seren left. Trystan and Beth went home too, and Keira drifted over to the bar to banter with the guys who'd won the quiz. Following a slightly awkward silence, Sylvie and Jago shuffled over to join Lowen and Pippa at their table. Mia had been on their team too but had gone over to sit with her boyfriend and his friends.

"What did you think of the quiz?" Pippa asked.

"I was glad I wasn't on Keira's team," Sylvie said quietly. "I think she'd have been very disappointed by my general knowledge."

Pippa leaned in and lowered her voice. "It's funny how enthusiastic Keira is about the quiz considering how terrible she is at it."

"It's nice that she likes to get everyone together," Jago remarked, then took a long swig of his pint. "It's strange being back here. I swear the pub hasn't changed since we were coming in here as teenagers."

"You're probably right about that," Lowen said, looking around fondly.

"I remember you talking about the Mermaid Inn," Sylvie said. "It almost feels like being on a film set. And meeting your family feels like meeting celebrities after I heard so much about them."

"How come you never came to visit before?" Pippa asked.

"I don't know," Sylvie mused. "We always talked about it, didn't we?"

Lowen's eyebrows twitched together. "Did we?"

"Yes!" She stared at him as she attempted to jog his memory. "You were going to take me swimming with seals, and out on the boat. You wanted to take me to the empty beaches where you could feel like you were stranded on a desert island miles from anywhere."

"I don't recall." Lowen scratched his jaw. "I suppose kids are always planning things that don't actually happen."

"I always thought it *would* happen," Sylvie said sadly.

"I guess if you were always together in school holidays it would have been difficult," Pippa pointed out. "You'd have been in school the rest of the time."

"How come you lost touch?" Jago asked.

Sylvie was about to reply, before realising she was keen to hear Lowen's answer, so looked to him instead.

He seemed to be waiting for Sylvie to reply, but eventually gave a subtle shrug. "There was university ... and then work ... life just got in the way I guess."

Sylvie forced a smile at his vague answer. She was sorely tempted to point out that it wouldn't have been that much effort to stay in touch, but she didn't want to make a scene.

"You're here now, anyway," Pippa said brightly. "Maybe it's even more special because it's been so long coming."

"You might be right," Sylvie said, appreciating the sentiment even though she wasn't sure she agreed with it. It occurred to her that if Lowen had really wanted her there, it would have happened a long time ago.

"How long can you stay for?" Pippa asked. "Hopefully long enough for Lowen to show you all the places he promised."

"I could stay for a few more days ..." Sylvie looked to Lowen for his reaction.

"You should hang around and explore the islands," he said. "Make the most of your trip."

Pippa gave Lowen's arm a nudge. "Can you take some time off and show her around?"

"I'd like to, but with the craft fair next weekend, I'm going to have a busy week."

"That's okay," Sylvie said quickly. "Maybe I could come over to Bryher again and watch you at work."

"I guess you could," he said unenthusiastically. "It's probably more fun for you to do some touristy things though. Make a holiday of it."

Sylvie smiled benignly. It didn't seem worth pointing out that she hadn't come for a holiday.

"Maybe you could stay for the week," Pippa suggested. "Then you could come to the craft fair."

"I should probably get back home before then," Sylvie said, noting the way Lowen was looking anywhere but at her.

"Do you want to head home?" he asked Pippa. "You need to be up early tomorrow."

"Yes, I do." She sat up straighter. "You'll have to come and visit the cafe sometime. Both of you."

"It's on the promenade, right?" Jago asked.

"Yes. I specialise in freshly baked cookies."

"That sounds like a dangerous place," Sylvie said lightly. "I'd love to come and see it."

"Make sure you do," Pippa said, standing when Lowen did.

Watching them leave, Sylvie reflected on how Pippa was far more welcoming than her own cousin. Lowen almost felt like a stranger. Feeling deflated, she declined Jago's offer of another drink. She insisted she was fine walking home alone if he wanted to stay longer, but he seemed happy to leave with her.

The air was crisp outside and Sylvie pulled her jacket tighter around her as they walked through the town. She wasn't sure if it was tiredness or alcohol that had heightened her emotions, but tears stung her eyes and it was an effort to keep them at bay.

"Are you okay?" Jago finally asked.

Discreetly, she caught a teardrop before it fell. "I feel like a bit of an idiot, to be honest."

"Why?"

The lack of surprise in his tone told her he knew exactly what was bothering her.

"I really thought Lowen would be happy to see me. But I feel as though I couldn't have got it more wrong."

"I'm sure Lowen's glad to see you again," Jago said.

Sylvie smiled sadly. "You don't have to try and spare my feelings. It's obvious he's not thrilled to have me here. I just don't understand why."

"Did you see a lot of each other when you were younger?"

"Yes," she snapped.

His head jolted sideways to look at her, surprise evident in his features.

"Sorry," she said, shaking her head. "I thought you would have known that. I saw him almost every school holiday. We were close. Or so I thought."

"He never spoke much about his time with his grandparents," Jago told her. "Apart from bragging about all the cool things he'd done while I'd been stuck at home."

She squinted, confused by the comment.

"It always annoyed me," Jago continued. "He'd arrive home full of stories about all the places he'd been to and all the fun stuff he'd done." The corner of his mouth jerked upwards. "The only good thing was that his grandma always bought him a whole new wardrobe, and quite often she got his size wrong so I'd get new clothes out of it too."

Sylvie stopped dead.

"What's wrong?" Jago asked, turning to her.

"N–nothing," she stammered. "I just ... Never mind." She set off walking again, deciding to keep her thoughts to herself. "Anyway, Lowen and I were close when we were younger. We had this connection ..." She shook her head. "I don't know how to explain it."

"It's a shame you lost touch."

"That's something else I don't understand." She took a deep breath, pushing down her emotions. "At first I really believed it was because he got caught up with university life, then it was his job. Back then I didn't question the fact that he genuinely had a lot going on. He used to reply to emails every now and again, but he shot down any attempt I made to meet up. Mum and I both kept trying to have a relationship with him, but the more time went on, the more it seemed he didn't want it. When he didn't come to my wedding, that was pretty much the final straw. I was sick of him rejecting my attempts to see him."

"How long ago was that?"

"About ten years. I'd hoped I might see him at Grandpa's funeral, but he didn't turn up, the same when Grandma died the following year. I think I pretty much lost all hope of seeing him again." Her chin twitched as her emotions threatened to overwhelm her. "I still thought about him often. When your mum got in touch this summer and said he was keen to hear from me, it felt like such a relief. I guess I was too excited to consider that it might not really be true."

"Mum wouldn't have said anything if Lowen hadn't told her to. At least I can't imagine she would."

"I guess he never expected me to turn up here. Maybe getting in touch was a nice thought, but he's not so keen on the reality of it."

Jago pulled the zip on his jacket higher. "Lowen and I were never close. And it's been so long since I spent any proper time with him that I couldn't even guess at what's going on in his head. But I know from my conversations with Mum and Trystan that Lowen hasn't been doing too well since Dad died. Apparently he fell out with most members of the family. From what I gather, he took himself away to Bryher and hardly saw anyone. I think it's only in the last couple of months that he sorted things out with everyone."

"I wish he'd talk to me," Sylvie said. "I feel as though if I could get some time alone with him I could figure out what's going on. But I get the impression he's avoiding being alone with me."

Jago remained quiet for a few steps before he spoke again. "He's also got a new girlfriend. Maybe Pippa is the jealous type and he's not allowed to be alone with other women."

Sylvie couldn't help but smile. "Pippa doesn't seem like the controlling type. She was even encouraging him to spend time with me. And I hardly think she'd feel threatened by his cousin."

They reached the far side of Hugh Town and left the lights from the houses behind. Pushing his hands into his pockets, Jago jutted his elbow out and Sylvie automatically slipped her arm through his.

"Maybe Lowen is genuinely busy and stressed at the moment with everything he's got going on," Jago said.

"I appreciate your attempts to make me feel better, but I don't think you believe that any more than I do."

"There's only really one way to test the theory." Jago pulled his elbow in, trapping her arm gently beside his body.

"What would that be?" she asked, ignoring the way her heart rate had notched up at his closeness.

"Stay until after his craft fair. With that out of the way, he should have more time. I'm sure he'll want to hang out with you then."

Sylvie wished she had his confidence, but she suspected it wouldn't be the case. She couldn't say the thought of staying wasn't tempting though. Since she was there, it would be a shame not to explore the islands more.

That was the temptation.

It had absolutely nothing to do with the way her heart was beating erratically at the warmth of Jago's body against hers.

CHAPTER ELEVEN

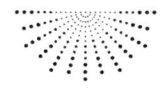

Mirren paused in wiping down the counter when Sylvie wandered into the kitchen the following morning. "Jago was just telling me that you might extend your stay."

"I don't know. I suppose I should decide."

"Stay for longer." Mirren shook crumbs from the dishcloth into the sink. "It would be nice to get to know you better. It's a great time to see the islands now that tourist season is dying down. The craft fair will be lovely next weekend as well. All the local artists will be showing off their wares."

"It's tempting," Sylvie admitted.

Jago leaned forwards in his chair, resting his forearms on the table. "You said yourself you have nothing to rush back for."

"That's true." She slouched against the sideboard. "Thanks for reminding me."

"I told your mum she should come over for a visit sometime," Mirren said. "I'd like to meet her in person. I know she's keen to see Lowen."

Sylvie suspected the feeling wouldn't be mutual but pushed the thought aside.

"I'm off to a meeting at the community centre," Mirren said, squeezing out the cloth and hanging it over the tap. "I'm not sure how long I'll be but they're putting lunch on so I may be a while. You two make yourselves at home." She patted Jago on the shoulder then collected her handbag and coat before heading out the door.

There was something about Mirren's house that made it very easy to feel at home. After only a couple of days Sylvie felt very relaxed. She filled the kettle for a cup of tea, then leaned back against the counter to wait for it to boil.

"Any chance you feel like coming on Kit's train with me today?" Jago asked. "After he mentioned it last night I feel as though I should show an interest. It feels slightly weird going on a tourist train though."

"Why?" Sylvie asked amused.

"It's like a kids' thing, isn't it?"

"I don't think so." She raised her voice slightly over the noise of the kettle. "I think it's aimed at all ages."

"It's also a bit strange to take a tourist train around the island I grew up on. I already know the place."

"I'm sure Kit would appreciate you going along."

"So do you fancy it?"

"Yeah, okay." She reached to take a mug from the cupboard above the kettle and dropped a tea bag into it. "I suppose it would be a good way for me to see more of the island."

∼

"It's definitely not just for kids," Sylvie said, feeling slightly awe-struck when she stepped out of the train at the end of the tour.

"No." Jago's eyebrows pulled together. "That was actually kind of amazing."

"Try not to sound so surprised when you tell Kit that."

He chuckled as they lingered on the promenade. At the front of the train, Kit chatted to a group of Canadian tourists. "I can see why he's done so well for himself. I knew it was a guided tour and not just a drive around the island, but he gives so much information and the way he delivers it is just ... I don't know ... he's so confident and funny. But also ..."

"He sounds like an old soul," Sylvie said, when Jago clearly couldn't find the right words. "If you could only hear his voice you'd have no idea he's so young."

"Yes." Jago looked along to the front of the train, where Kit continued chatting away to the group around him. "I'll be honest, I also didn't know about ninety per cent of the information about the island."

"That's a shame. I was going to rope you into being my tour guide for the week, but I guess I'll need to re-think that."

"I was actually thinking about that," he said seriously, then glanced around. "Kit's going to be ages," he muttered, catching Kit's eye and gesturing that they'd be down on the beach.

Sylvie automatically followed Jago and they settled themselves on a dry patch of sand. It was cold under her bum, but she was soon distracted by the waves washing onto the shore.

"So, I had this idea," Jago continued hesitantly. "How about you stay for the week and we do a tour of the islands together?"

"I was joking about you being my tour guide. You've got your family to catch up with."

"I know, but they have work and everything else going on. And it's so long since I spent a decent amount of time here – I'd like to take some time and look around. Pretend to be a tourist. It would be more fun with company."

Sylvie didn't have to think about her answer. There was a chance Jago was only offering out of charity, but she didn't think so. She also didn't really care. "I'd actually really like that."

"Great. I'll make us an itinerary. Is there anything you especially want to see or do?"

"I'd like to do more seal spotting. It's a good time of year for it, isn't it?"

"I'm not sure." Jago pursed his lips. "I can look into it."

"Hey!" Kit called out, striding towards them. "What did you think?"

"You were amazing," Sylvie told him.

Jago nodded. "Very impressive. I don't know how you do that, but I can see why you've made such a success of the train. Dad would be really proud." A muscle in Jago's jaw twitched and Sylvie got the distinct impression he'd surprised himself with the words.

Crouching in front of them, Kit's Adam's apple bobbed as he swallowed. "Thanks," he said, his voice only a whisper. "I enjoy it."

"You can tell," Sylvie said. "Your passion for the island and its history really comes across."

"Now you're making me blush." He pushed onto his knees to stand again. "Are we going for lunch or what?"

After hearing so much about Pippa's cafe from Mirren, Sylvie wasn't disappointed. She spent a while browsing Lowen's quirky pottery collection while they waited for their sandwiches. It was different from the creations at his studio – these were much more fun. A lot of it was aimed at kids, and she was sure it must sell well given how unique and eye-catching the items were.

"The pottery looks great, doesn't it?" Pippa said, arriving to stand beside her after delivering their food to the table where Kit and Jago were chatting away.

"It's gorgeous," Sylvie whispered.

"I recently went through a re-brand, focusing on cookies and making the place more child-friendly. Lowen created a pottery collection to match my vision for the cafe."

Sylvie turned to take in the cafe as a whole. "It's a really fantastic place."

"It's taken a while to get it to where it is now, but I'm finally happy with it."

"How long have you and Lowen been together?"

"A few months." Warmth radiated from her. "We were

working together for a couple of years. It took us a while to get together."

Sylvie smiled, unsure of how to respond.

"You really took him by surprise," Pippa told her. "How long is it exactly since you last saw each other? I tried asking him but apparently he has a terrible memory." There was something about her tone that made Sylvie wonder exactly what Lowen had said.

"We haven't seen each other for about fifteen years. Maybe a bit longer."

"But you used to go on holidays with him and your grandparents?" It sounded as though she was fishing for information rather than taking a casual interest.

"Yes," Sylvie replied. "We spent most school holidays together."

Pippa nodded. "Mirren gave Lowen a photo album for his last birthday. There are a couple of photos of you in there." Her smile tightened. "He doesn't talk much about his childhood though. I think the memories of the time with his grandparents are hard for him ..."

Clearly Pippa knew more than Jago on the subject of their grandparents. "It wasn't always easy for him."

"We're starving!" Jago called out to her. "We can't wait any longer. We're eating without you. You've been warned."

"I should go and eat," Sylvie said, reluctantly putting an end to their conversation.

They'd just polished off their sandwiches when a familiar face wandered into the cafe. Sylvie instinctively said hello to the curly-haired woman while her brain tried desperately to place her.

"Oh, hi!" the woman said to Sylvie, then shifted her focus to Kit as she hugged him in greeting.

"Do you two know each other?" Kit asked.

"Not really," Sylvie said. "I bumped into Holly at the tourist information when I arrived. She offered to help me out if I couldn't find a place to stay."

"How do you know each other?" Holly asked Kit.

"Sylvie is Lowen's cousin."

"No way!" She gasped. "That would have been hilarious!" Her eyes sparkled as she caught Pippa's eye. "If Sylvie couldn't find a place to stay I'd intended to send her your way, after you were saying the other week about maybe renting out your spare room."

Pippa beamed. "I wouldn't have turned you away," she told Sylvie.

"Are you staying with Mirren?" Holly asked.

"Yes. She took pity on me."

Holly's eyes roamed to Jago and she sucked in an excited breath. "You must be Jago?" When he nodded, she moved to give him a hug that clearly took him by surprise. "It's so good to meet you. Kit told me all about you. How long are you staying? Like a month, right?"

"Yes," he replied, looking slightly dazed.

"If you need suggestions of things to do just come by the tourist office and I'll help you out." Holly waved a hand in front of her face and looked slightly flustered. "You'll know everywhere, of course. You grew up here. Just ignore me."

"Coffees and cookies to go?" Pippa asked her.

"Yes." She turned and grinned. "Thanks."

"Can we get some cookies too?" Kit called as he checked his watch. "Then I need to go."

Holly asked Kit about his house while she waited for her takeaway order, then told them all to have a good day before leaving again.

"She's very chirpy," Jago remarked, watching her through the window.

"I went to school with her. She can come across as a bit manic but she's really sweet." Kit took a couple of cookies from the selection Pippa put in front of them, standing as he did. "I need to nip home before the next train trip," he told them as he clapped Jago on the shoulder. "See you both soon."

"The cookies are amazing," Jago told Pippa when she came over to them.

"Thanks. They've been my saviour. I was floundering for a little while, but the cookies draw in the customers."

"I'm not surprised," Jago said, munching away.

Sylvie tilted her head to meet Pippa's eye. "I decided I'm going to stay the week so I can see the craft fair."

"That's a great idea. I keep telling Lowen he should take some time to hang out with you but he's really stressed this week." The door opened and she greeted the new customers then went back to the counter to serve them.

"She definitely doesn't seem like the jealous, controlling type," Sylvie told Jago quietly.

"Nope. But she did confirm my other theory that Lowen is just busy with work this week."

"I hope that's all it is."

"You'll see. We'll have fun playing tourists, and then Lowen will have the craft fair out of the way and have time to hang out with you properly."

"What's on the agenda for tomorrow?" she asked, taking the last cookie from the plate, then breaking it in half when Jago stuck his bottom lip out.

"I was thinking of a trip to Tresco. I haven't been since I was a teenager but I have lots of good memories."

Sylvie licked cookie crumbs from her bottom lip. "I'm looking forward to some exploring."

CHAPTER TWELVE

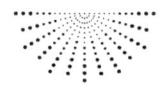

On the boat from St Mary's to Tresco, the early morning grey clouds shifted, leaving the sky a crisp clear blue. A breeze lifted Sylvie's hair from her shoulders as she stepped off the boat.

Taking Jago's hand for support felt natural, but the fizzing sensation in her stomach left her wanting to keep hold of it. There had been a definite lack of romance in her life in the years since her marriage had ended. Romance hadn't factored high in her marriage either. At least not since the very early days.

"You look miles away," Jago said, breaking her thoughts as they headed along the quay.

Her cheeks heated and she hoped he didn't have a talent for mind-reading. He was Lowen's brother and was showing her around since they were both at a loose end. That was all. Admittedly, they'd had their moments of flirting, but as far as she could tell that was just Jago's nature.

"I was daydreaming," she said, vaguely.

"You seem to spend a lot of time doing that." His mischievous grin made her cheeks heat up even more. The sparkle in his eyes made it seem as though he knew exactly where her mind had been.

"There's nothing wrong with daydreaming," she said archly. "Nothing at all!"

She stopped and glared at him. "How did you just make daydreaming sound dirty?"

"Well, was it?"

She shook her head and gave him a playful glare before setting off again.

"Wrong way," Jago called after her.

"I thought the Abbey Gardens were this way."

"They are, but who said we're going to the gardens?"

"I read up on things to do on Tresco and assumed we'd go to the gardens."

"I'm the designated tour guide," he said. "And I say we're going this way." He pointed in the opposite direction.

With a resigned sigh she changed course. "What's this way?" she asked, as they came to the coastal path and a long stretch of bright white sand.

"Cromwell's Castle. It's not far."

She remained silent for a few minutes, enjoying the sea view and fresh, briny air. "If you'd have told me we were going hiking, I'd have worn sturdier shoes," she finally said.

"This isn't hiking!" He caught her teasing smile and rolled his eyes.

Quickly, they reached the ruins of the cylindrical castle. Jago led the way inside the old stone structure and up an uneven staircase to reach the roof.

"That's Bryher, right?" Sylvie asked as they stood side by side, looking out over the turquoise water.

"Yes." He didn't say any more and since he looked deep in thought, Sylvie kept quiet too. After a few minutes they moved back to descend the steps, then walked out to the platform where a couple of large black cannons pointed out into the bay.

Jago slapped his hand against the one beside him. "Dad used to bring me and Lowen here when we were little. We'd pretend it was our castle and we had to defend it. We'd run around, calling out to each other about pirates on the horizon and pretending to fire the cannons to keep them away. Sometimes they'd breach our fortress and we'd have to fight them off with sticks as swords." His lips curled upwards. "Dad would get just as enthralled in our imaginary games as we did."

"That sounds idyllic."

"It was."

Sylvie leaned against the stone wall. "You must miss your dad a lot."

"I do." He nodded, the smile remaining at his lips as though he was still recalling their childhood adventures. "He was a great dad."

"You were lucky. Mine never took the time to play with me like that. Sometimes he'd play chess with me or backgammon, but it wasn't my idea of fun. Especially since he never let me win."

Jago cocked his head. "Seriously?"

"He claimed I'd never learn to play well if he let me win."

"That seems harsh."

"I think so too." She grinned. "Mum swears he was fun when they met, but it's hard to imagine. She claims it was the seriousness of the law office that rubbed off on him once he started working."

"He's a lawyer?"

"Yes. One of those people whose job is their entire life. I used to think that one day he might wake up and realise there are more important things than earning money and impressing your colleagues. But now I think he'll never change. Those are the important things for him. If that's where his self-worth lies, who am I to judge him for it?"

"I reckon you're probably the one person in the world who *is* entitled to judge him for it."

She shrugged. "I had a nice childhood. Being bitter about

him not being there for his family emotionally isn't going to help."

"That's a really rational way of looking at it."

"Don't be fooled," she said with a wicked grin. "I was bitter about it for a very long time." She rested her forearms on top of the wall. "My mum's great so I guess that makes up for it."

"You're an only child?" he asked, joining her and mirroring her pose.

"Yes. I was always jealous of Lowen when he talked about you and Trystan. I don't think it would have occurred to me that I was missing out on anything if it wasn't for hearing him talk about his brothers."

"Seriously? I'd have thought that would make you glad you never had siblings."

She cast him a sidelong glance. "It's sad that you aren't close any more. I imagined you'd always have stayed close to each other."

"I don't think we were ever close."

She turned to face him. "You must have been at some point."

"Maybe when we were still in our pirate adventure days."

"But not when you were older?"

He shook his head. "As teenagers we were at each other's throats most of the time."

"Huh," she said, frowning. "When we were kids, Lowen was always talking about you. He missed you when he was away."

"I'm kind of surprised he didn't spend the whole time slagging me off and being glad to be away from me."

She gave a slow shake of her head. "I don't think he ever had a bad word to say about you. I always found it fascinating because whenever he talked about you it sounded as though you were the older brother and not him."

He pushed off from the wall to stand up straight. "Really?"

She stifled a giggle as she recalled one particular story. "He told me about the time you punched a kid at school when they were teasing him. I remember laughing so much when he told me the story. He made you sound like a superhero stepping in to save the day."

"I never hit anyone," he said, looking genuinely puzzled.

Sylvie thought back to the story that she'd heard so many times. "He said some kid had been teasing him about his backpack and you hit the kid and shouted at him to stay away from your brother."

His eyes flickered with amusement. "I feel as though he made that into a way more dramatic story than it was. I was about ten, so Lowen must have been thirteen. The boy who was laughing at his backpack was bigger than me so I was terrified when I barged into the fray. I didn't hit the kid, just barrelled into him and pinned him against the wall while shouting a few garbled words, then fled with Lowen quickly."

"Lowen was so proud of you," she said quietly.

"Interesting." Jago raised an eyebrow. "I remember being embarrassed at my lack of finesse. I stuttered a lot while telling the kid to leave Lowen alone, and I hurt my own hand when I shoved him into the wall."

"Lowen made you sound very smooth and heroic when he told me the story. I heard it a few times." She turned into the wind and pulled a hair from the corner of her mouth. "He always had funny stories about you, and they were always told with affection."

Jago took a few steps back to the cannon, running his hand over the smooth black paint. "I hated that he got to travel the world and I never got to go anywhere."

"That's quite ironic since all he ever wanted was to stay at home with you."

"No, he didn't." Jago whipped his face to her. "He loved winding me up about all the places he'd been and all the cool things he'd done."

"I can't imagine that." She clearly remembered how homesick Lowen got while they were away and how much he looked forward to getting back home.

Jago stared straight ahead, seeming lost in thought for a moment. "Money was always tight when we were younger," he told her. "Mum and Dad were saving to renovate the cottages so they could charge more to rent them out. I know that was probably the main reason why we never went anywhere during the school holidays, but I remember one time begging Mum to go to Disneyland in Paris. Lowen had been and I was so jealous."

"What did Mirren say?"

"She said it would feel wrong for us to have a holiday without Lowen."

Sylvie winced but didn't say anything.

"It was just one of those throwaway comments. I remember it clearly – Mum was busy cooking dinner when I asked and I expect she didn't put any thought into the answer or how it would stick with me."

"This makes me glad I never had kids," Sylvie mused. "Your mum is great but even she says things to totally screw her kids up."

Jago laughed loudly. "Nice to know you think I'm totally screwed up."

"That's not what I meant." She slapped a hand across her forehead. "I can't believe I just said that."

"Don't you want kids?" he asked when the laughter died away.

"We tried for a while," she said with a shrug. "It didn't happen for us. We talked about IVF but the time was never right." She smiled tightly. "With hindsight it was probably more that the person wasn't right. If we'd really wanted it we'd have got on and done it." She paused for a moment. "What about you? Did you ever think about settling down and having a family?"

"I never found the right person." His gaze locked with hers

for the briefest moment, then he patted the cannon. "We should get going."

"Where to next?" Sylvie asked, following as he set off.

"The Abbey Gardens. Let's see which of my childhood memories we uncover there."

Chuckling, she fell into step beside him. "It's a unique approach for a tour, but I quite like it."

CHAPTER THIRTEEN

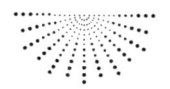

Sylvie could feel Jago's eyes on her while they waited at the harbour the following morning.

"Are you going to be annoyed with me all day?" he asked.

"No." She thought she'd been doing a good job of hiding her emotions but apparently not. It wasn't as though she even really cared what they did for the day, but when she'd asked him about going on a seal-watching trip that morning she'd expected him to readily agree. When he insisted they stick to what he had planned, she couldn't help but feel a little petulant.

Jago knocked against her. "We can go and look for seals tomorrow."

"The weather forecast for tomorrow isn't great."

"The weather will be fine." He took a step towards the approaching boat. "We might see seals on the way to St Agnes." He grinned at her, wiggling his eyebrows until the tension left her and she broke into a smile. "I promise you'll have a great day."

"I'd better," she said mock-sternly.

There were only a handful of people waiting for the boat, so they were all on board in no time. Despite how few passengers there were, the skipper seemed slightly stressed as he talked into his mobile phone, then left the boat to chat to the skippers of the other boats who were gathered at the harbour.

"What's so special about St Agnes?" Sylvie asked as she and Jago stood at the side of the boat. There were plenty of seats, but her eyes had been drawn to a school of fish beside the boat and she'd automatically lingered where she could watch them.

"It's especially peaceful and tranquil." His eyes sparkled. "But the best thing is the smaller island really close to St Agnes – it's called Gugh."

"Gugh?" she repeated. "Is that where you're taking me?"

"At low tide a sandbar appears between the islands. It's like this magical path that arises from nowhere."

"It sounds interesting. Probably not as much fun as the seal trip, but I'll go with it."

He beamed. "Things will be much easier if you relax and trust your tour guide." He tapped his foot against hers. "You really don't need those shoes."

She looked proudly at the hiking boots she'd borrowed from Mirren. "You're going to have to get over the fact that I'm with your mum on this issue. It's you who doesn't know the difference between walking and hiking."

"Yesterday wasn't a hike," he said, laughter in his eyes.

"It was a lot of walking on rugged terrain, and my legs ache today. In my book, that makes it a hike."

"We just strolled around the island."

"Maybe it was strolling for you," she said. "But my legs are shorter than yours. I wasn't strolling."

They exchanged an amused look, then turned and watched the skipper step back onto the boat.

"Sorry about the delay," he said loudly. "It seems there's been a bird sighting over on St Agnes so we're just waiting for a few more passengers who are keen to go over there."

"That's the real reason I wanted to go to St Agnes," Jago said in Sylvie's ear, more than a hint of mischief to his voice. "For the pretty birds."

In reply she rolled her eyes. Their amusement faded when they caught sight of the group of people walking purposely along the harbour. Everyone wore shades of green and grey, accessorised with binoculars and long lens cameras.

"Just to clarify," Sylvie said. "You said this trip was going to be peaceful and tranquil?"

"There should be barely a soul on the island." Jago shifted closer to her as the boat began to fill up.

"Surely all those people can't fit on the boat," Sylvie remarked, eyeing the bustling crowd still waiting to board.

"I don't think so." Jago moved closer still. "This might have been a bad idea," he said with a hand at Sylvie's elbow. "Do you want to abort the plan and do something else instead?"

"I'm not even sure that's a possibility." Sylvie took in the crush of people. It wouldn't be easy to fight their way through and off the boat. Thankfully, the skipper redirected the remaining crowd to a second boat.

"Sorry," Jago said, as the boat pulled away from the harbour.

"It's not your fault all these people decided to go to the same island we're going to."

He flashed a boyish smile and leaned in to whisper. "I meant I'm sorry I forgot to bring binoculars. Apparently it's the fashion."

"Let's not make eye contact with anyone," Sylvie said, standing squarely in front of him. "If anyone figures out we don't know anything about birds we might get thrown overboard."

Jago's eyes sparkled. "Speak for yourself. I know plenty about *birds.*"

She shook her head but couldn't help the way the corners of her mouth twitched upwards. "That joke wasn't funny the first time."

"You laughed the first time," he pointed out. "You look fairly amused now too.

"Sometimes I laugh when things aren't funny. It's a nervous

tic. The only thing that's amusing now is how terrible your sense of humour is."

It seemed as though everyone around them knew each other, and they chatted excitedly about the prospect of seeing a particular warbler.

Sylvie and Jago remained in their own little bubble, whispering and giggling about the people around them. When the boat docked at St Agnes, Sylvie automatically moved when the crowd did to disembark. She stopped when Jago took her arm.

"Let's hang back a minute. We need to see which way the birders are going before we decide on our direction."

"I thought we were going to some magical path across the water?"

"We were," Jago said, dipping his eyebrows. "But if everyone is going that way, we'll change the plan. Also, why are you mocking my description of the sandbar?"

She laughed. "Sorry. But you kind of made it sound like something from a fairy tale."

"That's because it is." He gave her a gentle poke to her side. "As long as these birders don't ruin my plans, you'll see for yourself. Then you'll owe me an apology."

Sylvie couldn't stop beaming. "I bet you're hoping everyone will go in that direction now. Just so you won't be proved wrong."

"I don't even know how you can question the magical aspect of a path that appears from out of the sea." He nodded towards the quay. "Come on. We're in luck. They're all headed in the other direction."

Jago looked fairly pleased with himself as they hopped off the boat. They walked briskly for five minutes before he stopped and pointed out to a smaller island across a thin stretch of water.

"So, where's the magical path?" Sylvie asked.

"Well, obviously it's not there. Did you by any chance bring a swimsuit?"

Sylvie laughed loudly. "You want to swim over there?"

"Walking seems to be out of the question. What with all that water."

"Did you even check what time the tide would be low enough to walk over there?"

"It's not an exact science." He walked from the path to a patch of grass overlooking the bay. After peeling his jacket off, he lay it down to sit on and patted the space beside him in invitation.

"What now?" Sylvie asked, joining him. "Are we going to hang around here, hoping a path appears?" To be fair, it wasn't a bad spot to pass the time, but the urge to wind Jago up was constant.

"There isn't a lot else to do, considering the rest of the island will be teeming with birdwatchers." He pulled his backpack between his legs and opened the zip. "I have snacks though."

Sylvie leaned back, resting her weight on her elbows. "Why didn't you say so before? If there are snacks, I'm quite happy to wait all day for this magical path of yours."

"Yeah," he said nervously as he passed her a packet of crisps. "The sandbar might not actually appear."

She shook her head as she chuckled. "I thought that was the whole point of us coming. Was this all a big ploy to avoid the seal-watching?"

"Nope." He tore open a bag of crisps. The way he avoided her gaze made her think he really was avoiding the seal trip.

"What's your problem with seals?" she coaxed. "Are you scared of them or something?"

"Of course I'm not scared of seals." He popped a crisp in his mouth. "I just thought you might like to see something different. You can see seals pretty much anywhere."

"Not really," she argued. "I never see any in Cambridge."

"You could go to the zoo and see them there."

She sighed heavily. "I can't believe I almost got excited about your magical path. I should've known you were lying again."

His laughter sounded far too loud for the peaceful surroundings. "I wasn't lying. I already told you it's not an exact science."

"Surely it is, though," she protested. "It's the tide."

"Well, yes," he admitted. "But there are other factors involved. Anyway, how about you relax and enjoy the view and the snacks."

"Fine," she said, taking a bottle of water from Jago and gulping it down.

Once they'd finished the snacks, she lay on her back to stare up at the fluffy white clouds.

"A nap would be good now," Jago said, settling beside her.

After a few minutes of silence she shifted onto her side to look at him. "I have a question," she said, ignoring the fact that he had his eyes closed and looked peaceful enough that he might be asleep.

"I might have known I wouldn't be able to get forty winks with you around."

She smiled down at him as he batted his eyes open. "I was wondering about the money that my grandparents gave Lowen."

"What about it?"

"I'm assuming Kit used his share to buy the train?"

"Yes," Jago confirmed.

She nodded. "Did someone use the money to buy the bus company on St Mary's?" she asked, thinking of the Treneary logo on the bus stop.

Amusement flickered in Jago's eyes. "That was Kit too. He owns the bus and the train."

"He's very unassuming, isn't he?" She couldn't say she wasn't impressed. "What did the rest of you do with the money?"

"Noah and Trystan each bought one of the cottages from our parents. Trystan was renting his out while he lived in London. He only moved back here recently."

"What about you? What did you use the money for?"

"Nothing nearly as sensible as my brothers." He dragged his teeth along his bottom lip, lines deepening on his forehead as he frowned. "I got myself into a precarious business situation."

Sylvie raised a questioning eyebrow as she waited for him to continue.

"A friend and I had gone into business together. I still had my main job, so this was just a side hustle ..."

"Oh my God. Please don't tell me you're a drug dealer or something?"

He laughed. "No, it was nothing illegal."

"If you don't want to talk about it, it's fine. Obviously, I'm very intrigued now and will spend the rest of my life wondering, but it's fine."

"It's not that I don't want to tell you. I'm just not quite sure where to start. It's kind of a long story."

"Just tell me the basics," she suggested. "What's your day job, by the way?" As much as she felt she already knew him well, it occurred to her that she knew very little about his life in New York.

"I work in software development."

"Okay. What was the side business?"

He released a steady breath. "I'm pretty good at brewing beer."

"Right," she said, dragging the word out. "That's a weird change of subject."

"Give me a minute ..." He turned onto his side to face her. "I was home-brewing beer. Just for fun. But it was good. Anyone who tried it said I could easily sell it. A friend of mine asked if I wanted to go into business with him. Scale up the brewing and distribute it." He paused, looking thoughtful. "The more we looked into it, the more it seemed like a good idea. We approached bars and restaurants and had a lot of positive feedback. Then we found a brewery that rented out space and equipment."

"I'm presuming this story is going to take a downward turn soon?"

He smiled sadly. "We moved forwards with everything. I sank all my savings into the business. The brewing went well and producing beer on a larger scale wasn't a problem. Naïvely that had been the only hurdle I'd anticipated." He winced. "What I hadn't considered is the number of independent brewers in New York. The beer was good, but so was everyone else's. We were competing in a market that was already saturated. By the time I realised we were on a sinking ship we'd already signed a lease with the brewery for five years. We couldn't find anyone to take it over, and we didn't have the funds to buy ourselves out of the contract. We were basically flailing around, heading quickly to bankruptcy."

"Is this where my grandparents' money comes into the story?"

He tilted his head back, staring up at the sky. "I used their money to buy us out of the contract. Obviously not having to file for bankruptcy was a relief, but it felt like an embarrassing use of the money."

Sylvie raised her eyebrows, trying not to judge. "So all of the money was gone, just like that?"

"Not all of it. But it was around 50,000 dollars down the drain."

"What did you do with the rest?"

He shrugged. "I'm saving it for a rainy day."

"That's not so bad then." She'd expected him to say he'd somehow squandered the rest of it. "If you still have the rest it gives you opportunities."

"I'm terrified to touch it." He looked at her intently. "I look at my brothers and everything seems to come easy to them. Look at Kit; he had a business idea and it took off in a way none of us would've predicted." He gave a small shake of the head. "I don't mean to sound bitter. I'm happy Kit has done so well. That all my brothers have. It just makes me feel a bit of a failure."

"Setting up your own business is always going to be a risk. It doesn't seem as though it was a bad idea, just that you didn't have a strong enough USP and the marketing let you down. Unique selling point," she explained when he looked vaguely confused.

"I know what it means. I just wasn't expecting you to have such an insightful response."

"Brains *and* beauty," she said smugly. "Some people really do have it all."

Laughing, he gave her arm a shove and sat up.

"Look at that," he said nodding towards the water.

After easing herself up, Sylvie's eyes widened dramatically. "Where on earth did that come from?"

"The magical path?"

"Yes, that."

"It rose up out of the sea." Jago gave her a smug smile. "*Magically.*"

She got to her feet, not quite believing her eyes. When Jago bumped his shoulder against hers she shifted her eyes to him. "You know it doesn't actually rise up out of the sea? The sea level has just dipped enough that the sand is visible."

"Are you really going to deny there's anything magical about what just happened?"

To avoid having to admit he was right, she chose to stay quiet.

Jago packed up their things, then pulled his backpack onto his shoulder. "Do you want to walk on the magical path or what?"

"Will it disappear as quickly as it appeared?" she asked. "Are we going to get stranded over on the island?"

"No," he said as he set off. "I checked the tide times. We're fine for a few hours. There *is* a science to it, you know?"

Sylvie hurried to catch up with him and gave him a playful slap on the arm when she did.

CHAPTER FOURTEEN

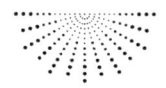

"Will you please admit that was a hike," Sylvie said, when they returned to St Agnes three hours later. They wandered in the direction of the pub, intent on grabbing some food while they waited for the boat.

"Okay. The uphill was pretty rough going. But you have hiking boots on so it only seemed right that we do some hiking."

"About that ..." She grimaced and leaned onto the stone wall beside the lane.

"What?" he asked dubiously.

"I've got a blister." The pub was in sight but the pain had just increased dramatically.

Jago helped her to hop up onto the wall, where she propped her foot up to remove the offending boot. A circle of blood had soaked through her sock and she peeled it back. "It's not so bad," she said while Jago swung his backpack from his shoulder.

"I've got plasters."

"You're very prepared, aren't you?"

A smile played at his lips. "I put them in when I saw you borrowing Mum's shoes."

"Thank you," she said, taking the plaster and sticking it over the wound.

"Are you going to be okay?"

"I'd imagine so," she said cheekily. "It's only a blister."

"I meant are you okay to walk?"

"Are you going to carry me otherwise?"

"Well ... I just ... do you need me to carry you?"

She eased her foot back into the shoe, then met his gaze. "I was only teasing."

"I know." He glanced away from her, his cheeks pinking slightly.

A lump formed in her throat as it occurred to her that he really would carry her if she asked him to. "You're very sweet," she said, touching his arm to draw his attention.

With a shy smile he took the laces of her shoe and deftly tied a bow. Watching him, Sylvie had the overwhelming urge to kiss him. In all the years they were together, her ex had never done anything as thoughtful as tying her shoelace.

Jago straightened up. "What's wrong?"

"Nothing." She took his arm and pulled him close. Their eyes locked and their faces were only inches apart when a bird sang loudly nearby.

With the moment broken, Sylvie relaxed her hold on Jago and glanced over to the nearby bush. A small bird with a yellow head darted out to join them on the wall.

"She's friendly," Jago remarked, pulling his phone out and snapping a picture.

"*She?*"

The smile crept slowly over his face. "Yes. It's clearly a bird."

Sylvie reached out to hit him, the action causing the bird to fly away and stirring what sounded like a collective gasp.

Her eyes widened as she spotted the large group of birdwatchers at the other side of the field, the sea of green clearly upset with her.

"Oh dear," Jago said. "I think you're about to be set upon by an angry mob."

"Do you think that was the bird they were looking for?"

"I'd say so."

"But it was just a tiny little thing."

"Not everything is about size." Jago let out a comical sigh and helped her down from the wall as the crowd approached them. "I think it flew into that bush," he told them.

The guy nearest them shook his head. "It flew off again. I can't believe you got so close to it." He extended his hand to shake Jago's. Apparently after the initial shock of Sylvie scaring the bird away, the group were just happy about the sighting and huddled round to congratulate Jago and Sylvie while firing a bunch of questions at them and demanding to see the photo Jago had taken.

"This calls for champagne," a young guy said, slapping Jago on the back. "Are you coming up to the pub?"

"We were actually heading up there before the bird waylaid us," Jago told him. They got swept up in the crowd and Sylvie had lost Jago by the time they reached the Turk's Head. Inside the door, she scanned around for him, then felt a hand on hers and turned to find him behind her. Keeping hold of her hand, he led her to a table at the back of the pub.

"This is Philippe," he said, introducing her to the guy at the table. "He's bought us champagne."

Sylvie thanked him as she sat and took the flute of bubbly he offered her.

"It is not every day you see a Blackburnian Warbler, is it?" he said with a thick French accent.

"I suppose not." She smiled at the guy, who must only have been in his twenties.

He wasn't the only one keen to buy them a drink. By the time they left the pub they had about sixty new friends and were both pretty giggly.

A guy with a furry microphone approached them while they waited for the boat at the quay.

"You're the ones who got up close with the warbler, aren't you?" he asked.

"That's us." Jago grinned at Sylvie. "I finally have my claim to fame."

"Would you mind if I ask you a few questions? I'm with BBC Radio Four."

"Sure," Jago said, clearly entertained by the fact that there was so much interest.

When the guy asked how Jago felt about seeing the warbler, he leaned close to the microphone. "Having such a pretty bird right beside me was incredible." He shot Sylvie a look of glee. "To be close to that kind of beauty is really a privilege. It's just a shame it's so noisy. It never stopped twittering away the whole time it was near me." He gave the reporter a curt nod, then put a hand at the small of Sylvie's back to lead her away to the boat. "I was talking about you," he whispered in her ear.

"I realise that," she replied. "But the joke is on you because while you were trying to wind me up by referring to me as a bird, all I heard was how beautiful you think I am."

She expected a blush from him but when his response was a one-shouldered shrug it was her who flushed.

On the boat, tiredness hit Sylvie and she remained silent while Jago chatted to a group about the warbler. She zoned out of the conversation, her mind drifting to how close she'd come to kissing Jago earlier, and whether or not that would have been a good thing.

Since her divorce she hadn't had the remotest interest in romantic relationships, but spending time with Jago made her realise it was something she'd like to have in her life. Especially considering how he made her realise there could be a relationship which didn't resemble her marriage.

She told herself not to get too attached. Jago would be back in America in a few weeks and she'd be back in Cambridge in a few days. At least her time with him might spur her into giving dating a go once she was back home.

"We didn't even get food," Jago said, patting her leg and breaking her trance. "Do you want to stop off at the Mermaid Inn before we head home or are you done in? You look tired."

"It was all that hiking," she said, leaning her head against his shoulder. She could blame it on the alcohol dulling her inhibitions but it wasn't only that. Being around Jago just felt so comfortable and easy.

"We can go straight home if you want?"

"Pub food sounds good," she said. "Just don't let me drink any more alcohol."

"It might be fun to see you drunk."

"Me being drunk will only entail falling asleep on the table."

"Maybe not then. I don't actually want to carry you home."

She closed her eyes, only opening them again when Jago nudged her to say they were at the harbour.

"It looks as though I've worn you out," he said as they made their way off the boat. "Maybe tomorrow's plan should be a little gentler."

"Yes," she agreed, perking up. "How about a leisurely boat trip and some seal-watching?"

He rolled his eyes. "If we must."

CHAPTER FIFTEEN

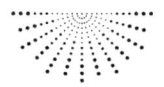

It was evident as soon as Sylvie woke on Friday morning that she probably wasn't going to get her boat trip. Rain tapped steadily against the windowpane and she buried her head under the pillow in annoyance. She couldn't say what was more frustrating: that she wasn't going to get her boat trip or that she'd have to deal with Jago being smug about it.

Once she'd showered, she made her way down to the kitchen, frowning as she went. Her irritation intensified when she caught sight of Jago sitting at the table.

"Why are you so against seal-watching anyway?" she asked.

He peered over his coffee at her. "How come it sounds as though we're already mid-argument?"

"Because I've been arguing with you in my head since the moment I woke up." She plonked herself in the chair beside him. "You're happy about the rain, aren't you?"

"Why would I be happy about rain?"

"Because now we can't go seal-watching."

"Maybe the question shouldn't be why I'm against looking for seals but why you're so excited by the idea. If you've seen one seal you've seen them all. And we already saw two the other day."

"But they're so cute!" She pouted. "I wanted to see more."

"Well I would have gone with you if it wasn't raining."

"I guess we'll never know if that statement is true."

"I think you have trust issues," he said, chuckling.

Sylvie was about to tell him he was probably right but was interrupted by Mirren's arrival.

"What are you two up to today?" she asked brightly.

"We're hoping a few seals swim into the bay," Jago said. "That way we can watch them from the comfort of the kitchen window to make up for the boat trip we're missing out on."

"Do you think that might happen?" Sylvie asked.

"No." Mirren shook her head. "I'm afraid not."

"It *could*," Jago said. "I've definitely seen seals from the kitchen window before."

"Have you looked out of the window?" Mirren tutted. "You can't even see as far as the water today."

"I guess I'll just give up on my hopes of a seal-watching expedition," Sylvie said, aiming a dramatic pout in Jago's direction.

"There's always next week," Mirren remarked "The weather's changeable at this time of year but I can almost guarantee there'll be one day that will be suitable for a boat trip."

"Hopefully at the beginning of the week. I've booked a flight for Wednesday. I need to get home and start job hunting." She looked out of the window at the unrelenting downpour. "I could probably get started on that today actually."

"Have *you* got plans for today?" Mirren asked Jago.

"Not really. I've got a bit of work I should be doing."

"You're supposed to be on holiday."

"No rest for the wicked," he said, his smile not quite reaching his eyes.

"How about we all go up to the Castle for lunch? I promised Beth I'd speak to Carol again about the food for the wedding. I can't believe it's only a week away."

"It's exciting," Sylvie said wistfully.

"Beth's panicking about everything. I'm certain they have it all under control at the castle though. It's not the first time they've hosted a wedding."

"I love that they're getting married in the castle." Sylvie had read about the hotel and restaurant in a star-shaped castle in Hugh Town. "It's so romantic."

"It's where they had their first date," Mirren said. "And where they went the night Trystan proposed."

"I love that." Sylvie smiled at the quaintness of it. "When I got married it was in a random hotel that we chose because it had picturesque grounds for the photos. I love the idea of getting married somewhere significant to your relationship."

Jago grinned. "Lucky for Beth they had their first date at the Castle restaurant and not in the Mermaid Inn."

"It is a bit more special," Mirren agreed. "But we've had just about every other celebration in the Mermaid Inn and it's never disappointed."

Smiling, she bustled around the kitchen, making coffees for them all before Jago went off to do some work and Sylvie went and got her laptop out for a half-hearted job search before lunch. There were plenty of accounting jobs she could apply for, but nothing that sparked much enthusiasm. Since she was living with her mum and had the money from her grandparents, she had the luxury of not desperately needing a job, which made her long to find something she was passionate about rather than working to pay the bills as she'd been doing before.

∼

Having Sylvie around meant Jago had barely had time to think about the decisions he was supposed to be making about his future. He'd put it all out of his head and focused on exploring the islands and having a good time.

Trawling through online job postings brought him fully back to real life. It became increasingly clear he wasn't going to get everything figured out in the next few weeks and he felt a stab of guilt for telling his mum he was working. Technically, he hadn't lied – job hunting definitely felt like work. It just clearly wasn't the kind of work his mum assumed he was doing.

He should probably let his family in on his altered job and living situation. After pondering it for a while he decided to wait until after the wedding. He didn't want to cause any drama and steal the attention, after all.

The job search had been utterly fruitless and it was a relief when his mum called up to him about lunch. A distraction was welcome. Especially as Sylvie was going too. As far as distractions went, she was a particularly pleasant one.

Over lunch at the hotel – while his mum spent most of the time chatting to the owner – his gaze flicked to Sylvie's lips numerous times. The previous day he could have sworn she'd been about to kiss him before they'd been interrupted by the bird. Since then he'd hardly been able to stop thinking about it.

With the rain still falling lightly when they returned home, he challenged Sylvie to a game of chess. It ended up being slightly embarrassing when she won three games in a row. She teased him mercilessly the whole time, which he thoroughly enjoyed.

"I give up," he said after the third defeat. He pushed himself up from the floor where they'd been playing across the coffee table. "Your dad taught you too well."

"I'm sure he'd be very proud of me," she said, flopping beside Jago on the couch.

He pushed his head back into the cushions. "Can I ask you a personal question?" When she nodded, he hesitated for a moment. They'd only known each other a matter of days so maybe he shouldn't be prying into her personal life, but he had the feeling that nothing was off-limits between them.

"Did your husband really divorce you straight after you inherited the money?"

"Yeah," she said sadly. "With hindsight things hadn't been

good for a long time, but I still think it was a crappy thing for him to do ... or at least I did for a long time."

"And now?"

"Now I think he probably did me a favour. Things were okay between us but when I look back at my life with him it was all very ordered and safe. That's about the best that I can say about it. I didn't particularly feel I was missing much, but breaking up made me stop to think about what I want out of life."

"Which is?"

Her lips twitched upwards. "I've no idea but it's nice to think about it rather than just plodding along."

"It was pretty crappy of him to take half of your inheritance."

Sylvie looked thoughtful. "I think it would have been decent of him to at least offer not to take half of it, especially since ..."

"What?" he ventured when she trailed off.

"When we got married we lived in Cambridge, but after a couple of years his dad died. His mum wasn't coping well so we moved up to Manchester to be near her. Don't get me wrong, it was the right thing for us at the time and I was fond of his mum, but I gave up a good job to move up there. I feel as though I spent our entire marriage making sacrifices and even when we split up he still wanted to take from me."

"That sounds really rough."

She blew out a breath. "It's actually not. He was entitled to half of the money."

"Legally, maybe, but morally?"

"That may be questionable," she admitted. "But it doesn't matter. I have a new life. I get to live with my mum again, which is pretty awesome. And it's not as though he left me with nothing. Financially, I have more than enough. I live a privileged life and I don't intend to let Julian turn me into a bitter old trout."

Jago smiled at her choice of words, then subtly shifted his leg so it rested against hers. "I know this is absolutely none of my business and it's possibly inappropriate for me to comment, but I think your ex-husband is a complete idiot."

She pressed her leg a little harder against his. "Oh you do, do you?"

"I do," he said without looking at her. "Although, I guess I should be thankful that he divorced you and took half your money …"

"Why?" she asked, her voice turning serious.

"Because if he hadn't you might not be here, or maybe you'd be here with him …"

"And that would be a problem for you?"

He rolled his head on the couch cushion so he was looking right at her. "Yeah," he said, deadly serious. "Think about it … We wouldn't have gone to St Agnes yesterday, you wouldn't have got a blister and therefore I'd never have spotted that warbling thingy and become a celebrity."

Her eyes danced as she laughed. "You're a celebrity, are you?"

"The photo I took is all over social media," he declared proudly. "And there was a soundbite of me on the radio last night."

"I'm not convinced that makes you a celebrity."

"Let me have my moment in the spotlight, will you?" His smile fell away as their eyes locked. "Even if I hadn't spotted the bird, I'd still be very glad you're here." And *single,* he wanted to add, but couldn't bring himself to.

Sylvie's phone buzzed in her pocket, the vibrations startling Jago and breaking their intense gaze.

"It's my mum," she said, looking at her phone in her hand. "I should answer it."

∼

Sylvie couldn't decide if her mum's timing was impeccable or terrible. Yet again, she suspected she'd have kissed Jago if they hadn't been interrupted.

"How is everything?" her mum asked as Sylvie ascended the stairs.

"Good."

"I'm glad you decided to stay longer. Gives you time to properly catch up with Lowen. Is he more relaxed now that he's over the shock of seeing you again?"

"I've hardly seen him. I went to the pub with him on Monday night but the rest of the family were there too."

There was a pause in the conversation and Sylvie walked into her bedroom and closed the door behind her.

"I thought the whole reason for you staying for longer was to spend time with Lowen?" Confusion was evident in her mum's voice.

"He's busy getting ready for a craft fair on Saturday. I'm staying longer so I can hang out with him once it's over."

"So you've been exploring by yourself this week?"

"Jago's been showing me around."

"That's nice." She snorted. "Do you remember shopping for that bloody football shirt for him?"

"Yes." Of course she remembered – she and her mum had reminisced about it many times over the years.

"Did you mention it to him?"

"No." She rubbed at her eyebrow and stared out of the window at the peaceful bay with the boats bobbing gently on the water. "I almost did but …"

"But what?" her mum prompted when Sylvie debated whether to say more.

"It's kind of strange … Jago doesn't know that Lowen picked clothes out specially for him. Apparently Lowen told him that Grandma bought the wrong size."

"You know what boys can be like – Lowen probably didn't want his brother to know he cared."

"If that's the case, he succeeded." She crossed the room and sank onto the bed. "Jago said he and Lowen aren't close and never really were."

"That's odd. I always got the impression they were very close."

Sylvie leaned back against the headboard, not wanting to dwell on all her confusion around Lowen. "The islands are gorgeous," she said, to change the subject. "We went to Tresco on Wednesday, and St Agnes yesterday." She gave a quick rundown of the bird incident and told her all about Jago ending up on the radio.

"What have you done today?" her mum asked, once Sylvie wound the story up.

"It's raining so we went out for lunch with Mirren, then I've beaten Jago at chess a few times this afternoon."

The ensuing silence felt loaded. "Is Jago cute?" her mum asked slowly.

"What?" Sylvie sat up straight.

"I'm just wondering if he's attractive ... he's about your age, isn't he?"

"Yes, he is ... but ..." She sighed loudly. "Where are you going with this conversation?"

"Just wondering if you have a thing for him ..."

"Mum!" she said indignantly.

"I'll take that as a yes. Isn't that a bit awkward?"

"I don't have a thing for him ..." She winced at the lie. "I mean we've been hanging out. He's just visiting so he's got time on his hands while everyone else is working." She flopped back again, hearing how defensive she sounded. "Anyway, why would it be awkward?"

"I just wondered how Lowen would feel about it."

"I don't suppose he'd care considering he can't even be bothered to spend any time with me."

"You said he was busy working."

"So he says."

"What's going on?" her mum asked.

"I don't know. Maybe he really is busy working, but I can't shake the feeling that he just doesn't want to see me."

"I'm sure that's not true."

Her mum's words weren't particularly convincing, but Sylvie supposed she'd soon find out. The craft fair was tomorrow, and with that out of the way, Lowen should finally have time for her.

CHAPTER SIXTEEN

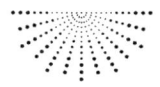

Sylvie was chatting to Mirren in the kitchen the following lunchtime when the back door burst open. Having only ever seen Beth looking calm and collected, it was a shock to see her rosy-cheeked and flustered. Her hair was also oddly styled in tight curls.

"I know I'm being very vain," she said, not bothering with a greeting, "but is it really so wrong of me to want my hair to look nice on my wedding day?"

"Is that your wedding style?" Mirren asked without bothering to hide her grimace.

"It's awful, isn't it?" She sat heavily at the table. "I called Trystan and told him we'll have to put the wedding back to later in the day so I can fly to the mainland in the morning to get my hair done."

Mirren tilted her head. "That seems drastic."

"I know. But I can't let Susan do my hair. She's sweet and everything, but what on earth was she thinking?" Beth attempted to pull her fingers through her hair but ended up getting in a tangle and tugging them out again. "I said loose waves. Does this look anything like loose waves to you?" Finally, she caught

Sylvie's eye, only then seeming to register her presence. "Sorry. Hi. How are you?"

"Fine." On autopilot, Sylvie moved behind Beth to take a closer look at her hair. "It's not so bad."

Beth huffed out a breath. "Thanks for being polite, but you don't need to be."

"Your hair always looks gorgeous," Mirren said. "You don't even need a hairdresser. It's lovely the way you do it."

"That's what Trystan said. I'll have to do it myself. It's just disappointing, that's all."

"The colour is gorgeous," Sylvie remarked, lightly running her fingers over the roots. "Is this your natural colour?"

"Yes."

Sylvie reached for her handbag which sat at the end of the table. "If you run a brush through it, the curls should loosen up." She retrieved one from her bag and held it up. "May I?"

"Be my guest." Beth's shoulders sank. "It's not as though you could make it any worse."

Sylvie gripped the hair at the roots while she worked her way down the length with the brush. "Do you usually wear your hair down?"

"Yes. Almost always."

"Have you thought about wearing it up for the wedding?"

She shook her head. "I look kind of stern when I wear my hair up."

"Will you be wearing a veil?"

"Yes. At least for the ceremony. I'll probably take it off later."

Frowning, Sylvie continued to drag the brush through her hair. "She really went to town with the styling products, didn't she?"

"I'm fairly sure she used an entire can of hairspray."

"It certainly seems like it." After a little more wrangling the tight curls admitted defeat and hung loosely around her shoulders. Delving into her bag again, Sylvie scooped up the errant kirby grips which lined the bottom. "I think it could look really good in an updo. Nothing tight or harsh, but a nice smooth bun, and a few loose strands around your face." She'd already begun styling but was hindered when Beth turned her head.

"You sound as though you know what you're talking about," she said quizzically.

"Not really. When I was a teenager I had a Saturday job in the local hair salon. I picked up some tips. When I was at university I started cutting hair for a few friends and it escalated. Word got around that I would cut hair for cheap and I suddenly had a lot of willing practice subjects."

"Did you continue after university?" Mirren asked.

"No." She stuck another grip into Beth's hair. "At least I've never done it professionally. Just for friends and family."

"Did you ever want to do it for a job?" Beth asked.

Pausing, Sylvie tilted her head. "I never really considered it. It was expected that I'd go down an academic route at school. I was strong in maths so I ended up in accounting. Not as glamorous as hairdressing, but my dad and my grandparents approved."

"And your mum?" Mirren asked.

"I think she'd have approved of anything really. When I was younger she tended to go along with whatever Dad said. Since they split up she's much more of a free spirit. If it was up to her she'd probably steer me away from accounting now. In fact, she's always telling me to try something new. I just have no idea what else I'd do so I'm a bit stuck in a rut."

A slow smile spread over Mirren's face. "Hairdressing seems like the obvious answer to that."

"I'd have to get proper training and qualifications. I don't think I have the energy for it."

"You're very good though," Mirren said, looking pointedly at Beth.

"Thanks," Sylvie said while Beth got her phone out and switched on the front camera to look at herself.

"Oh, that does look good. Can you take a photo of the back for me?"

"Just a sec." Sylvie wrangled a few stray strands into place then took the phone from Beth. "It actually looks really good, even if I do say so myself."

Once she'd taken a picture, Beth turned in the chair to look at the shot on the phone screen. "That's lovely. How did you do that so easily?"

"Probably because the hairdresser put enough product into your hair that it had no choice but to stay where I put it."

"It's really lovely." She twisted to show Mirren the back.

Returning her gaze to Sylvie, Beth's eyes widened. "Would you please do my hair for the wedding?" She pressed her hands together in a prayer-like gesture. "You should come to the wedding too." She grimaced slightly. "We should have invited you anyway. I don't know why I didn't think of it. My head's been all over the place."

"You don't need to invite me to your wedding," Sylvie said, amused.

"We'd like to have you there. You're family."

Sylvie couldn't help but laugh. "So you're inviting me because you consider me family ... not because you want me to do your hair?"

"Maybe a bit of that too," Beth admitted.

"I'd have loved to come to your wedding, and I'd have been more than happy to do your hair, but unfortunately I won't be here. My flight back is on Wednesday."

"I can't tempt you to stay an extra few days?"

"Sorry." She twisted her lips to the side. "If I can get my hands on a pair of hairdressing scissors I can give you a trim before I leave. That way your hair will be nice and healthy so it'll be easier to style on the day."

"Thank you," Beth said, not quite hiding her disappointment. "That would be great."

The back door opened again, bringing a gust of cool air.

"Hello!" Ellie said as she skipped inside. "Your hair looks very pretty, Mummy." She stood in front of Beth, grinning widely.

"It does," Trystan agreed, following her in. "I'm not just saying that to make you feel better. It looks great. What's the problem with it?"

"This isn't how it looked when I walked out of the hairdresser," Beth told him. "This is all Sylvie's handiwork."

He flashed her a smile. "I guess you get an invite to the wedding then. We should have invited you anyway."

"I just said the same," Beth told him.

"Can you do my hair for the wedding too?" Ellie asked, gazing up at Sylvie.

"Unfortunately I'm leaving before then so I won't be able to."

"Can't you stay longer?" Trystan asked.

"I can't – my flight is booked. I've already stayed for longer than I intended."

Ellie pouted. "That's a shame."

"It really is," Beth agreed before changing the subject to ask about the craft fair.

Ellie let out a comically loud sigh as she propped her hands on her hips. "Lowen and Mia were too busy to talk to us, so it wasn't much fun at all."

Trystan pulled up a chair beside Beth. "I'd say Lowen is making a killing. He'll have to put up with Mia being even more smug with him since he kept telling her it probably wouldn't be worthwhile doing it."

"I think I'll head down there now," Sylvie said. If it was busy she probably wasn't going to get time to speak to Lowen, but she loved craft fairs and was keen to check out all of the other artists' work too.

"I'll come with you," Mirren said.

Sylvie was about to mention that Jago was planning on going too, but he arrived in the doorway at that exact moment.

"Hello," Ellie said to him brightly. "I saw a photo of a bird that you took. It was a very nice yellow bird."

Beth scowled playfully. "Don't get any ideas about entering it into the photography competition. I'm the photographer in the family and I'm determined to win this year."

"You're tempting me to enter," Jago told her.

"Are we going to this craft fair?" Mirren said. "They'll be nothing left if we don't go soon."

After a brief discussion about how to get there they opted to walk into Hugh Town. A few groups of people were gathered outside the community centre and Mirren lingered to chat to a couple of friends while Jago and Sylvie mooched around the various stands. Things seemed to be winding down – many of the tables were low on stock as Mirren had predicted. When Jago was accosted by a little old lady who'd apparently been one of his schoolteachers many years ago, Sylvie slipped away and approached Lowen's table.

"It looks as though you've had a successful day," she commented after waiting for a group of customers to move away from the table.

"Yes," Lowen replied with a smile.

"It was definitely worth the hard work," Mia said, while rummaging through cardboard boxes behind the table. "Wouldn't you say, Lowen?"

His eyes flashed with mock irritation. "I suppose so."

"I'm glad it was worthwhile. Hopefully you can take it a bit easier now. Have you got tomorrow off?" Sylvie had checked the opening times for the pottery studio and knew it was always closed on Sundays and Mondays.

"Yes." He shifted his weight. "We could do something if you have nothing planned."

"I have nothing planned until my flight on Wednesday."

"Is there anything you still want to see or do?"

She smiled, thinking of the one thing that Jago wasn't keen to do with her. "What I'd really love is to go seal-watching. I heard there are a lot around at the moment and a lot of baby seals too."

"Okay. We can take Mum's boat and cruise around the Eastern Isles ..." His eyes slid to Mia, who was standing with her hands on her hips. "Why are you looking at me like that?"

"You can't go tomorrow," Mia said. "You're busy. Have you seriously forgotten?"

He grimaced. "I totally forgot."

"How can you forget?" Mia pouted. "I swear your brain doesn't function properly half the time."

He gave a small shake of the head and turned to Sylvie. "Sorry. I've started offering pottery classes and the first one is tomorrow afternoon."

"Pottery classes sound great." For a moment Sylvie was impressed by his business acumen, but it didn't take long for disappointment to settle over her.

"We could go out on the boat on Monday." He glanced at Mia, seemingly looking for permission. When she gave a subtle nod, Lowen flashed Sylvie a quizzical look.

"Monday's good. It'll be good to get some proper time together before I leave."

"Yes." His lips twitched to a weak smile. "I'm looking forward to it."

CHAPTER SEVENTEEN

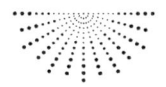

Sylvie felt a little lost on Sunday when Jago told her he was going over to Kit's place with Trystan and Noah. Apparently Kit wanted help planning which renovations they could realistically do on the house and which he'd have to hire someone else to do.

Apparently Jago sensed Sylvie's disappointment at losing her tour guide and half-heartedly offered for her to join. Of course she declined. As welcoming as the Trenearys had been, she wouldn't be comfortable foisting herself on their sibling get-together.

Mirren was off getting one of the cottages ready for more guests and adamantly declined Sylvie's offer to help. Since the weather was decent she explored St Mary's a little more, going for a ramble along the coast and discovering sandy stretches of beach that she hadn't seen yet.

At a particularly inviting bay on the eastern side of the island, she plonked herself on the sand and revelled in the solitude. Closing her eyes, she marvelled at the feel of the cold breeze across her cheeks while enjoying the sound of the waves rushing onto the shore and the occasional squawk of gulls overhead. The time alone cleared her head, and by the end of the day she'd convinced herself that all her worries about Lowen had been for nothing.

Certain that everything would be better when they'd spent some time together, she woke the next morning with a tingle of excitement about the day. The weather was perfect for a boat trip too.

Sylvie was finishing off a cup of coffee when Lowen arrived. She wasn't sure she managed to hide her surprise when Pippa walked into the kitchen with him. She'd understood that it would just be her and Lowen for the trip. The disappointment at not getting him to herself rippled through every part of her body.

"You don't mind Pippa tagging along, do you?" Lowen asked.

"Of course not." She forced a smile and could've sworn the look she received from Pippa was equally as pained. When she caught the way Pippa glared at Lowen, it seemed fairly obvious she was furious with him.

"The more the merrier, right?" Lowen said, resting his hand on the small of Pippa's back.

"Is the cafe closed today?" Sylvie asked.

"It's open." She moved away from Lowen and took a seat. "Mia's looking after the place since it looks like it'll be quiet today."

"That's nice," Sylvie said, not sure why she felt suddenly panicky about the trip. "Jago said he might come with us too ... that would be okay, wouldn't it?" He hadn't said any such thing, but she was sure she could convince him.

When Lowen nodded she told him she'd go and check. In the living room, Jago was slouched on the couch, flicking through TV channels.

"Are you heading off?" he asked, glancing up at her.

"Yes." She sat sideways on the couch, facing him. "Pippa's coming too."

"I thought it was just you and Lowen."

"Me too." Instinctively, she grabbed his hand, clutching it in both of hers. "I need you to come with us."

He muted the TV. "What?"

"Please. Come with us."

"Why do you need me to come?"

"Everything just feels a bit weird. There's a strange atmosphere between Lowen and Pippa."

"How so?"

She slouched, knowing she'd sound like a crazy person if she continued.

"You're not making a lot of sense."

Her chest heaved as she sighed. "It'll sound ridiculous but I could swear Pippa doesn't want to be here. It's like Lowen has forced her to come."

"Yeah, it sounds ridiculous."

"Please will you humour me and come with us?" Squeezing his hand, she smiled sweetly. "I promise I'll protect you from the scary seals."

He scratched his forehead. "I don't want to," he said, with weight to his voice.

"Oh." She'd fully expected him to agree and felt overwhelmingly pathetic for begging him. "Okay." She pulled her hand from his and stood up.

"Sorry," he said as she backed away.

"It's fine. I'm being daft anyway. Hopefully the sea air will blow away my neuroses."

He started to speak but she turned and left the room quickly. Entering the kitchen, she opened her mouth to tell Lowen it was just the three of them when she felt Jago behind her.

"Do you want to start getting the boat out?" he called to Lowen over her head. "I just need to get changed and I'll be right behind you."

Sylvie barely had time to register what had happened before he was off up the stairs. Only as she was climbing into the boat did she have time to mouth her thanks to him. He smiled in reply and sat at the back of the boat with Lowen while Sylvie and Pippa squished onto the bench at the front.

"You're not from Scilly, are you?" Sylvie asked Pippa as the engine purred to life.

"No. I moved from Brighton a few years back."

Sylvie peppered her with questions as the boat bounced over gentle waves. Conversation came naturally and by the time they reached the Eastern Isles Sylvie was convinced she'd overreacted earlier. Maybe the tension between Pippa and Lowen had been about something else entirely. Or maybe she'd imagined it.

Lowen slowed the boat and pointed to a strip of sand on the nearby island where a collection of dark shapes lay. From a distance the seals could easily be mistaken for rocks. Sylvie couldn't take her eyes off them as they lolled on their blubbery stomachs and let out the occasional barks and grunts.

Eventually, Sylvie turned her attention back to the boat. Pippa and Lowen were as entranced by the seals as she was, but Jago was staring at the water beside him with an expression that sent a jolt to Sylvie's heart.

"Are you okay?" she asked.

His stricken gaze met hers and she resisted the urge to reach out and take his hand.

"What's wrong?" she asked, registering how pale he'd gone. "Are you seasick?"

"No." He straightened up, seeming to physically pull himself together under the weight of three pairs of concerned eyes.

"You're not going to puke, are you?" Lowen asked.

"No." His smile looked painful but some colour returned to his cheeks. "I'm fine." Raising a hand, he pointed behind Sylvie and she twisted in her seat in time to see the slick black head of a seal disappearing under the water nearby.

Pippa tilted her head. "I love how they're not scared at all." Her eyes stayed on the water and they all watched the seal reappear and swim around the boat. "We should have brought wetsuits."

"Can you just get in and swim with them?" Sylvie's gaze switched to Lowen, who nodded. "I remember you telling me that you used to swim with seals as a kid, but I since convinced myself that you were just telling a little girl stories."

"It was all true," Lowen told her.

"Lowen would spend hours telling me stories when we were kids," Sylvie told Pippa, feeling a wonderful pang of nostalgia. "Now that I think of it, my parents must have had such an easy time of it while we were on holidays with Lowen. He always kept me entertained and looked after me."

Briefly, Lowen returned her smile, then pointed to the seal which had reappeared again. They watched it playing for a while, then continued on, moving slowly around the islands and spotting several more groups of seals, along with a few babies, which thrilled Sylvie. In between the nature spotting, Pippa and Sylvie chatted away while the men stayed pretty quiet. Jago seemed fine but certainly wasn't as relaxed as he usually was.

"How long do you want to stay out?" Lowen asked after an hour.

Since the question felt loaded, Sylvie said she was happy to head back whenever.

Pippa rubbed her hands together and suggested they go and find a hot drink somewhere. "Where haven't you been yet?" she asked Sylvie. "We could stop off at one of the off islands and find a cafe if you want?"

"I'd love to." Sylvie looked to Jago. "Where haven't we been?"

"St Martin's," he suggested.

"That's close," Pippa said. "And they have a few options for places to grab food and drinks."

"Don't you need to get back and check on Mia?" Lowen asked, frowning at Pippa.

"No. She'll be fine." Her jaw tensed and she glared at Lowen. "Weren't you just saying this morning how I should take more time off?"

He raised an eyebrow. "I was only checking you didn't want to get back."

"If I was rushing to get back I wouldn't have suggested more exploring, would I?"

Silence hung heavy and Pippa looked mortified for snapping at Lowen.

"What's the pub like on St Martin's these days?" Jago asked in a blatant attempt to ease the tension.

Sylvie hadn't been imagining it before – clearly Pippa had been strong-armed into coming along.

As they walked from the quay on St Martin's to the pub, they naturally split off with Pippa and Sylvie leading the way and the men following along behind. Sylvie reminded herself that Lowen and Jago hadn't seen much of each other in recent years and would be keen to catch up too.

"Sorry about earlier," Pippa said out of the side of her mouth. "I think Lowen and I are probably in need of some time alone to scream at each other."

"Is everything okay between you?" Sylvie asked quietly, already feeling a kinship with Pippa.

"I think we've both been working too hard recently. The craft fair really stressed Lowen out. Hopefully he'll relax again now it's over."

Sylvie was tempted to confide in Pippa about her worries around Lowen being so standoffish with her, but with the men close behind them she didn't feel she could.

Over lunch in the pub the conversation meandered pleasantly.

When they were leaving again, Pippa slipped her arm through Jago's. "I need you to tell me all about New York," she said happily. "And when the best time would be for us to visit."

Given the width of the path Lowen and Sylvie were excluded from the conversation as they fell into step behind. Sylvie strongly suspected that Pippa had engineered the walk back so Lowen had no choice but to speak to Sylvie. She should prob-

AN UNEXPECTED GUEST

ably have been grateful to her, but all it did was confirm that the issue with Lowen wasn't only in her head.

"Are you enjoying your trip?" Lowen asked, shoving his hands into his pockets.

"It's been great. The islands are beautiful." She pushed her hair from her face. "They're just like you described."

"Sorry I haven't been able to show you around. I hear Jago stepped in as tour guide."

Her eyes drifted to the back of Jago's head and she smiled. "It's strange getting to know him after hearing about him from you. He's not how I expected."

"Well, he's an adult now, so it's probably a good thing he's not how I described him."

"In my head he was kind of tough and scary." She grinned. "I guess because of that story you used to tell me about him beating up the kid at school."

He shot her a sidelong glance. "What story?"

"Remember, when the kid was bullying you and Jago stepped in and shoved him against the wall?"

"Oh, yeah." He shook his head. "You have a good memory."

"You told me several times! You always sounded so proud of him."

"It was a very long time ago," he said quietly.

Anger pulsed in her veins and once again it felt as though she was conversing with a stranger. "Why didn't you come to their funerals?" she asked, not bothering to specify who she was talking about.

"Why would I?" he asked, his tone utterly confused.

"Because they were your grandparents."

His jaw tightened and a vein pulsed at his temple. "We might have been related by blood, but that doesn't count for much in my book. It's certainly not a determiner of whether I spend my time and energy on people."

"Clearly," Sylvie said bitterly, her voice louder than she'd intended.

"What's that supposed to mean?"

"Never mind," she said through gritted teeth.

Pippa turned back to them. "I think New York in the spring would be good," she called to Lowen, grinning.

"Sounds great." He pulled his hands from his pockets to zip up his jacket. "What did you mean?" he asked again, when Pippa returned to chatting with Jago.

Sylvie didn't trust herself to speak. She knew exactly what Pippa had meant about needing time alone to scream at each other. If she continued the conversation she was sure that was where they were headed.

To her relief, the jetty came into view and she increased her pace to catch up with Jago and Pippa. As she took Jago's hand to steady herself onto the boat, he caught her eye and raised a quizzical eyebrow.

She squeezed his hand – silently telling him she was okay, while trying to convince herself of the same thing.

CHAPTER EIGHTEEN

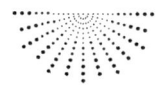

For the journey back to Old Town, Sylvie kept her eyes on the horizon, trying to focus on the breath-taking surroundings rather than the heaviness in her heart. Lowen attempted to catch her eye several times on the boat and on the beach, but she avoided looking at him until they were on the path up to Mirren's house.

"What did you mean earlier?" he asked quietly, taking her elbow to draw her close.

She resisted the temptation to shrug him off and instead waited a moment so that Jago and Pippa were out of earshot. "I was referring to the fact that you cut me and Mum out of your life as though we meant nothing to you." Tears stung the back of her eyes but she fought them. "I can understand why you wouldn't want to see Grandma and Grandpa, but what did me and Mum do to deserve the cold shoulder treatment?"

He kept his hand on her arm as though she might bolt. "It wasn't like that. I didn't want to see our grandparents, but it was different with you and Bess. I was busy and—"

"Oh, come on!" she snapped, removing her arm from his grip. "That's crap and you know it. At least have the decency to tell the truth."

"I am." He looked indignant and she wondered if he genuinely believed his own lies. "I thought of you and your mum often. I always assumed we'd catch up again, but time just seemed to slip by."

"I'm here *now*," she said. "And you still have zero interest in spending time with me."

He shook his head, but she wasn't keen to hear more of his lies, especially since Jago and Pippa had stopped at the back door and were watching their exchange.

"It doesn't matter," she said, as she began to walk away. "I'll be gone in a couple of days and you can go back to pretending I don't exist."

"It's not like that," he said, following her. "I'm glad you're here."

"You have a really weird way of showing it," she hissed.

"I'm sorry."

Ignoring his apology, she smiled as they reached Jago and Pippa.

"Everything okay?" Jago asked.

Sylvie told him everything was fine, then walked quickly inside. Thankfully Lowen and Pippa only stayed for a quick coffee, and with Mirren around the atmosphere was much easier. Once they'd left, Jago disappeared upstairs. Sylvie very much felt like doing the same but she'd volunteered to help Mirren cook dinner. Maybe being alone with her thoughts wasn't such a great idea anyway.

She went into a trance while she cut the veg, then had to focus when Mirren's voice cut through the silence.

"He was fine," Sylvie said, answering the question about how Jago had been while they were out on the boat. "It really seems as though he grew out of the seasickness."

"I didn't mean that." Mirren's eyes glazed over while she peered into the fridge. "Never mind. Ignore me."

Sylvie's curiosity was well and truly piqued. "What did you mean?"

"I thought it might be hard for him to go to the Eastern Isles." Mirren hesitated, looking thoughtful. "I wonder how he's feeling generally about being here. It's the first time he's been back since his dad's funeral. I guess it's hard for him, but he doesn't say much to me."

A sliver of dread sneaked its way into Sylvie's stomach. "I think he's doing okay," she said vaguely.

"It's great timing that you're here. All the sightseeing will be a good distraction for him."

"Yes." The knife in her hand remained hovering over the carrot on the chopping board. "What did you mean about the Eastern Isles?"

Mirren closed the fridge door without removing anything. "I didn't mean to be cryptic. Do you know how my husband died?"

Sylvie gave a sympathetic smile. "Jago mentioned it."

"His body was found over on the Eastern Isles. That's why I thought it might have been difficult for Jago. But he was okay, was he?"

The sliver of dread intensified as Sylvie thought back to that morning when Jago had told her he didn't want to go with them, and then to her teasing about him being scared of seals. She pressed her lips together as the knife clattered out of her hand.

"What's wrong?" Mirren asked.

"Nothing. I just think I might have been really insensitive with Jago ... I didn't know the significance of the Eastern Isles." She pressed her palm to her forehead and let out a low growl. "Bloody men! Why didn't he say something?"

"I'm sure it's fine."

Sylvie stepped away from the chopping board. "Do you mind if I leave you to it for a little while? I think I need to go and apologise."

On the upstairs landing, Sylvie paced a few times before finally working up the courage to knock on Jago's door. When he shouted for her to come in, she pushed at the door.

"Everything all right?" he asked, sitting on the bed and looking over his laptop at her.

"You tell me." She went and perched beside him.

He closed the laptop, looking at her with a bemused smile. "As far as I know everything is fine."

"Why didn't you tell me the reason you didn't want to go seal-watching?"

He squinted at her.

"It was because of your dad, wasn't it?" she asked.

"Oh." He squeezed his eyes shut. "You've been talking to Mum?"

"Yes. And now I feel terrible for teasing you and for not taking no for an answer. If you'd told me why you didn't want to go I never would have kept on at you to come."

"It's fine." He covered her hand with his. "You weren't to know."

"Why didn't you tell me?"

"Because you'd already teased me about being scared of seals." His lips hitched upwards. "I knew if I told you after that you'd feel bad about it."

"So you just let me keep going on?"

"It all worked out in the end. I felt a bit weird being out there, but maybe it was better to face it."

"I wish I'd known."

His eyes sparkled. "So you could have held my hand?"

"Yes." Her heart rate increased as she became hyper aware of the way their hands were touching now. After a moment he removed his hand from hers.

"What happened with Lowen today?" he asked. "You looked upset or angry or something."

"I was both of those things," she said sadly. "Still am actually."

He looked at her questioningly, clearly wanting to know more but not wanting to pry.

"He said something that upset me," she told him. "He apologised after, but I can't help but think it was probably a mistake for me to come here."

Silence filled the room for a moment. "Who would have kept me entertained?" Jago asked wryly.

"That's a good point." Her heart fluttered under the intensity of his gaze and she felt the intimacy of sitting on his bed with him. She stood abruptly. "I should go and help with dinner."

"Good idea. I'm starving."

She stopped at the door, remembering the reason she'd gone up there in the first place. "Are you okay?"

"Yes. Thanks."

Her palms were sweaty and she smiled awkwardly before pulling the door behind her.

CHAPTER NINETEEN

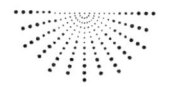

On Tuesday morning Sylvie was contemplating what to do for the day when the noise of the back door made her turn.

"Morning!" Trystan said, wandering into the kitchen in jeans and a crisp blue shirt under a lightweight puffer jacket.

"You've already missed Mirren," Sylvie told him. "She said she wouldn't be back until the afternoon."

"I was actually looking for you." He flashed her a dazzling smile as he held out an envelope in fancy ivory paper. "I wanted to deliver this."

"My flight is tomorrow," she said, taking the wedding invitation but not bothering to open it.

"I know, but I heard you're between jobs and don't have anything pressing to rush back for so I was hoping I might be able to convince you to stick around a little longer."

She opened her mouth to speak but couldn't get a word in.

"I'll cover the cost of changing your flight. I'm happy to cover any costs, and you can bill me for hairdressing services too."

"What's going on?" she asked, taking in the desperation in his eyes. "I feel as though there's more to this than Beth's hair."

Trystan sank into a chair. "It's not just the hair. It's the pregnancy hormones and the morning sickness, and missing her mum and feeling guilty about her dad ... lots of things that I can't do anything about. The only thing I *can* do is beg you to stay and do her hair on Saturday."

Sylvie pulled out the chair beside him. He was right that she didn't have any reason to rush home. Part of her desperately wanted to stay longer.

"I don't know if I can," she said, scratching her eyebrow. "I need to think about it."

"So that's a maybe?" he asked, eyes shining with hope.

Nodding slowly, she wished circumstances were different and she could tell him that she'd stay for the wedding, but given the way things were between her and Lowen she suspected extending her stay again would be a very bad idea. In fact she should probably tell Trystan she definitely couldn't instead of getting his hopes up.

An image of the entire Treneary family all dressed up in wedding attire and in full celebratory mode tugged at her. Being invited to join them felt special, even if it was mostly because of her hairdressing skills. It would also mean an extra week of exploring. She was sure there were plenty more places she and Jago could visit. Her stomach felt fluttery at the thought of spending more time with him.

Trystan was looking at her quizzically and she shook her thoughts away.

"Let me think about it and I'll let you know later," she told him.

"Thank you." He stood, eyeing her pleadingly. "It would be so great if you could stay."

She smiled at his efforts to persuade her.

"One more thing," he said when he reached the door.

"What is it?"

"Can we keep this conversation between us? If you decide to stay can you let Beth believe it was all your own decision?"

"Okay," she said slowly, not sure why that would be an issue for Beth. It was actually very sweet how he'd intervened. She didn't get a chance to quiz him on it since he was apparently in a rush to get to work.

She remained sitting at the table for a while, trying her best to ignore the twinge of excitement at the idea of staying longer. A creak of floorboards overhead brought her thoughts to Jago. When the water rattled through the pipes she imagined him getting into the shower, then immediately cursed her wandering mind. Picking up her phone she slipped out of the back door, hoping the fresh, sea air would bring her to her senses.

She pulled her cardigan around her and paced the patio with her phone pressed to her ear. A conversation with Lowen would surely quash any ideas about staying for the wedding. That was if he even answered the phone. She was about to give up when his voice finally greeted her.

"Hi," she said nervously, wracking her brain for what she was going to say.

"Hey. I was going to call you later. We should hang out again before you leave."

To say she was surprised was an understatement. "That would be good."

"Your flight is tomorrow, right?"

"Yes." She stopped her pacing as she decided her best approach was a direct one. "Except I was wondering how you'd feel about me staying for another week."

"What?" he muttered.

"Beth found out I have some talent as a hairdresser and wants me to stay and do her hair for the wedding. I said I'd think about it. I'll probably say I can't. I should get home, I suppose."

"You could stay longer if you want to," he said, the slightest tremor to his voice.

"I don't want to outstay my welcome. And yesterday ..." She trailed off, not quite sure what to say on the subject.

"I'm sorry about yesterday. I've been working a lot and the

house renovations have been stressful. I should have made more effort to spend time with you."

"Oh." It was the exact opposite she expected from the conversation and she felt unusually speechless.

"You should stay for the wedding, if you want. I'm sure you'd enjoy it."

"I think I would too," she agreed.

"Okay. Good. In that case why don't you come over to Bryher again tomorrow? I can show you around the pottery studio properly."

A warm glow started in her chest and spread around her body. "That would be great."

He told her he'd see her tomorrow before ending the call. In a daze, Sylvie went back into the kitchen, where Jago had just wandered in. His hair was damp from the shower, making it appear darker than usual.

"Did I hear Trystan before?" he asked.

"Yes. He brought me a wedding invitation." She slipped it from the envelope and scanned the gold calligraphy with the details.

Jago hovered behind her. "Are you going to stay for it?"

"Yeah."

"Really? I thought you were adamant you were leaving tomorrow."

"I was." She stood up and grinned at him. "But I got a better offer so I changed my mind. I love weddings."

"Where are you going?" he asked when she picked up her bag and headed to the door.

"Just to the shop."

"Do you want company?"

She smiled at his eagerness. "Nope, that's okay thanks."

"I don't have anything else to do."

"I have no plans for this afternoon," she told him. "We can hang out then."

"What exactly are you shopping for that you don't want me to know about?"

She shot him a playful look. "Did it ever occur to you that I might be getting sick of you?"

"No." His eyes twinkled. "That seems highly unlikely. Now tell me what embarrassing items you're buying?"

"I'll see you later," she called over her shoulder as she waltzed out of the door. Her smile remained while she walked into Hugh Town, and she was still feeling a tingle of warmth from her surprising morning when she knocked on Beth's door on the way back.

Beth answered the door dressed in a pair of black leggings and what looked to be one of Trystan's hoodies. Her skin was pale with dark circles under her eyes.

"Are you okay?" Sylvie asked automatically.

"I thought the morning sickness would be easing up by now, but it's dragging on."

"I heard you were having a rough time of it." She pulled out her purchase from the chemist and handed it over. "I don't know how effective these are, but a friend of mine swore by them when she was pregnant."

"Travel sickness bands," Beth said, a line appearing between her eyebrows as she looked at the packet.

"They target pressure points on your wrists which is supposed to alleviate nausea. I don't know if they'll help but it's worth a try."

"Thank you." Beth looked a touch emotional. "That's really thoughtful of you."

"I was also thinking about the wedding ... would it be okay if I changed my mind about coming?"

"Yes." Her eyes widened. "Of course. Please tell me this means you'll do my hair."

"I'd love to."

Beth stepped forward to embrace Sylvie. "Thank you so much."

"It'll be my pleasure."

"I'm sorry," Beth said, taking a step back. "I don't know why I'm keeping you on the doorstep. Come in."

"If you're not feeling well I'll leave you to rest."

"Please come in." She ushered her with her hand. "I'm mostly feeling sorry for myself. Everything feels a bit too much these last few days. I completely bit Trystan's head off this morning over nothing. Now I feel terrible because all he ever tries to do is make me feel better and I take everything out on him." She led the way to the kitchen. "I wouldn't be surprised if he changed his mind before Saturday."

"I would," Sylvie said. "The man worships you. It's my mission in life to find a man who looks at me the way Trystan looks at you."

"I'm very lucky to have found him," Beth said as she set about making drinks. "I wish I could focus on the positives in my life instead of being so stressed."

"Weddings are stressful," Sylvie said, hopping up onto a stool at the breakfast bar.

"You were married, weren't you? Was your wedding stressful?"

"Very. And afterwards I was annoyed with myself that I couldn't relax and enjoy it."

"I wish I could relax. It's not so easy when I feel sick all day every day." Her eyes brightened slightly as she wrangled the acupressure bands from their packaging.

"I hope they work," Sylvie said.

"Me too." She smiled lightly and put them on. "I'm really grateful that you can stay longer. I know it seems vain to be hung up on my hair …"

"It's your wedding day," Sylvie pointed out. "Of course you want to look good. And you should have someone pampering you."

"That's exactly it. I want to feel special."

"You will. I'll make sure of it."

Beth sighed. "I said to Trystan this morning that I just need one thing to go right." Her eyes bulged before her features softened dramatically. "He convinced you to stay, didn't he?"

Sylvie was a terrible liar and stuttered some random words.

"What did he do? Bribe you, or beg you? Hopefully he didn't resort to threats of kidnapping or anything ... I wouldn't entirely put it past him."

"What are you talking about?" Sylvie asked.

"I'm assuming Trystan somehow got you to agree to stay for the wedding and do my hair ... and then he made you promise not to mention he had anything to do with it?"

Sylvie caved and gave a subtle nod. "I don't understand why he didn't want me to let on that he'd spoken to me."

Beth rested her forearms on the counter. "Because he suggested it this morning and I told him it wasn't fair to guilt trip you into staying just to do my hair. I had a rant at him for even suggesting it."

"He's really concerned about you." Sylvie tilted her head sympathetically. "He just wants to make you happy."

"I love that man so much," Beth said, adjusting the strap of her acupressure band. She straightened up abruptly. "Right, that's it. Enough of feeling sorry for myself. It's the week before my wedding, I should be excited."

"You do have a lot going on," Sylvie said. "Don't be too hard on yourself."

"My best friend arrives from Plymouth on Friday with her husband and little girl. I can't wait to see them. I'm sure I'll feel better once Dee is here."

"I'm sure you will. Do you have much you need to do this week? If there's anything I can help with let me know. The only thing on my schedule is going to Bryher tomorrow ... oh and doing my washing every three days when I run out of clean clothes." She gasped and slapped a hand to her mouth. "I've got nothing to wear for the wedding. Are there any clothes shops around here?"

"Not where you could get anything suitable for a wedding."

"Do you mind if I come in jeans and a jumper? I promise to hang back and not get in any of the photos."

"I don't care what you wear," Beth told her, picking up her phone. "I'm sure we can find you something nice though."

"What are you doing?" Sylvie asked when Beth began to tap on her phone.

"Messaging Seren and Keira to ask if they've got something you can borrow. They'll be about the same size as you."

"Do you think they'll mind?"

"No." She watched her phone. "I need to add you to this group chat about the hen night. It's on Thursday night in the Mermaid Inn … Keira and Seren are now arguing about who has a dress for you to borrow." She fell silent, a smile playing at her lips as she messaged them back. "They're both going to bring clothes over on Thursday before we go out. It sounds as though you might have to do a fashion show for us … it's turning into a hen night activity. A contest to see who can dress you the best."

Sylvie chuckled. "I suppose it might be fun."

"Keira's going to make her famous frozen margaritas, so yes, it will definitely be fun."

CHAPTER TWENTY

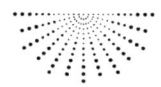

Sylvie's phone conversation with Lowen gave her a glimmer of hope that they could sort out the awkwardness between them and properly reconnect. Sadly, her positivity dwindled overnight and she woke on Wednesday with a feeling of dread lodged deep in her stomach. She lingered in bed, considering the ways in which the day might disappoint her.

When she messaged Lowen to check what time she should go over to Bryher, she half expected him to reply with some excuse for why they couldn't hang out after all.

In fact, he told her he was around the pottery studio all day, and she should come over whenever she felt like it. He added that he'd be going to Trystan's stag party that night so he'd get the boat back with her late in the afternoon.

After chatting to Mirren and Jago over a leisurely breakfast, Sylvie finally forced herself to get on her way. They told her to have a good time, and Jago gave her a reassuring smile that made her wish she was spending the day with him so she wouldn't have to worry about how the day would go.

As she left the house, she checked her watch. Either she needed to hurry to get to the boat or take her time and get the next one in a couple of hours. Not feeling like rushing, she fired off a message to Lowen, telling him she had a couple of things to do before she got the boat.

It was easier than she expected to find hairdressing scissors in Hugh Town, and she stocked up on grips and a few new combs and brushes too.

Feeling like time alone, she avoided places where she thought she might bump into someone she knew and headed to the Harbour Café for lunch. Sitting at a table by the window, she ate a toasted sandwich and watched the boats coming and going, then lingered over a couple of cups of coffee while she waited for the ferry to take her to Bryher.

The door to the pottery studio was slightly ajar when Sylvie arrived. Mia was sitting by the till, and immediately put a finger to her lips when she caught sight of Sylvie.

"Lowen is working on the pottery wheel," she whispered. "If you go quietly you can watch him work. I know it sounds a bit creepy but I like to secretly watch him. If he knows he's being watched he stops."

She tipped her head to the archway at the back of the room and Sylvie walked hesitantly over there. The idea of watching him in secret was definitely a little creepy, but as soon as she caught the look of contentment on his face, she was mesmerised. His hands seemed to move instinctively over the wet clay. With the gentlest touch, it bent to his will, shifting gradually from a lumpy ball of clay into what she assumed would end up being a mug.

When he eventually pressed the foot pedal and the wheel slowed to a stop, she cleared her throat to make her presence known.

"Hi," he said, a smile flashing on and off his face as he turned on the stool. "How long have you been there?"

"A few minutes. I didn't want to interrupt."

"Do you want a turn?" He switched his attention back to the

clay, running a piece of wire under it to remove it from the board.

"On the pottery wheel?" she asked, confused.

"Yeah. Everyone seems to like to have a go."

"Yeah, okay." She moved further into the room, then lowered herself onto Lowen's stool when he offered it.

"I have no idea what I'm doing," she told him.

"It's okay." He used the same piece of wire to cut a chunk of fresh clay, then slapped it onto the wheel in front of her. "Mia reckons I'm a good teacher."

For the next half hour, it was as though there'd never been any issue between them. Things were exactly as Sylvie had imagined when she'd had the idea to come and surprise Lowen.

Conversation was all about the clay, and how to work it, and the different techniques Lowen used. He was completely at ease while Sylvie questioned him about how he'd come to own the pottery studio, and how he'd grown his business.

After two attempts, Sylvie managed to create what Lowen insisted was a passable attempt at a mug. She was washing her hands at the sink in the corner when Mia came in.

"There's a rumour going around," she said, leaning against the sideboard, her eyes fixed on Sylvie.

It flashed into Sylvie's head that Mia was about to say something about her and Jago spending so much time together. It wasn't as though anything had happened between them, and she definitely hadn't done anything wrong, so the guilt which stirred inside her was illogical.

"You've got that look on your face," Lowen told Mia. "It's easy to tell when you want something. Why don't you just spit it out so I can say no and you can get back to work."

Mia laughed. "In case you haven't noticed I'm not exactly snowed under out there. Anyway, this conversation has nothing to do with you."

"So you want a favour from Sylvie?" Lowen asked.

"When exactly did I say I wanted a favour?" She lifted her chin in defiance of Lowen.

"Go ahead, then," Lowen said, raising his eyebrow cockily.

Mia shrunk a little as her gaze flicked back to Sylvie. "I heard you're a hairdresser."

"I knew you were after a favour," Lowen said, chuckling

"Not a *favour*," Mia said. "A *haircut*. Which I'm more than happy to pay for."

"Of course," Sylvie said. "I'll definitely do it as a favour."

Lowen ran a hand through his hair, ruffling the back of it.

"You could do with a haircut too," Mia said.

"I was planning on going to the barber's this week, before the wedding, but I'm not actually sure when I'll have time."

"I can do it," Sylvie said.

"Really?"

"I have scissors with me if you want me to do it now."

Mia's eyes widened. "That is so cool. Do you just always carry your hairdressing things with you?"

"No." Sylvie beamed. "I was at the shop this morning buying them. I should also tell you that I'm not actually a qualified hairdresser."

Mia waved a hand in the air. "Do hairdressers even need qualifications?"

"I think they do, actually," Sylvie pointed out. "At least if you want to claim you're a professional. I have plenty of experience though."

"That's good enough for me," Mia said.

"I don't suppose we'll be missing out on much business if we shut up shop for the afternoon," Lowen said. "Shall we go up to the house and play hairdresser there?"

Having something to focus on made the afternoon go by in a blink, and they were getting the boat back to St Mary's together before Sylvie knew it. On the ferry she was introduced to Gareth, who she'd also spoken to briefly on the trip over but hadn't realised he was Mia's boyfriend. He hung around chatting to them for the quiet crossing, then was apparently nipping home to get changed before joining the stag party in the Mermaid Inn.

Outside the pub, Sylvie said goodbye to Lowen while wondering if Jago was already inside. She found herself longing to see him and spent the walk through Hugh Town thinking exclusively of him.

With her mind elsewhere, she didn't spot him walking towards her at Old Town Bay until he was almost in front of her.

"How was your day?" he asked cheerfully.

Her eyes roamed over his jeans and white shirt, the sleeves of which were rolled up to show off his toned forearms. "Good," she said forcing her eyes to his face.

"Yeah?"

She nodded, liking how it wasn't just a perfunctory question. He genuinely wanted to know, which made her reflect on the afternoon too. It *had* been good.

"You look unsure," Jago prompted.

"It was good," she said, trying to pinpoint what it was that niggled at her. "I had a play on the pottery wheel. Oh, and I gave Lowen and Mia haircuts. It was all pretty chilled out."

"That's great. I told you he'd be happy to hang out with you when he wasn't so busy."

"Yeah ... I suppose you were right." She rolled her eyes. "As painful as it is to say!"

"I'm sure." He smiled widely. "I have to hurry. I'm already in trouble for being late."

"Lowen's just got to the pub," she told him.

"I know. I'm getting abuse on the group message for being the last." He checked his watch. "To be fair, I'm not even late. The rest of them are early."

"I'll let you get on." Sylvie stepped to the side. "I'll see you in the morning."

"You'll probably see me tonight. I don't think it's going to be a wild night."

"Famous last words," she said cheekily.

CHAPTER TWENTY-ONE

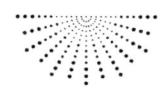

A loud crash pulled Sylvie back from sleep not long after she'd drifted off. Adrenaline pulsed through her, getting her up and out of bed before she was even fully awake. Her instincts had her concerned for Mirren, and the bright light dazzled her when she stepped into the hallway.

Across the landing, Mirren stood in her pyjamas. "Jago Treneary!" she growled, standing over him. "What on earth are you doing?"

Face down on the carpet, he lifted his head a little then dropped it again. His entire upper body was shaking in silent laughter. "Are you ever going to get those stairs fixed?" he asked, rolling onto his back.

Mirren folded her arms across her chest. "Please tell me you're not going to use the same excuse as the last time you fell up my stairs?"

"The stairs are wonky!"

Mirren glanced over at Sylvie. "He was always very giggly when he was drunk – even as a teenager."

"I don't giggle!" he said, then did exactly that.

As her heart rate settled down, Sylvie smiled. "That was definitely a giggle."

"Oh, hello!" Jago turned his head in her direction. "Where did you come from? And why are you upside down?"

"It might be you who's upside down," she told him.

He grinned adorably. "You look very nice when you're upside down."

"Oh, god," Mirren groaned. "I think I'll go back to bed if you're going to start flirting." She gave him a gentle tap with her foot. "You're not injured, are you?"

"I might have bruised my forehead." He pressed between his eyebrows. "You should get softer carpet up here if you're not going to fix the wonky stairs." He set himself off laughing again but made no effort to get up.

"Go to bed, Jago," Mirren said before heading back to her room.

Sylvie took a couple of steps towards him. "Do you need help?"

"I really like your pyjamas," he told her with a lopsided smile. "Especially the top because it's a bit see-through."

Her arms shot across her chest and she glared down at him as he launched into another fit of giggles.

"Don't do your angry face!" He pouted and made a wobbly attempt to get up.

"How much have you had to drink?" Sylvie asked, reaching down to help him.

"I had to drink for Trystan." With her support he managed to get to his feet and stumble along the hall.

"Surely Trystan can manage his own drinks." She grimaced as he wobbled.

"Trystan doesn't drink," he said, flopping onto the bed and almost pulling Sylvie with him.

"So you had to drink for him?" she asked, pulling her vest strap back onto her shoulder.

"Yes. Noah had this great idea that for every round, one of us would drink Trystan's drink for him. Because we're good brothers." He crawled up the bed and settled his head on the pillow, his eyelids drooping. "I have the best brothers."

"I'm glad you had a fun night," Sylvie said, resisting the urge to run her fingers over his hair.

"Do you know what's really good?" he asked, gazing up at her.

"What?" she whispered.

"It's really good that Lowen didn't want to hang out with you."

She managed to keep her mouth in a straight line even as her heart sank.

"It *is* good," he said firmly. "Because it means I got to hang out with you." He smiled lazily. "I really like hanging out with you."

"I like hanging out with you too."

His eyes fluttered closed and Sylvie lingered for a moment after his features relaxed into a picture of contentment.

The following morning, Sylvie ate breakfast with Mirren while joking about the state that Jago had come home in. Unsurprisingly, there was no sign of him. When Mirren went out after breakfast, Sylvie was tempted to go and wake him.

Ignoring the impulse, she took advantage of the mild weather and sat out on the patio, enjoying the autumn sun on her face and the fabulously peaceful view over the bay. She strained to hear sounds from the house but the only thing that stirred her ears were the noisy gulls circling on the gentle breeze and the hush of the sea as it caressed the shore.

Eventually, she went back in to make another coffee and heard movement upstairs. When Jago failed to appear, she made him a coffee and set off up the stairs. She knocked lightly on the door to his bedroom, then turned the handle at a grunt from inside.

"I'm asleep," he muttered, face down on the bed with only a pair of tight black boxers on.

"I wondered if you might like coffee." She stayed in the doorway, cringing slightly as it occurred to her that she might be crossing boundaries. What was she doing going into his bedroom while he was still sleeping?

"You're an angel," he said, opening his eyes but not managing to move. "I thought you were going to be my mum asking me to do something around the house."

"Like fix the wonky stairs?" she asked, placing the steaming mug on the bedside table.

Sitting up, he shot her a puzzled look, then touched his forehead and groaned. "Please tell me falling up the stairs and landing on my face was a bad dream?"

"I'm afraid not."

He looked fairly sheepish and picked up the coffee. "Thanks for this."

"You're welcome." She took a couple of steps towards the door, trying not to let her gaze linger on his barely clothed body. "Do you feel like going for a walk today?" she asked, hoping she sounded casual.

He stretched his neck. "I think my day is mainly going to be spent nursing my hangover and feeling sorry for myself. Walking probably isn't on the agenda."

"It's a gorgeous day. The fresh air and exercise will soon cure your hangover. I can make us a picnic."

"Have you ever had a hangover? Because you don't seem to have any clue about how to deal with them."

"I promise you, you'll feel better in no time."

"You just don't know what to do with yourself, do you?"

"What?" Her voice came out in a higher pitch than she'd intended.

"If you don't have me to hang out with, you don't know what to do."

"I'm perfectly capable of going for a picnic alone," she

said primly. "I just thought you might like to come. Lying around in bed isn't going to do anything to help your hangover." She gave him a smug look. "If you want to stay there and wallow, that's up to you. I'm off to enjoy the day."

"Fine!" he shouted as she pulled the door behind her. "Give me five minutes to shower, then I'll prove to you that you know nothing about curing hangovers."

"I'll make the picnic!" she called happily, then went back downstairs with a spring in her step.

∼

"I think I feel worse," Jago groaned, face down on the picnic blanket on Pelistry Beach. "Cheese and tomato sandwiches definitely don't help hangovers. Though I really think that was obvious."

"The fresh air must be helping," Sylvie said, amused.

"What was wrong with the stuffy air in my bedroom, that's what I want to know."

"Your room stank like a brewery."

"Exactly." He grinned at her as he sat up. "I love breweries." After looking up and down the deserted stretch of golden sand he turned to her. "Close your eyes."

"What?"

"Close your eyes," he repeated. "Please."

After a moment of him beaming at her, she did as he asked. "Why am I closing my eyes?"

"Because I need to go skinny dipping. Don't open your eyes unless you want to see me naked."

Her eyes opened automatically and he let out a rumbly laugh while he whipped his hoodie off and then his T-shirt. "I knew it!" he said mischievously.

"Are you seriously getting naked?" she asked, feeling a tingle of excitement as his hand went to his belt buckle.

"Yes. Now stop being a perv and close your eyes. Unless you want to come with me?"

"Skinny dipping?" she asked, putting a hand over her eyes.

"Yes. Since your hangover tactics are useless I'm going to have to resort to swimming. That water's freezing, by the way. This is what you've reduced me to."

"Are you serious?"

"The shock of it will fix my hangover in seconds. Right, I'm off. No peeking!"

She waited about half a second before opening an eye and sneaking a look through her fingers. Since he had his back to her, she dropped her hand and let her eyes rove over the deliciously taut skin of his back and the paleness of his backside.

She didn't have time to look away when he glanced back over his shoulder. "Pervert!" he shouted, making her laugh loudly.

The sight of him prancing around as he forced himself into the cold water kept her laughing until he was fully submerged.

CHAPTER TWENTY-TWO

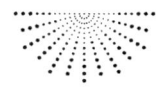

Seren and Keira were in especially high spirits when they arrived at Mirren's house that afternoon laden down with dresses, shoes and accessories for Sylvie. Her protests that she could try on outfits in private the following day were brushed aside, mainly by Keira, who insisted the fashion show was now part of the hen night itinerary.

Sylvie fell in love with one of Keira's dresses before she even had it on. In the downstairs bathroom, she pulled the maxi dress over her head and shuffled the soft, clingy material into place. The green and white flower pattern was wonderfully unique, and she adjusted the low neckline as she stepped out into the hallway. She paused, tugging on the skirt to reposition the slit which ran up her thigh.

She was about to go and show it off to her waiting audience in the living room when she glanced along the hall and realised she also had an audience in the kitchen. Jago sat at the table, his eyes wide as they travelled up and down the length of her body. If she hadn't already been sure it was the dress she'd wear for the wedding, the look on his face cinched it. He was practically drooling, and the longing in his eyes made butterflies dance in her stomach.

Clearing her throat got his attention and his eyes darted up to meet hers. A smile cracked across his face, and he gave her a definitive thumbs up that had her grinning as she sauntered into the living room to a round of gasps and gushing.

Since she'd been wearing the same three outfits for the past week and a half, she borrowed a shirt dress from Seren for the pub that evening too. When she nipped back into the bathroom to change again, Jago was nowhere to be seen, but the image of him looking her up and down stayed with her over the course of the evening.

The Mermaid Inn wasn't busy – a fact that most members of the hen party were grateful for since Seren had arranged karaoke for after dinner. The twist was that no one was allowed to choose their own songs. Watching Mirren sing "Barbie Girl" was pretty entertaining. As was Keira's rendition of the Ghostbusters theme tune.

"It's great that you could stay for longer," Pippa said, standing beside Sylvie by the bar while Seren took to the microphone with Keira, laughing their way through an ear-splitting rendition of "Sex Bomb".

"It's been really lovely getting to know everyone." Sylvie's thoughts went to Jago's remark the previous night about Lowen not wanting to hang out with her. Except Lowen had been perfectly fine with her when she'd been to the pottery studio, so she should just forget about the previous awkwardness. "It's a shame Lowen's been so busy," she found herself saying.

Sympathy flickered in Pippa's eyes. "I'm not sure it's just that."

"How do you mean?" Sylvie asked, her heart rate notching up.

"I'm not entirely sure." Pippa shook her head. "Ignore me."

"Sylvie!" Keira's voice in the microphone was impossible to ignore. "You're up!"

"No." She let out a nervous laugh. "I haven't had enough to drink to get up and sing." Honestly, there'd been plenty of drinks flowing with the meal, not to mention the margaritas they'd drunk prior to leaving the house. Even so, she still didn't feel like getting up to sing.

"Here," Noah said, handing her a shot across the bar. "That should help."

Mirren patted her on the shoulder. "If I had to do it, you're going to have to do it. No one's allowed to leave before they've sung."

Resignedly, Sylvie knocked the shot back with a grimace then made her way to the tiny stage in the corner.

"*I'm* not singing!" Beth declared from her seat at the table. "It's my hen night so I'm exempt."

"That's definitely not how it works," Keira said as she handed the microphone over to Sylvie.

"I'll be exempt on the grounds of pregnancy then," Beth said, smoothing a hand over her stomach, which was still pretty flat.

Seren plonked herself down at the table. "That's no excuse either, I'm afraid."

As the first bars of "Dancing Queen" sounded, Sylvie caught Pippa's eye and called for her to join her. She shook her head emphatically until Sylvie pointed out that it would be better than singing alone. That got her to relent, and she'd just picked up the other microphone as the song began.

The shot that Noah had given Sylvie seemed to kick in about halfway through the song, and she lost any self-consciousness and swung her hips as she belted out the familiar lyrics.

Beth dutifully got up to sing after them, but then complained that she was tired and needed her bed. Mirren seemed happy at the excuse to leave too and there was a round of hugs before the two of them left.

"Maybe I should have gone with them," Sylvie said as Noah brought over another tray of shots.

"Half an hour until last orders," he told them.

"I'm never going to get up in the morning," Pippa mumbled,

pulling her phone from her bag. "I'm messaging Mia to warn her she'll need to open the cafe for me."

"That's the spirit!" Seren said.

"No." Keira giggled as she pushed a shot glass filled with golden liquid across to Pippa. "*That's* the spirit!"

"I'm going to curse you tomorrow," Pippa said holding the drink aloft.

"Me too." Sylvie clinked her glass against Pippa's and drank it in one go. While Seren and Keira pored over the karaoke song book again, Sylvie shuffled closer to Pippa. "What were you saying earlier? About Lowen?"

"Oh." She pressed her lips together. "Nothing."

"You said it's not just that he's busy at the moment ..."

"Yeah. I don't know. He's quite stressed. Maybe it's the best man thing. He's nervous about the speech." She smiled lightly. "I think it's good you're staying longer, that's all. It's nice to have you here."

"Thank you."

"Do you want to sing again?" Seren asked Sylvie.

"No. I'm happy to watch you though."

Pippa leaned onto the table. "Whose daft idea was karaoke anyway?"

"Mine!" Keira put her hand up in the air like an excited child. "It's how I met the man of my dreams." She grinned at Noah, who rolled his eyes at her across the bar, then she turned back and launched into a long tale about how she used to frequent a pub where Noah worked in Bristol. Apparently karaoke night was always her favourite. Her meandering story about the start of their relationship kept them entertained until Noah rang the bell for last orders.

"No!" Seren whipped around to look at him. "It can't be closing time. The party is only getting started."

"Ooh look!" Keira called as the door swung open. "The stripper has arrived!"

"I was actually planning on keeping my clothes on," Jago said, amusement twinkling in his eyes.

"That's not allowed." Seren sidled over to him and tugged at the hem of his hoodie. "If you're gate-crashing a hen night, you have to get your kit off. That's the rule, I'm afraid."

Chuckling, he pushed her hand away. "I'm not gate-crashing. Mum sent me to drive Sylvie and Keira home."

"I'm going to wait for Noah," Keira declared.

"I have to cash up and clean up," Noah told her, coming over to them.

"I know." She draped her arms around his shoulders. "I'll help you."

"I'm sure it'll go much quicker that way," he replied, his voice dripping with sarcasm.

"Are you going to strip then or what?" Seren asked Jago.

His face scrunched up in amusement. "No!"

"Don't be boring. We all want a look, don't we?"

Noah raised his hand as he went back behind the bar. "I don't."

"I've already seen it all," Sylvie said, then slapped a hand over her mouth. The looks on Seren and Keira's faces had her cracking up too much to explain.

"I went skinny dipping this afternoon," Jago told them. "Sylvie was supposed to have her eyes closed, but apparently she couldn't resist looking."

Sylvie snorted a laugh. "That's not even what I meant. I was thinking about this morning in bed."

"What?" Seren screeched.

Again, Sylvie couldn't speak for laughing. This time it was the look on Jago's face that had her gasping for air.

"She brought me a coffee because I was hungover," he explained. "That's all. And I wasn't naked. Now, I think I should take you home before you start any more sordid rumours."

"Aw!" Seren gave his stomach a friendly pat. "Jago wants to take Sylvie home."

While the women cracked up into fits of giggles, Jago exchanged a look with Noah.

"I don't even see how that's funny."

"That's because you're about eight drinks behind them," Noah said.

"Are we going then?" Jago asked Sylvie.

She gave Keira and Seren hugs, then followed him outside.

"Thanks for coming to drive me," she said, putting a hand in front of her mouth as she hiccupped.

"I take it you had a good night?"

"It was really good."

On the drive home, she told him all about their karaoke performances, and even treated him to a short rendition of "Dancing Queen".

When she stepped out of the car and into the cool night air, she felt her smile fade away and a wave of melancholy washed over her. She stared out at the water, the surface of which glimmered under the silver light of the moon.

"Let's get you inside and into bed," Jago said, rubbing between her shoulder blades when she failed to move.

Slowly, she turned to face him. "When you said Lowen didn't want to spend time with me, was it because he'd said something or just because it's obvious that he doesn't want me around?"

Jago gave a quick shake of the head. "What?"

"Last night you said that he doesn't want to hang out with me, so I wondered if he'd said something to you."

"No." He chewed on his bottom lip. "Last night I was drunk. I have no idea what I was saying."

Sylvie tilted her head, refusing to break eye contact. "You said you were glad Lowen didn't want to spend time with me because it meant you got to hang out with me. Which was nice, in one sense ... But now I'm worried that Lowen said something to you ... or that everyone knows he doesn't want me around and I'm making a fool of myself just by being here."

"You're not." He moved his hands to her upper arms and gently rubbed her biceps. "Everyone likes having you here." His smile brightened. "In fact, from the conversation among the men last night I suspect you're going to have a queue of people wanting haircuts tomorrow."

"Really?" she asked, falling into step with Jago as he discreetly ushered her towards the house.

"Will you give me a trim?" he asked.

"Yes. I've been dying to get my hands on your hair."

"Have you now?"

"I might be drunk," she said, flashing him an over-the-top grimace.

He laughed loudly. "I hardly noticed!"

"You do have lovely hair. It's all thick and silky. Makes me want to sink my fingers into it."

"I'm already looking forward to teasing you about this conversation tomorrow."

"We have to be quiet now," she said as they reached the door. "I don't want to wake your mum up."

"Just be careful on the wonky stairs."

The comment kept her amused as Jago guided her through the house.

"Thank you for bringing me home," she said, resting a hand on his chest as he lingered in her bedroom doorway.

"You're welcome." She wanted him to kiss her, but all he did was give her hand a quick squeeze before he crossed the landing and disappeared into his own room.

Sylvie changed into her pyjamas before stumbling into bed. The evening had left her with a smile on her face. Lowen may not have been as pleased to see her as she'd expected, but she was still glad she was there.

His family had made her feel welcome, even if he hadn't.

CHAPTER TWENTY-THREE

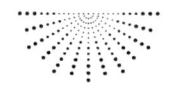

The knock at the bedroom door made Sylvie groan as she came slowly out of sleep.

"Good morning!" Jago said, far too loudly and far too brightly. To make things worse, he clapped his hands. Sylvie winced and pulled the covers over her head.

"What do you want?" she mumbled.

"Time for a walk!" He pulled the covers back and grinned at her. "Fresh air and exercise is what you need. Up you get while I pack a picnic."

"You're really enjoying this, aren't you?" She attempted to hide again but he kept hold of the duvet.

"Do you want to fix your hangover your way or my way?"

"I'm not getting out of this bed," she told him, snatching the duvet and plunging herself back into blissful darkness beneath it.

"My way it is then."

Sylvie breathed a sigh of relief when his footsteps retreated across the room. Ten minutes later the smell of fried food almost roused her, but her body refused to move from the comfort of the bed.

"Picnics don't cure hangovers," Jago announced when he returned with a tray in his hands.

"Is that a bacon sandwich?" Sylvie asked, hauling herself to sit up.

"It is indeed. And a Coke. You'll feel better in no time." He placed the tray on the bed, then moved to sit beside her, stretching his legs in front of him and picking up the remote from the bedside table. "All we need now is some brainless TV."

Sylvie ignored him as she concentrated on the deliciously greasy breakfast.

"I'll admit that was better than a cheese sandwich," she said, settling back on the pillows when she'd finished. "I still feel pretty rough though."

"Watch some mindless TV and have a nap, then you'll be all set to play hairdresser this afternoon."

She let out a moan of disapproval. "I don't know if I can."

"I thought you were dying to get your hands on my hair," he said, smirking as he leaned into her.

"Oh, god." A wave of nausea swept over her. "I said that, didn't I?"

"Yep." He poked her in the ribs. "You also announced to the pub that you'd seen me naked."

She put a hand over her face. "I'm never drinking again."

"That doesn't ring true. Especially since we're going to a wedding tomorrow."

"I might not be able to move from the bed by tomorrow."

"Now you're being dramatic."

Thankfully he was right. The hangover faded over the next few hours, and by the time Noah, Kit and Trystan arrived for haircuts she felt almost normal. Their banter revived her even more.

∼

With a good night's sleep behind her Sylvie was raring to go for the wedding the following morning.

The door to Peswera Cottage was opened by Ellie. She wore

pink pyjamas and beamed at Sylvie, then excitedly introduced her friend Ferne, who stood beside her, also sporting pyjamas.

"Are you the lady who's going to do our hair?" Ferne asked while Sylvie closed the door behind her, then slipped her shoes off.

"That's right," she replied.

"Me and my mummy bought lots of pretty slides and little flowers to go in our hair," Ferne told Sylvie. "Mummy says we just have to choose a few each, but we can't decide."

Ellie's eyes sparkled. "We want to wear them all."

"I think picking out a few is probably a good idea." Sylvie looked towards the kitchen, but there was no sign of Beth. "I can help you pick some out if you'd like. We'll find the nicest ones." She looked to Ellie. "Where's Mummy?"

"Upstairs with her friend Dee. You can go up there."

At the top of the stairs, Sylvie followed the low voices to Beth's room where the door was slightly ajar. She knocked on the door frame and went in.

"Oh, gosh, sorry," she said, immediately feeling the tension in the room. "Have I interrupted?"

From the chair at the dressing table, Beth gave her a small smile. "No, of course not. I'm just having a bit of a wobble."

The other woman rose from the end of the bed, offering her hand and introducing herself as Dee, Beth's best friend.

"Could you please tell Beth that it wouldn't be weird for me to give her away?" Dee said.

"Oh, erm …"

"See," Beth said. "It would be weird."

"I was just surprised by the question," Sylvie said in a rush. "I don't think it matters who gives you away."

"Obviously it should be my dad." There was a slight tremor to Beth's voice and Dee moved beside her to squeeze her shoulder.

Sylvie didn't know what the story was with Beth's dad and wasn't sure how to ask.

"He's in a care home, in Plymouth," Beth told her without prompting. "He has Alzheimer's so he couldn't be here. Obviously I knew this before. I told myself I didn't need anyone to give me away. It's just a stupid tradition. But now ... I don't know. It's hard, not having either of my parents here." She reached for a tissue and dabbed at her eyes.

"I think it would be fine for me to walk down the aisle with you," Dee said. "It's not as though it's actually about somebody giving you away these days. It's more like moral support as you walk in. I can do that."

Beth rolled her eyes. "It will look weird, and I don't want you taking any attention from me."

"Well that's the first good point you've made in this discussion." Dee sat back down on the bed. "What about Hugh? He'd do it. My husband," she clarified for Sylvie's benefit.

"I know he would," Beth said. "Kit offered as well."

"Take him up on it," Dee said firmly.

"Having Trystan's little brother give me away would be odd too."

"Only because you seem to be approaching this tradition in a fairly archaic way," Dee said.

Beth shook her head. "I don't need anyone to walk in with me. It's not as though it's even a long aisle. I'll be fine on my own." Her eyes flicked to Sylvie. "You look gorgeous, by the way. That dress is perfect on you."

"Thank you. Now what's the plan regarding hair? Should I do the girls first? Or you?"

"I think the girls," Beth said. "I'll get ready last."

"I made the mistake of letting Ferne pick out hair accessories," Dee told Sylvie. "It would be good if you could give them some direction about that. I think they'll take the advice of a professional hairdresser easier than their mothers."

Sylvie winced. "I'm not actually a professional hairdresser."

"You are today," Dee said with a grin.

The girls ended up being fairly pliant when it came to

choosing hair things. As soon as they saw Sylvie's array of brushes, combs, hairdryer and hot iron, their eyes widened in awe. They barely moved a muscle when they took it in turns to have their hair done.

The atmosphere became much more relaxed, and the girls' excitement was infectious. Dee brought up two glasses of champagne and three glasses of fizzy grape juice when Sylvie was putting the finishing touches to Beth's hair.

Clinking glasses together seemed to raise excitement levels even further, and Sylvie felt giddy after just a few sips of champagne. They were still up in Beth's bedroom when the knock came at the front door. Dee opened the window and leaned out to shout hello. She pulled herself back in with a huge grin on her face.

"It's a hot guy in a suit," she said, eyes twinkling.

"I think that's for you." Beth caught Sylvie's eye in the mirror. "Thank you so much for everything."

"You're welcome." She gave her a hug, careful not to mess up her hair. "I feel very honoured to have spent this morning with you." Grinning madly, she squeezed Beth's hand and told her to have a great day.

Downstairs, the sight of Jago in a suit took her breath away.

"You look amazing," he said, making her self-conscious as she crossed the room.

"Thank you." She slipped her feet into the heels she'd borrowed from Keira. They were higher than she'd usually wear but the added height gave her a confidence boost. "You look pretty good yourself," she told him, then automatically adjusted his tie.

With a grimace he loosened it again.

Sylvie shoved his hand out of the way and tightened it.

"Are you trying to kill me?"

"Nope. Just trying to make you look presentable." She slapped at his hand when he reached for his collar. "You can loosen it after the ceremony."

"You're a menace." He stretched his neck from side to side but left the tie as it was. "Ready to go?"

"Yes." She picked up her handbag and stepped outside, taking Jago's arm to steady herself.

In the lane, Keira and Noah were waiting in the golf cart.

"That dress looks like it was made for you," Keira said, reaching back to squeeze Sylvie's hand in greeting when they settled themselves on the back seat.

"I love it. And I'm so excited."

"Me too." Keira shifted in her seat to look back at Sylvie as the cart pulled away. "How's Beth doing?"

"Good."

"I can't imagine how excited I'd be if it was my wedding day. I get hyper at other people's." Keira leaned towards Noah. "Imagine if it was our wedding day. How excited would you be?"

Noah kept his eyes on the road. "Even the thought terrifies me."

"Hey!" Keira glared at him until he cracked a smile.

"I felt sick on the morning of my wedding," Sylvie said as her mind took her back to the day. "Maybe that should have been a sign."

"Was it nerves?" Keira asked eagerly.

Sylvie pursed her lips. "Nerves, excitement, stress ... I hadn't been sleeping because of all the worry of organising everything."

"Did you have a good day though?"

"Yes." Her features relaxed. "It was a really great day."

She turned in time to catch Jago looking at her intently, but he shifted his gaze and they continued in silence to the Star Castle Hotel.

When Jago took her hand to help her out of the golf cart Sylvie had to force herself to release it again. She stuck by his side while people mingled in the car park and foyer, and stayed with him when they were ushered into the conservatory where rows of elegant white seating were set out. At the front of the room, Trystan stood with Lowen under a trellis archway, entwined with vines and beautiful white blooms. The entire ceiling was covered in grape vines too.

"It's a beautiful setting," Sylvie said, following Jago along the front row. Only when she sat down did she panic and lean close to him. "Is this row for family? Should I go and sit at the back?"

"No. There isn't a specific seating arrangement. Besides, you *are* family."

"Not really," she murmured, smiling as she caught Lowen's eye.

Keira and Noah sat with them, while Seren and Kit took seats with Pippa and Mirren at the other side of the aisle. In the row behind them, Mia sat hand in hand with Gareth.

"Hi," Sylvie mouthed to Holly from the tourist office when she slipped into the seat beside Mia.

"You know more people than I do," Jago said in her ear when she faced the front again.

She shifted in her seat, scanning the room and taking in the almost palpable thrum of excitement in the air. Trystan looked amazingly relaxed as he and Lowen chatted quietly.

Ten minutes later a hush fell and music filled the room. Trystan stepped to the centre of the aisle, a smile blooming on his face as Ellie and Ferne appeared, both looking adorable in matching white dresses with blue belts. While Ferne almost immediately bolted to her dad, Ellie confidently skipped down the aisle, grinning at everyone as she went.

"Hello!" she said loudly when she reached Trystan. "I don't know where I'm supposed to sit."

He crouched to her. "Do you want to wait with me for a minute and look for Mummy?"

"Okay."

With practised ease he lifted her on his arm. She leaned her head against his shoulder while Dee walked slowly down the aisle in a stunning midnight blue dress.

When Beth stepped into the back of the room, emotions rose in Sylvie's throat. The sleek ivory dress flowed to the floor, and the light veil framed her face beautifully. Her eyes shone with tears, and it only took a moment for Sylvie to register that they didn't seem to be tears of happiness.

"Is she okay?" Jago whispered in her ear.

"I don't know." The entire room seemed to hold their breath and Trystan took a step into the aisle, his face a picture of concern.

From the back of the room, Beth made a subtle hand gesture, seemingly warning Trystan to stay put. She caught a tear at the corner of her eye and Dee looked all set to go to her when Kit moved Trystan to the side and strode down the aisle.

"What's going on?" Jago asked Sylvie quietly.

"Beth was upset about not having her dad to give her away. She didn't want to ask someone else, but I guess she's regretting that decision."

Kit carried out a quiet conversation with Beth and handed her a tissue. After a moment, he turned to face the front, jutting his arm out for Beth to take.

Leaning his head close to Beth's, he spoke in a stage whisper. "Why's everyone looking at us?"

Laughter rippled around the room taking all the tension away. It got Beth smiling and she pulled her shoulders back as Kit escorted her slowly down the aisle.

"Sorry," she said when she reached Trystan.

"Are you okay?" he asked, taking her hand.

"Yes. Just had a moment."

"Don't be sad, Mummy," Ellie said loudly when Trystan set her down. "You look like a princess."

"You do," Trystan agreed.

Ellie swung her hips, making her dress swoosh around her legs like a bell. "I do too."

Kit moved to take Ellie's hand. "Do you want to come and sit with me?" he whispered.

"No, thank you," she said, with absolutely no awareness that she had the attention of everyone in the room. "I'm going to sit with my friend, Ferne. I'll sit with you later though. Why don't you sit with Seren now?"

"I'll do that," he said, winking at Beth before slipping back to his seat.

The celebrant stepped up behind Beth and Trystan, welcoming them before launching into the ceremony, which seemed to go by in a blink.

Sylvie dabbed a tissue at her lower lids when Trystan and Beth made their way back down the aisle as husband and wife. "That was beautiful," she murmured, tilting her head in Jago's direction. "Isn't Kit the sweetest?"

"It's Trystan's wedding day and now everyone will be talking about Kit jumping in to save the day. I'm not entirely sure I'd call it sweet."

"Aw." Sylvie pouted dramatically. "Poor old Jago ... jealous of his baby brother getting all the attention. Is this a new issue or a deep-rooted one?"

He rolled his eyes, then glanced pointedly at the other guests moving out of the room. "There's a champagne reception on the ramparts. Are you still sticking to your conviction about never drinking again?"

"I suppose I might manage one in honour of the happy couple."

Jago beamed at her. "I'm willing to bet you'll manage more than one."

CHAPTER TWENTY-FOUR

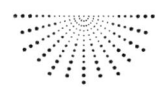

While the guests sipped champagne and enjoyed panoramic sea views, the conservatory was rearranged for the wedding breakfast. Given how much time Sylvie had spent alone with Jago in the previous two weeks, it felt a little odd to have other people vying for his attention.

Over the course of the afternoon she occasionally caught his eye across the room and felt a flutter in her stomach. She didn't let herself think too much about the implications of that. It was likely the champagne was to blame.

"This might be one of the best weddings I've ever been to," Sylvie said to Lowen, sidling up to him as Trystan and Beth were called for their first dance. Tables had been rearranged to make space for a small dance floor.

He gave her a sidelong glance. "I heard Beth is very grateful to you for staying longer."

"It wasn't exactly a hardship. The islands are gorgeous. It's such a beautiful place." She fell silent as the music kicked in, then beamed at the boyish grin on Trystan's face as he waltzed Beth around the room. He spun her a couple of times, then slowed down and swayed with her for the remainder of the song.

When the DJ invited the guests to join the dancing, Sylvie

looked nervously up at Lowen. As other couples took to the dance floor she waited for him to ask her to dance, but when he opened his mouth it was only to ask if she wanted another drink.

Sylvie didn't even have time to answer before Pippa appeared.

"Don't you dare slink off to the bar," she said, sliding her arms around Lowen's waist. "You're dancing and that's all there is to it."

He draped an arm around her shoulders. "I'm thirsty."

"You're dancing with me," Pippa told him. "Argue all you want but it's happening. I'm not letting you spend the evening propping up the bar and being grumpy."

"I won't be grumpy if I'm propping up the bar. I'll be quite happy."

Pippa pushed on her toes to kiss his cheek. "Just dance with me, please."

Reluctantly, he did as he was told. They were out of Sylvie's hearing when Pippa said something in his ear that made him break into a smile. It was good to see him relax, even if he didn't always seem to be able to do so around her. Glancing around the room, Sylvie searched for Jago only to find him looking back at her. He quirked his eyebrow while his mum led him to the dance floor.

"You look as though you're at a loose end," Kit said, appearing beside Sylvie and holding his hand out in a formal gesture.

"Not any more." She took his hand and they joined the busy dance floor, then chatted easily while following the music. When the song ended, Mirren appeared to steal Kit, insisting she was on a mission to dance with all her sons.

"Looks as though you're stuck with me," Jago told her, stepping in front of her. His hand landed on her hip, before slipping around her back. The sensation made her stomach flip. As they moved around the dance floor she relaxed in the comfort of his arms and soon found her mind shifting to Lowen.

"What's wrong?" Jago asked.

She focused her eyes on him. "Hmm?"

"You're all pensive. As though you're deep in thought."

"Nothing's wrong," she said weakly. Nothing she could pinpoint anyway. Lowen had been fine with her on Wednesday, but she still had the feeling he was being elusive with her.

She probably shouldn't take it personally. She had the impression he might be that way with most people. Come to think of it, the only times she'd seen him truly at ease was around Pippa and Mia – both of whom had no qualms about bossing him around. Maybe Sylvie ought to do the same. Or at least be a little more direct with him.

"You're definitely a bit melancholy," Jago said. "Is it the champagne?"

"No!" She smiled, impressed by how well he could read her. "I'm fine, honestly."

"Can you put a bit more effort into acting like you're enjoying dancing with me?"

"Sorry." She inched closer to him. "I am enjoying dancing with you. I might just be a bit tired."

Jago raised an eyebrow, clearly not buying her excuse. He let it drop anyway and twirled her under his arm to make her laugh. They danced for two more songs before Noah cut in. After that she danced with Trystan and then a guy who worked with Trystan. Finally, Sylvie excused herself to the bathroom. On entering the conservatory again, she caught Lowen alone at the table at the back of the room.

"Are you going to dance with your cousin or what?" she asked, injecting confidence into her voice when she approached him

"I think I might be all danced out."

Her confidence wavered, but only for a second. "You can't be," she insisted, taking his hand. "You haven't danced with me yet."

For the briefest moment she had an awful feeling he was

going to decline, but then his shoulders relaxed and he gave a small nod of acceptance.

"I've really loved getting to know your family," she said softly as they swayed together. "I understand why you always missed them so much when you were away." She felt his shoulders tighten. It seemed as though anytime she attempted to engage him in conversation about anything other than the mundane he tensed up on her. The problem was she wanted to reminisce about their childhood holidays. She had so many memories that only he knew about. "Do you have a favourite holiday?" she asked him eventually.

A frown wrinkled his forehead. "No."

"I think mine was when we stayed in that huge, converted barn in Italy. The one with the housekeeper who'd witter on at us in Italian and we had no idea if she was angry with us ... except then she'd smother us in kisses and give us sweets." She smiled as she tried to recall the name of the woman whose face she could picture as clear as day. "She was funny, wasn't she? Do you remember her name? I can't think of it ..."

His frown deepened. "Do I remember the name of some random woman we met on holiday thirty years ago? Oddly enough, I don't."

"But we were there for about three weeks. We spent a week being terrified of her, and then we figured out that Italians are just loud and expressive."

"I really don't remember," he said, releasing her as the song came to an end. "I've definitely danced enough for one day."

He strode away, leaving Sylvie more than a little stunned. She didn't have time to dwell on her confusion since Jago swooped in and wrapped his arms around her waist, making her laugh at his confidence.

"You're supposed to ask people if they want to dance," she told him as he raised her arm to twirl her. "Not just inflict it on them."

"Don't be silly, I could see you were dying to dance with me."

"Is that the vibe I was giving off?"

He smiled bashfully. "Actually, I just saw my chance and jumped in quick."

"You seem as though you might get giggly on me soon."

"I don't giggle." His eyes sparkled. "I have a deep and manly laugh."

"Just not when you're drunk?"

"I'm not drunk. I'm happy!" His eyes drifted over her shoulder and his smile slipped. "Which is more than I can say about some people."

His gaze was locked on Lowen and Pippa, standing close together by the door. From their body language and facial expressions they appeared to be mid-argument. After a moment, Lowen moved quickly out of the room. Pippa paused before following him.

Sylvie barely had time to wonder what their exchange was all about. Laughter drew her attention to Kit and Seren, who waltzed their way over to them.

"Help me out here," Kit said. "I think the music needs a tempo change … liven things up for the end of the evening … what do you reckon?"

Seren glared at him. "Everyone is enjoying the slow dancing. It's romantic. If you have a word with the DJ I'll …" She squinted, thinking.

"You'll what?" Kit asked.

"I'll tell your mum on you!"

He stuck his bottom lip out. "That's mean. She always sides with you."

"Because I'm always right."

As Seren steered Kit away again, he mouthed to Jago that he should go and talk to the DJ.

"What do you think?" Jago asked, pulling Sylvie closer and sending a shiver down her spine. "Slow music or party music?"

"Slow," she whispered.

He touched his cheek to hers. "That would be my choice too."

Sylvie could happily have slow danced with him all night, but the DJ apparently had similar ideas to Kit and switched to a half hour of more upbeat songs to end the evening on a high.

While everyone headed off in their different directions, Sylvie and Jago lingered in the lobby with Keira, waiting for Noah so they could all go home together.

"How are we getting home?" Noah asked, swaying slightly as he appeared beside Keira. "Did you know Mum's staying in the hotel tonight?"

"Yes." Keira yawned. "We're walking with Jago and Sylvie."

Noah shook his head. "I thought Mum would drive us. I assumed she'd be taking Ellie home with her."

"Nope. Beth and Trystan are staying in the hotel. Beth's friends are staying at their place so Ellie's gone back with them. Your mum booked into the hotel so she could drink without worrying about getting home."

"Why didn't she tell me this?" Noah demanded. "Did she even consider how we'd get home without her driving us?"

Keira rolled her eyes. "I assume she decided you could figure it out yourself ... what with you being a grown up."

"Why didn't we book into the hotel?" Noah asked as Keira steered him towards the door. "That was a sensible idea. Are either of you sober enough to drive?" he asked Sylvie and Jago over his shoulder.

"Not even close," Jago replied.

Stepping outside, Noah slung an arm around Keira's shoulder. "You might have to carry me."

Tiredness swept over Sylvie and she quietly listened to Noah and Keira's playful banter while she and Jago followed them. The air was crisp and cool, making Sylvie automatically pull her cardigan tighter around her.

"Here," Jago said, slipping his suit jacket off and placing it around her shoulders.

"Aren't you cold?" she asked while slipping her arms into the sleeves and savouring the warmth of it.

"Big, buff men don't feel the cold."

Sylvie bumped against him, then hooked her arm through his, partly for the body heat and partly to steady herself on the dark walk home. Mainly it was because she just enjoyed being close to him.

While Noah and Keira joked around ahead of them, Sylvie's mind drifted to Lowen, wondering what was going on with him and why he'd left the party so abruptly, without saying goodbye to anyone.

"You worry me when you go all quiet," Jago remarked when they reached Old Town Bay and the lane which led to the cottages and Mirren's house.

Her reply was delayed as Keira and Noah called goodbye to them from their doorstep.

"I'm just tired," she eventually said.

"Really? So Lowen didn't say something to upset you?"

She shook her head and felt a lump swell in her throat. "He hardly says anything to me at all."

"I thought things were better when you went over there on Wednesday."

"They were, but it all seemed kind of superficial. We didn't really talk, and he still seems to have an issue with me being here."

"It's probably not personal. I think he's distant with most people."

While Jago moved to open the door, Sylvie was distracted by the blanket of stars overhead. She took a few steps to the patio, then craned her neck to look up at the fantastic display above her. The vast darkness punctuated by so many glittering stars was something she never experienced in city life.

"It's stunning, isn't it?" Jago remarked, close behind her.

"Beautiful," she whispered, feeling the heat of his body and instinctively leaning back against his chest.

His arms circled her waist, the intimacy of their stance feeling completely natural.

When he spoke softly, his breath tickled her cheek. "How long do you think you'll stay?" There was an edge to his voice as though he wasn't even sure he wanted to ask the question.

At the thought of leaving, a heaviness settled in her chest. "I changed my flight to next Wednesday."

Jago's arms tightened around her, intensifying her sadness. The thought of saying goodbye to him and going back to her everyday life filled her with dread. But he wasn't the only reason she didn't feel ready to leave.

"Things feel unfinished with Lowen," she said quietly. "Which is silly. I came to see him and I've done that."

"You were expecting more from him?" Jago murmured.

"Yes. But maybe that was unfair to him. I think what I really wanted was to spend time with the Lowen I knew when I was a kid. It's not as though I was expecting him to still be a child, but I also wasn't expecting him to be *so* different. It's like there's nothing left of the person I knew."

"Sorry," Jago said, holding her closer still.

Slowly, she turned in his arms and brought her hands up to his face. "You've made everything better. I can't imagine how I would have dealt with the last couple of weeks without you around."

"I'm sure you would have managed fine," Jago said bashfully.

"I'm going to have to disagree with you on that one."

Her hands remained at his face, and she moved a thumb to gently caress his cheek. In response he lowered his face to hers. Sylvie felt as though all the breath was sucked from her body in the moment before their lips met. The kiss was soft and lingering. Her heart forgot to beat as she savoured the taste of him.

Too soon, Jago pulled back, lifting his hands to brush her

hair from her face. "Can I see you again?" he asked, more than a hint of desperation to his voice. "When you go back to Cambridge? Can we still see each other?"

Her heart felt as though it swelled, before deflating rapidly. "You'll be back in New York," she pointed out, the thought of there being so much distance between them like a blow to her chest.

"I won't," he said, with a small shake of the head

For a moment, Sylvie thought he was about to offer to stay for her, before realising just how ridiculous that was.

"What do you mean?" she asked, a spark of hope igniting low in her belly.

"My employer sponsors my visa." He smiled uncertainly. "It has to be renewed every three years. This time the application was denied."

"How long have you known?" She was certain his family didn't know, so she wondered whether it was recent news.

"I found out about a week before I got Trystan's wedding invitation. It was good timing. Since I had to leave the country anyway, a longer trip home made sense."

"So you're staying here permanently?"

"My plan was to go back to London. I have a friend who I left a bunch of my stuff with before I came out here."

"So you've already left America? You don't even need to go back and pack up your life?"

He shook his head. "It's all done. I sold my furniture and gave up my apartment. I'm not going back."

For a moment she stayed silent, letting the information sink in. If he wasn't going back to America, she'd definitely be able to see him again.

He touched her nose with his, then caught her lips in a brief kiss. "I probably should have told you sooner."

"Probably," she agreed, then realised that the last thing she wanted to do was make this about her. "None of your family know," she stated.

"No. Not yet."

"Why not?"

"I wanted to make a plan first. Figure out what I'm going to do next."

"Mirren will want you to move back here."

"That's one reason I didn't say anything. I didn't want to be subject to a lot of nagging and guilt trips."

"I don't think Mirren would …" She stopped herself, a slow smile creeping over her face. "Yeah, you're right. She'd absolutely do that. You'd never get a moment's peace."

"You're shivering," he remarked, taking her hand to lead her inside.

He kissed her again when they reached her bedroom and she pulled him close, a hand gripping the back of his neck as she deepened the kiss. Her insides turned to mush when he took a step, pinning her between him and the doorframe. A groan escaped her and all she wanted to do was move into her bedroom and pull him onto the bed.

"I should …" She drew back, fighting to get her breathing under control. "I mean, you should. We shouldn't …"

"You're not making a lot of sense," he said, then caught her lower lip between his teeth.

Her eyes rolled back in her head and she felt as though she was about to lose all control. "You really need to stop that," she murmured.

"I know." He lowered his head to kiss her neck and it felt like torture. "I need to go to my own room. That's what you're trying to tell me?"

She tilted her head back, savouring the sensation of his lips trailing over her collar bone. "I think you probably should." His eyes came up to meet her gaze, the longing in them shaking her resolve. "I don't actually want you to."

"I don't either." He touched his forehead to hers. "I think you're right that I *should* though."

"This all feels kind of weird and messy …"

"Careful, you might overwhelm me with compliments like that."

She trailed her fingers over the back of his neck. "I meant with Lowen and everything."

"I know." He sighed heavily. "Are you going to make this easier for me and let go of me?"

She wrinkled her nose. "I don't really want to."

"Same here." His lips caressed hers one last time before they moved apart as though by some mutual agreement. From his bedroom doorway, he gave her a heartfelt smile and wished her goodnight.

CHAPTER TWENTY-FIVE

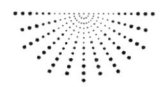

Despite the late night and excessive alcohol, Sylvie was awake early the next morning. Creeping around the house to avoid waking Jago wasn't purely out of courtesy, but also because she wasn't sure she was ready to face him. Presumably they'd continue as though nothing had happened. They could blame it on the romance around the wedding and nothing more. It couldn't really be anything more. Except that Jago wasn't going back to America after all.

The thought made Sylvie's heart beat faster as she stared out of the kitchen window at the choppy water throwing itself against the rocks on the headland. If Jago was going to be in London, it would be easy to see each other again. Could whatever was between them continue? Could it develop into something more? She wanted it to, she realised, as the bitter aroma of the coffee in her hands invaded her nostrils.

While Jago slept on, Sylvie took herself off for a walk, hoping to clear her head. All her thoughts came back to one thing – she needed to speak to Lowen again. If nothing else, she wanted to see if she could gauge how he'd feel about her continuing to see Jago. That would no doubt be an awkward conversation. One that she should have soon, though.

Hugh Town was especially quiet on that blustery Sunday morning, and as Sylvie strolled along the empty streets, she realised that Lowen must have stayed at Pippa's place the previous evening. He'd probably still be there and it seemed as good a time as any to speak to him if he was around.

The Pottery Cafe wasn't due to open for another half an hour, but the lights were on and Sylvie decided to try there before ringing the doorbell for Pippa's flat and potentially waking people up.

It only took a moment for Pippa to emerge from the kitchen at the back after Sylvie knocked on the glass in the door.

"Hi," Pippa said tightly. "How are you?"

"I'm okay. I'm looking for Lowen but thought I'd check in here before the flat. I presume he didn't go back to Bryher last night."

Pippa's shoulders were bunched and her jaw tight. "He stayed at my place but he's not there now. He's gone to the mainland."

"What?" Automatically, Sylvie stepped inside. "Why?"

"Something about talking to clay suppliers." The harshness of Pippa's tone made Sylvie nervous.

"Are you okay?" she asked.

Pippa's shoulders slumped and she closed the door and locked it again. "Not really. Sorry. I didn't mean to take it out on you. It's Lowen I'm annoyed with."

"What happened?"

"He got up early and said he needed to go and speak to his clay suppliers. Completely out of the blue. He got on the ferry an hour ago."

"When will he be back?" Sylvie asked.

"Your guess is as good as mine." A timer beeped in the kitchen and Sylvie followed Pippa back there, then watched her pull a tray of cookies from the oven.

"Is Lowen's sudden trip to do with me?" Sylvie asked.

"I guess so," Pippa said, while quickly and methodically

transferring the cookies to a cooling rack. "But I couldn't say for certain what's going on with him."

"I'm sorry if I've caused issues." Sylvie chewed her bottom lip while debating what else to say. In the end she decided that since her presence was clearly unwelcome she shouldn't start quizzing Pippa. "I'll leave you to it," she said and made for the door.

"Wait," Pippa called, then offered Sylvie an apologetic smile. "I'm sorry. It's not your fault." Pulling a stool from under the large table in the centre of the room, she indicated for Sylvie to do the same.

"He's been out of sorts since you arrived," she began. "I know he has some painful memories from the time he spent with your grandparents. I guess seeing you brought all that back. The problem is, Lowen tends to keep everything to himself. If he's upset, he shuts everyone out. He'd previously been quite open with me but now he won't talk to me. When I try to talk to him he snaps at me."

"I'm sorry."

Pippa shrugged. "He's also snapped at Mia several times recently, which really isn't like him."

"I shouldn't have just turned up like I did." Sylvie paused and blew out a frustrated breath. "I definitely shouldn't have stuck around so long, but I wanted to believe he really was busy with work and not using it as an excuse not to see me."

"He *has* been busy with work," Pippa said. "Apparently that's what he does when he's stressed. Mia said he's been like a machine, the way he's turning out pottery. He gets pain in his hands, so he really shouldn't be working that much."

Sylvie felt an intense surge of guilt but still couldn't get everything straight in her head. "I don't understand it," she told Pippa. "We were close as kids."

"I suspect his problem is more to do with his grandparents than with you."

"They weren't *that* bad," Sylvie said idly.

"Really?" Pippa squinted. "That's not the impression I got."

"Well, they weren't particularly pleasant people, and they could be hard on Lowen, but we had a lot of fun on those holidays too."

"I've never had that impression from Lowen."

Sylvie felt a stab of irritation at Pippa's words but swallowed it down. "I feel terrible for causing issues. I've definitely outstayed my welcome."

"I didn't mean to take my bad mood out on you," Pippa said. "Will you try speaking to Lowen again when he gets back?"

Sylvie was surprised by the question. "Do you think that's wise?"

"I think you're probably the only person who can get him to open up. Whatever's going on in his head is going to eat away at him until he figures out how to let it go."

"Did he give you any indication about when he'd be back?"

"Nope. He just left."

Sylvie grimaced, angry with Lowen on Pippa's behalf.

"I wouldn't be surprised if he comes straight back again this evening, or tomorrow morning. Mia isn't working this week, so theoretically he needs to be at the pottery studio. I know he has customers coming to pick something up tomorrow, so he'll need to be there then."

"Will you let me know when he turns up?"

Pippa nodded, then surprised Sylvie by embracing her tightly.

Sylvie's phone rang almost as soon as she stepped out of the café, and she hesitantly answered the call from her mum.

"How was the wedding?" Bess asked in a rush. "I messaged you yesterday evening but you were obviously having too much fun to reply. I've been dying to hear how it was."

Automatically, Sylvie crossed the promenade and walked down onto the long stretch of sandy beach. "It was great." She injected more enthusiasm into her tone. "Really great. Beth looked amazing, and she and Trystan seem so happy." She strolled near the water's edge, her shoulders hunched against the cold wind while she gave her mum a brief rundown of the day, choosing not to mention the part about Lowen being offhand with her.

"How are things with Jago?" her mum asked eventually.

"Fine." Sylvie rolled her eyes heavenwards. "Why do you ask?"

"Because I know what weddings are like – all that romance in the air, and the champagne and the dancing …"

"Mum," Sylvie said with an exasperated sigh.

"Come on," her mum said. "Has something happened between you two or what?"

"No." Sylvie was glad her mum wasn't in front of her, certain she'd be able to tell she was lying. Her mind instantly went to the end of the evening. If the wind hadn't already made her cheeks bright red, the thoughts of kissing Jago would have done.

"Really?" her mum asked suspiciously. "Mirren said you two have been getting very close."

"Oh my goodness. Have you two been talking about us?"

"Just the odd comment."

"Well there's nothing going on," she said again. "But …" She trailed off, not quite sure how much she wanted to share.

"But what?" her mum asked.

"You can't mention this to Mirren," Sylvie said firmly. "None of the family know yet, but Jago isn't going back to America. He's looking for a job in London."

A tiny, excited gasp hit Sylvie's ear. "So you'll be able to see him again," her mum said.

"Maybe." Sylvie stopped on the sand and looked at the waves rolling towards her feet. "I'm not sure."

CHAPTER TWENTY-SIX

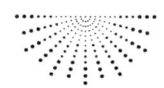

Waking up on Sunday to no sign of Sylvie induced a niggling feeling of unease in Jago. He couldn't help but think she was regretting the events of the previous evening. As it turned out, when she appeared all she could talk about in the ten minutes before his mum joined them was how she'd wanted to speak to Lowen but couldn't since he'd flitted off to the mainland.

Her usual cheery banter had turned manic, and she seemed close to tears as she ranted. The interruption of his mum was almost welcome. Sylvie pulled herself together and switched to rehashing the wedding with Mirren. They were still chatting about it when Trystan and Beth arrived, along with Beth's friends.

The day ended up being an extended celebration with the whole family and a few friends arriving over the course of the afternoon. Lowen and Pippa were noticeably absent, but no one commented on it.

With no chance to speak to Sylvie privately, Jago had no idea how things stood between them. When he fell into bed that evening, he still had no idea if they'd continue to see each other once Sylvie was back in Cambridge.

The buzzing of his phone on Monday morning made him sit up straighter in bed. He'd been awake for an hour but had been checking his emails and making another fruitless trawl through the job listings. He stared at the phone screen, his brother's name on the display seeming ominous. Lowen never called him.

"Hi," he said, forcing himself to answer and half expecting it to be a pocket dial.

"Hey." Lowen sounded unsure of himself. "How are you?"

"Good, thanks. Are you back? I heard you went over to the mainland."

"Just a quick day trip to straighten out a few things with my clay supplier."

"On a Sunday?"

"Yep."

Jago felt his jaw tighten and tried to keep his irritation in check. "Does Sylvie know you're back? She was keen to see you again before she leaves on Wednesday."

"That's why I was calling. I wanted to ask you a favour... is there any chance you could watch the shop for me today? Mia's taken the week off and everyone else is working so …"

"So I'm not your first choice, but your only choice?"

"I didn't mean it like that."

"I know. I'm messing with you. I didn't even think you opened on Mondays."

"I don't usually, but I'm expecting customers from the hotel." Silence hung down the line for a moment. "So do you think you could? That way I can get over and spend a bit of time with Sylvie. You and I could go for a drink at the hotel this evening if you fancy it. Maybe dinner? I feel as though I've hardly had time to see you either."

"I guess I could watch the studio for a bit." Jago didn't know anything about working in a shop but he figured he'd manage. If it meant Sylvie got to spend more time with Lowen before she left he'd do it.

After ending the call, Jago put his laptop away and wandered downstairs, intending to ask his mum about the ferry times. By the time he reached the kitchen, he'd had a change of plan.

"Is it okay if I borrow the boat?" he asked.

"Words I never thought I'd hear from you." She smiled lightly and he forced himself to return it. "Of course you can. Just don't forget to wear a life jacket."

"I won't," he said with a slight eye roll.

She gave him a look that made him wish he could take the eye roll back. "I know you all think I'm a big nag," she said. "But I don't care. I only care that you're safe."

"I know." He put an arm around her shoulders and gave her a side hug. "You know we all feel as strongly as you about life jackets though, right?"

"Yes, but I'm your mother. I like to remind you." She glanced out of the window. "It's looking a bit foggy. You might be better getting the ferry."

"I'll be fine."

She seemed to be biting her tongue to stop from getting into further safety discussions. "Where are you off to anyway?"

"Bryher. Lowen asked me to watch the studio for him."

Now it was her turn to roll her eyes. "One week without Mia and he's completely lost."

"I think he just needs a bit of time off." He pursed his lips. "Have you seen Sylvie?"

"She went for a walk."

He nodded slowly. "I should get going."

Mirren checked her watch. "I better get showered and organised too. I'm having lunch with Carol up at the hotel later."

He told her to have a good day, then went to get the boat out of the garage. Being alone out on the water felt utterly exhilarating. Jago could see why his dad had been such a fan of taking off on the boat on his own. With the wind in his hair and the sea stretching out in front of him, he felt completely free. Breathing in the briny air, he revelled in the sense of peace he felt. If it weren't for the fact that he'd promised

Lowen he'd help out, he might have stayed out on the boat the entire day.

It occurred to him that if he'd enjoyed being out on the water this much as a kid, his life might have turned out completely differently. Maybe he'd have felt more connected to the islands and wouldn't have spent his adult life keeping away from them.

He could change that now if he wanted. It had been in the corner of his mind while he'd been job hunting. He could move back to Scilly and set up his own business, brewing local beer. Get himself a boat and take off on the water whenever he needed to clear his head. The idea felt absurd one moment and completely natural the next.

Sylvie popped into his mind and he couldn't help but imagine how she might fit into his plans. After spending so much time with her in the past weeks, it seemed automatic to imagine her in his hypothetical future.

He slowed the boat on the approach to the quay, then hopped onto dry land as he pulled up beside it. Grey clouds lurked at the horizon and rolled closer as he wandered across the island. He zipped his jacket up against the chill in the air.

"It's getting pretty wintery out there," he remarked when he stepped into the pottery studio with his arms across his chest, rubbing at his biceps.

Lowen was leaning on the counter with his phone in his hand. "Yeah," he said. "That might be a slight problem. You may have had a wasted trip."

"How come?"

"I just checked the forecast. It looks as though the fog is set to get worse. You might want to get back to St Mary's while you still can. The ferries will stop running if it gets too bad."

It irritated Jago that Lowen talked to him as though he was completely clueless. As though he hadn't grown up on the islands as well.

"I've got Mum's boat," he said.

"You still won't be able to go back in the fog. It's not worth the risk. Plus if Mum finds out you've been on the boat when the weather's bad you'll never hear the end of it."

"I know ... I didn't mean ... I was just saying I came with the boat." He shook his head. "Are you still going over to St Mary's?"

"I don't know."

"If the boats stop running, surely you won't have customers anyway. You can close up and we can ride back together. If you get stuck you can stay at Pippa's place, right?"

He tapped a pen on the desk. "There's a woman staying up at the hotel who's coming down later to pick up a vase. She couldn't decide which she wanted, so was going to come in this afternoon and browse some more."

"She might not even turn up," Jago pointed out.

"She's a regular customer. Every year she comes and picks out something new. And she always picks the higher priced items. I don't want her to turn up and find the place closed. I can go over to St Mary's tomorrow instead."

Jago thought of how badly Sylvie wanted to smooth things over with Lowen. "I don't mind staying here today," he said. "The weather forecast might not even be right."

"If it is, you'll be stuck here for the night."

He shrugged. "As long as you leave me the keys to your house it's not a huge issue." He'd miss out on time with Sylvie but with any luck they'd be seeing a lot more of each other in the future.

"Are you sure?" Lowen asked, cocking his head.

"Yep. Show me how to use the till before I change my mind."

Fifteen minutes later, Lowen thanked him profusely and headed for the door.

"The keys to your place?" Jago reminded him.

"Probably on the kitchen counter."

"You don't lock up?"

"Not unless I'm leaving the island. Even then I sometimes forget."

Jago chuckled and told him to have a good day.

It turned out that Lowen was right about the woman coming to buy the pottery. The older woman arrived with two friends, all of them in their sixties and slightly glamorous. There was more than a hint of disappointment when they found Lowen wasn't there, but Jago turned on the charm and had them fawning over him in no time. When one of them couldn't decide between two vases, Jago suggested she buy them both and, given the price tags, was fairly shocked when she went ahead with his suggestion. The amount of cash they parted with made him understand why Lowen wasn't keen to miss out on their custom.

Once they left, Jago turned the sign to closed, then grabbed his jacket and locked up on his way out. The wind had dropped completely and the fog hanging low over the island was eerie and unsettling.

He was halfway to the quay when he met Sylvie coming the other way.

"What are you doing here?" he asked, realising how unfriendly he sounded when she raised her eyebrows at him. "Sorry. That came out wrong. I thought you were hanging out with Lowen today."

"That's my plan. I'm on my way to his place to force him to speak to me."

"He's not there," Jago said, puzzled. "He asked me to watch the studio so he could go over to St Mary's and hang out with you."

She pulled her chin back. "He didn't mention anything to me. When did he leave?"

"A good few hours ago."

She planted her feet squarely and let out a low growl. "I'm

stuck here. You are too, by the way. The boats aren't running in the fog, so there won't be another one going until the morning."

"I've got Mum's boat," Jago said. "If the day tripper only just set off back to St Mary's, we should be fine to get back too."

"They left a while ago," she told him. "I've been hanging around on the beach while I try to figure out what to say to Lowen. I guess that was a waste of time."

"So you knew you were going to be stuck here?"

She nodded. "The guys on the boat told me it was likely before we set off. I thought it seemed like a good way to force Lowen to spend time with me."

"Your plan didn't work out so well," he mused, looking around at the thick fog, which seemed to be closing in by the minute.

Irritation flickered in Sylvie's eyes. "I really thought I could finally figure out what's going on with Lowen."

"Where on earth is he?" Jago said. "He definitely said he wanted to catch up with you."

"I hope he's okay." Sylvie pulled her phone from her pocket and Jago did the same, but neither of them had any signal.

"Let's head over to the hotel," Jago suggested. "We can grab dinner there. At least there's plenty of space for us to stay at Lowen's house."

"Yes," Sylvie murmured, but worry lines wrinkled her brow. "I'd really like to get hold of Lowen and check everything is okay."

"I'm sure he's fine," Jago said. "We'll no doubt pick up a phone signal somewhere along the way to the hotel."

~

Sylvie barely spoke as they walked back to the western side of the island. They were about to enter the hotel when her phone rang.

"It's Lowen," she said, relief flooding through her as she swiped the screen and moved the phone to her ear.

"Hi," Lowen said cheerfully. "What are you up to? I've just left Pippa and thought I could come and hang out if you're not doing anything."

"I'm on Bryher," she told him, a sizzle of anger deep in her stomach. "Why didn't you call me earlier if you wanted to do something? I came over here to see you."

"You should have said."

She almost snapped at him that she hadn't wanted to give him the chance to make up an excuse to avoid seeing her. Instead she took a steady breath through her nose. "Jago said you asked him to look after the studio so you could spend time with me."

"That was the plan. I just had to see Pippa first."

"I see," she said tersely. "Well, I guess we won't get to hang out today. It seems I'm stuck on Bryher thanks to the fog."

"I already told Jago to stay at my place. Stay with him and I'll see you tomorrow."

"Will you?" she asked, unable to keep her irritation to herself.

"Of course. Why?"

"It seems as though you're avoiding me, that's why."

"I was literally on my way to see you," he said, sounding as irritated as she was. "How was I to know you were going over to Bryher? This is hardly my fault."

"No. Just quite convenient for you."

When he didn't respond, she told him to have a nice evening and ended the call.

She took a deep breath before finally facing Jago, who'd been hovering by the door to the hotel. "Lowen spent the afternoon with Pippa," she told him. "And was just on his way to your mum's place to see me. Or so he says."

Jago's eyebrows dipped sympathetically as he pulled on the door handle. "Let's get you a glass of wine."

CHAPTER TWENTY-SEVEN

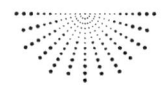

Once her annoyance at Lowen subsided, Sylvie relaxed into the evening with Jago. Several times during the meal she caught herself thinking of their kisses after the wedding and longing for a repeat. She also wanted to discuss what the future might hold for them but wasn't sure how to bring it up.

On leaving the restaurant Jago smoothly slipped his hand into hers for the walk home. The gesture felt utterly natural, as did the way he sat so close beside her on the couch in Lowen's living room. There wasn't an inch between them as he eased his arm behind her and drew her to him.

Still, conversation remained light and easy as they sat snuggled up. Only while they were making up the bed for Sylvie in the spare room did the conversation turn serious.

"You never answered my question the other night," Jago said, while battling the pillow into its pale blue case.

"Which question?" She fluffed up the duvet and walked around the bed to him.

"About whether we can see each other again when you go back to Cambridge." His tone was casual, but Sylvie was willing to bet his heart was beating furiously. She could tell by the way he was so focused on the pillow.

"I'd like to."

His eyes met hers. "Really?"

Taking the pillow from him, she tossed it onto the bed, then placed her hands against his chest before creeping them up to circle his neck. "I can't imagine not seeing you. I know it's only been a few weeks, but it already feels strange to think there was a time I didn't know you." She winced and dipped her head. "That sounded really cheesy."

His arms tightened around her waist. "I know exactly what you mean. I feel the same."

"Do you really think you'll move to London?"

"I'd imagine so." His cheek twitched and his eyes shifted away from her. "I haven't spotted any jobs that appeal yet, but I'm sure I'll find something."

She nodded, choosing not to dwell on the uncertainty in his voice. "If you're in London it will be easy to meet up." Her fingers explored the short hairs at the back of his neck. "We can play it by ear. Keep in touch and see how things go."

"I think that's a good plan." He lowered his face to hers and kissed her softly.

With his tongue exploring her mouth and his hands slipping under her top to stroke the skin at her back, it was difficult to worry about the future.

"I suppose I should probably go and make up a bed for myself somewhere," he said, pulling back slightly, his beautiful blue eyes regarding her questioningly.

"You could always sleep in here," she suggested. "You did help make the bed after all."

Relief flashed in his eyes. "That's true, and the bed is definitely big enough for two."

"Are you going to promise to stay on your own side?"

"I'm not sure I can manage that," he whispered, his face so close that his breath tickled her lips.

"Good," she replied. "I definitely won't manage it."

AN UNEXPECTED GUEST

∽

Her ex-husband had never been a cuddly sleeper so the feeling of waking with Jago's arms wrapped around her and his head snuggled on her shoulder felt completely foreign to Sylvie. Also utterly glorious. She didn't dare move for fear of waking him, so closed her eyes again and focused on the feel of his breath across her collarbone and all the places where their bodies touched. Which turned out to be a lot. Her entire left side was wonderfully ensconced by his naked body.

"Morning," he finally muttered, without moving a muscle or opening his eyes.

"Good morning," she murmured happily while running her fingers through his hair.

He dropped a hasty kiss on her forehead before easing his arm out from under and slipping out of bed. Having expected some cuddling – and possibly a repeat of the previous evening's activities – Sylvie felt a rush of disappointment and a pang of rejection as he crossed the room.

"Where are you off to?" she asked, hoping her voice didn't betray her emotions.

He turned in the doorway, apparently unconcerned by his nakedness. He flashed her a reassuring smile that told her she'd sounded exactly as insecure as she felt.

"Bathroom," he said. "I'll be right back. Don't go anywhere."

With a rush of relief she flopped onto the bed again. Before she knew it, Jago was back and snuggling into her. His now cold feet against her legs made her squirm, which amused him greatly. Once their laughter settled down, she curled into his chest and rested her head under his chin.

"I thought you might freak out this morning," he whispered as he stroked her hair.

"Because of Lowen?" It was the only reason she could think that he'd imagine her freaking out.

"Yeah. I didn't know if you'd feel weird about it."

"I feel very weird about it."

"Me too."

She lifted her head, propping herself on her elbow to look at him. "Really?"

"Yes. He's my brother. You're his cousin."

"You realise that doesn't make *us* related," she teased.

He pushed his fingers gently into her side to tickle her. "I know that!" he said, chuckling as she swatted his hand away. "It just feels like we're in some weird territory. Lowen would surely have something to say about it."

"I'm not even sure he'd care." She trailed her fingers over Jago's chest and felt a stab of hurt deep in her gut. "I might be his cousin, but it's definitely starting to seem as though he has absolutely no affection for me."

Jago's hand swept up and down her spine before settling at her lower back. "I don't see how that could be true."

"You're kind of a charmer, you know that?"

He didn't reply but kissed her instead.

"Maybe we should get up in case Lowen comes back early," she suggested, trying half-heartedly to untangle herself from him.

"Soon." His eyes twinkled as he pulled her back to him.

In an instant she lost all thoughts of anything except Jago and the tug of desire low in her stomach.

~

They didn't linger too long, the fear of Lowen arriving home forcing them out of bed to get coffee and toast for breakfast. Once they'd tidied up after themselves, Sylvie messaged Lowen to see what his plans were. She'd lost all motivation to try to spend more time with him. If it happened, good. If not, she wasn't overly concerned. Chasing him was getting her nowhere, and being subjected to his unpredictable moods was exhausting.

When he didn't reply to the message, Jago suggested they head back to the boat and catch up with him on St Mary's. They stepped outside into a dazzlingly bright morning. The sky was a heavenly shade of blue and Sylvie automatically took Jago's hand to lead him down to the beach. The scenery was too glorious to miss out on a stroll along the sand.

A cold wind stung their cheeks and had Sylvie zipping her coat up further. Strong waves rolled onto the shore and the golden sunshine cast a warm glow on everything. The screech of gulls filled the air while a variety of sea birds dove into the waves. Some flew in their direction, landing close by before taking off again, no doubt hoping for an easier breakfast.

Releasing her hand, Jago picked up a flat stone, then launched it in a low arc over the water. He beamed proudly as it skipped across the surface, bouncing in long leaps at first then turning to a fast staccato before finally being swallowed up by the sea.

Sylvie made a half decent attempt at skipping a stone, then gave Jago a shove when he tried to give her tips.

"What was that for?" he asked, laughing as he darted out of the way of a wave rushing close to his shoes.

"I thought I did quite well," she told him.

"You did!" He slung an arm around her shoulders.

"There was no need to tell me how to improve then." She gave his ribs a playful dig with her elbow, then rested her head against his shoulder as she gazed out to sea. "It really is beautiful here."

"Yeah," he breathed, resting his chin on the top of her head.

"Are you tempted to stay?"

"Huh?"

His attempt to sound confused by the question didn't fool her for a moment, and her heart sank a little.

"You said you hadn't had any luck finding jobs to apply for in London …"

"Something will come up," he said, straightening his spine.

Part of her wanted to nod and smile and drop the subject, but in the end she couldn't resist digging deeper.

"Do you think you haven't found any jobs because you don't actually want to be in London?"

"I think it'll probably just take a bit more time," he said slowly.

"Really?" She kept her gaze on the horizon, certain she didn't want to look Jago in the eyes at that moment. "So you never think about moving to Scilly?"

"What would I do here?" he said, his voice betraying him.

"You have the money from my grandparents." She forced herself to turn and look at him. "You could do whatever you want."

The small shake of his head didn't do anything to reassure her.

"You could set up a brewery here," she said, hating herself for suggesting it.

His laugh was unconvincing. "What the heck are you talking about?"

"You've never thought about it – moving back here and setting up your brewery?"

"It may have crossed my mind," he admitted. "But in a bucket list kind of way. It's completely unrealistic."

"It's not. It's a great business idea."

"It's too risky," he said, the vulnerability in his voice making her ache for him.

"You could easily make a go of it."

He shook his head again. "I'm not even sure I could come back to Scilly permanently."

"Why not? You clearly love it here."

He tilted his head, gazing down at her intently. "What I've loved is being here with you."

"I've loved it too," she said, an ache in her chest at the thought of leaving.

"See." He gazed down at her lovingly, his lips turning

upwards at the corners. "I can't move back here because it's too far from Cambridge."

She tilted her head and let out a sigh. "*Jago ...*"

He didn't let her continue and instead silenced her with a kiss that made her knees feel weak.

"Well this is cosy." At the sound of Lowen's voice, Sylvie instinctively jolted away from Jago.

"Hi," Jago said, somewhat awkwardly.

"I take it you two had a good night?" Lowen remarked, a bitter tone to his voice.

Sylvie smiled nervously. "I'm not sure I'd ever get used to living on an island where you can get cut off any time."

Lowen held her gaze for a moment, the disappointment in his eyes both upsetting and irritating her. Considering that he didn't seem to want anything to do with her, it felt wrong that he should take issue at something going on between her and Jago.

After an uncomfortably long silence, Lowen shifted his eyes to Jago. "Thanks for looking after the place," he said curtly, before turning and walking briskly away.

Jago tipped his head back and cursed quietly.

"I need to go and talk to him," Sylvie said.

When she took a step, Jago did too. "I'll come with you."

She shook her head. "Stay here. It'll be better if I speak to him alone."

"No way. He's absolutely fuming with me. I need to speak to him."

"And say what exactly?"

"I've no idea. But I still need to talk to him."

He took another step and Sylvie put a hand on his arm to stop him. "Please wait here," she said desperately. "I've barely had a moment alone with him since I got here. I need to have this out with him. It's not just about you and me. There are other issues too." At least she assumed there were. "I need to figure out what's going on with him once and for all."

Jago's features softened. "Okay. I'll wait here."

Grateful for his understanding, she hurried up the beach towards the studio, where Lowen had just disappeared inside.

CHAPTER TWENTY-EIGHT

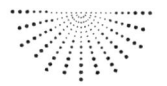

It wasn't only the brisk walk that had Sylvie breathless when she reached the door, but also a burst of nerves and adrenaline. With no sign of Lowen in the studio she continued swiftly to his workshop. She could hear his shuffled footsteps before she entered, so wasn't surprised to find him pacing the room.

Tension radiated from him, and when he swung around and glared at her, his eyes were so full of rage that she felt as though she was standing in front of a stranger.

"I take it you're sleeping with my brother?" he growled at her.

She gritted her teeth. "Apparently that's what I have to do to get your attention." She regretted the remark immediately, but it felt as though all the emotions of the previous weeks had bubbled up to boiling point. She had no option but to explode.

"Are you serious?"

"No." Her hands balled to fists at her sides. "Of course I wouldn't do that. But it's true that it's the only thing that's got your attention where I'm concerned."

"Surely you knew I wouldn't be okay with you sleeping with my brother."

She matched his glare with a steely one of her own. "This

isn't about Jago. Don't try and make it about him when you know as well as I do that it's not."

"I'm not sure how you can say it's not about Jago," he insisted. "You turned up here unannounced, wormed your way into my family, spent all your time with Jago and then ... What? Are you a couple now?"

She almost choked on a humorless laugh. "The only reason I was spending time with Jago is because you didn't have time for me." Tears threatened, but she refused to let her emotions get the better of her now that she finally had a chance to have it out with him.

"I spent time with you," he said. "We hung out several times. We went for a day trip. I'm not sure what else you want from me."

Her chin twitched then, and it occurred to her that they really *were* strangers. Her anger faded to sadness as she thought of her cousin who she'd once idolised.

"I don't understand," she said, her heart feeling as though it was breaking in her chest. "We're family."

"I guess that depends on your definition," he said coolly. "But considering we haven't seen each other for almost twenty years and you've only just met any other members of my family, it doesn't feel as though we're particularly closely related."

She was so stunned it felt as though she'd had all the breath sucked out of her. "We have the same grandparents," she murmured.

He turned away from her, gazing out of the window. "I didn't consider them family either."

A tear slid effortlessly down her cheek and onto her lip, the saltiness taking her by surprise.

"What about all the time we spent together as kids? All that shared history. There aren't many people in the world who I felt as connected to as I always did to you, but now I think I either imagined the connection or it was just one-sided."

Lowen stood straighter, pulling his shoulders back, but didn't turn to look at her. "Maybe we have different memories of the times we spent together."

Again it took her a moment to find words. "I guess so," she whispered as she turned to leave. Tears streamed freely down her cheeks as she stopped in the archway. She suspected it would be the last time she ever saw him, and as confused and angry as she was, the thought of never seeing him again tore at her insides. Lifting her chin, she took a deep breath to relax her throat enough for her to speak, but when no words came she turned and walked out.

"What happened?" Jago asked as soon as she stepped outside.

She didn't reply but took his hand to lead him up the beach.

"*Sylvie.*" He tugged on her arm to stop her while the Marram grass on the sand dunes swayed in the wind and reached for her legs. "Stop and talk to me. What happened?"

With his hand gripping her arm, she didn't have much choice but to stop. "He doesn't want me here. He never did. In his eyes I'm nothing to him."

Anger flashed in Jago's eyes. "I need to go and talk to him."

"No." She clamped her hand on his arm. "Don't. It won't help."

"He's pissed off with me though."

"Let him calm down and talk to him when you're both feeling more rational."

He looked over her head and she had the distinct impression he was going to ignore her and go back there.

"Please." She touched his jaw to draw his gaze. "I just want to get back to St Mary's."

The lines around his eyes faded as his features relaxed. "Sorry," he said, engulfing her in a bear hug.

"It's not your fault."

"I feel as though I've made things more difficult for you."

She smiled at how wrong he'd got that. "You've only made

things easier," she whispered against his neck. "I just hope I haven't caused issues between you and Lowen."

"There have always been issues between me and Lowen." He kissed the side of her head. "It'll all be okay."

She didn't feel quite so optimistic as they made their way across the island. The boat trip only seemed to intensify her melancholy, and by the time they arrived back at the house she was getting increasingly irritated by all the concerned looks Jago was casting her.

"I'm fine," she said tightly, giving his hand a quick squeeze outside the door.

"I don't believe you."

"Well there's nothing you can do."

"I can talk to Lowen."

"You can talk to Lowen about your own issues with him. I'm done with him."

He tilted his head and opened his mouth to say more but Sylvie cut him off.

"I am," she insisted. "That's all there is to it."

To further end the conversation, she opened the door and entered the warmth of the homely kitchen.

"You made it," Mirren said, while continuing to unload the dishwasher.

Sylvie forced a smile. "It's amazing how quickly the weather changes around here."

"It's all part of the charm of island life." Mirren took glasses from the top rack and placed them away in the cupboard. "You got the full Scilly experience – stranded on an island for a night."

"I'm just thankful it was only a night," Sylvie said automatically while wondering how long she could keep up the idle chit chat.

"That's true. Although I wouldn't have minded if you missed your flight tomorrow." She smiled fondly at Sylvie. "Your mum wouldn't be too happy though. She was messaging me earlier to say how excited she is to have you back."

"I might go and give her a call." Sylvie was mostly looking for a reason to excuse herself, but the thought of talking everything through with her mum was appealing too.

As she ascended the stairs she could hear Jago's low voice as he chatted to his mum. Sylvie couldn't help but wonder what – if anything – he'd tell her about the situation with Lowen. Presumably he wouldn't be too keen to discuss the details of their relationship, but at some point Mirren was bound to find out about any tension between Lowen and Jago.

In her bedroom, she flopped onto the bed, feeling a pang of anticipatory nostalgia at the thought of leaving. Given the way things were with Lowen, she couldn't imagine being back anytime soon.

Tears threatened at the thought and she plugged her phone in to call her mum.

"I heard you got stuck on Bryher with Jago last night," her mum said with a glimmer of glee to her voice.

"Yeah." Perched on the edge of the bed, Sylvie rubbed at the side of her face.

"I was expecting you to sound a little more enthusiastic about that."

"Things are really weird with Lowen," Sylvie said, not even sure how to explain.

Surprise was evident in her mum's reply. "From your messages I thought things were better. You said you'd had a good time over at his pottery studio."

"That was because I avoided mentioning anything about the past. He was really short with me at the wedding, then he disappeared off to the mainland." She closed her eyes as she tried to get her thoughts in order. "I had a big argument with him this morning. Apparently he doesn't consider me family."

"He said that?"

"Yep. He claims he never considered Grandma and Grandpa to be his real family either."

"That makes some sense at least …"

"Does it?" Sylvie sat up straight.

"They were so cold towards him. Holidays with them were always hard for him."

Sylvie squinted in confusion. "Pippa is also under the impression he had a terrible time when he was on those holidays with us. She thinks that's why he doesn't like me being here. I know Grandma and Grandpa could be a lot to deal with, but it wasn't all bad."

The silence down the phone felt loaded, and Sylvie wondered what her mum wasn't telling her.

"I'm not sure how much you remember," she finally said, her voice a low whisper in Sylvie's ear. "Those trips definitely weren't all fun for Lowen. Your grandparents threw money at him, and there were all those private tutors and nannies, but emotionally he wasn't really taken care of at all. At least when we weren't there."

A memory started at the edge of Sylvie's mind, though she couldn't be sure how real it was.

"I do remember one time," she began as the memories came clearer in her mind. "I'm not sure if I remember properly, but we arrived somewhere, late at night, and …" She stopped, shook her head. "Was he alone in the house?"

"That huge house that they rented for a summer in France," her mum said. "There was supposed to be a nanny with him that evening. Your grandparents had gone out somewhere. I'm not sure what happened with the nanny, but Lowen was on his own when we arrived."

"There was a storm," Sylvie mused. "I remember we got soaked running from the car to the house."

"It was thundering and lightning like crazy," her mum confirmed. "There was a power cut so the whole place was in darkness. Even I would've been scared all alone in a dark house in the middle of nowhere. But for an eight-year-old." Her voice trembled and she took a steadying breath. "After that, I tried to make sure we were there as much as possible. When your grandmother was hard on Lowen, I'd step in, but I'm not even sure she realised she was doing anything wrong. To her, that was just the way children should be treated. She thought she was doing him a favour by making sure he got a good education."

"I never thought it was that bad," Sylvie said.

"I always wondered if that was why he drifted away from us as an adult."

"I still don't understand. It was so long ago."

Her mum sighed. "I've spoken to Mirren about it recently. She didn't know what it was like. Apparently Lowen came home telling them all what a great time he had."

"Why?"

"I guess it was his way of dealing with it. But I can't imagine the scars it left if he never spoke to anyone about it."

"That explains why Jago was jealous of Lowen's trips. And why he had no idea what Grandma was like."

"Do you think you can talk to Lowen again? Smooth things over before you leave?"

Sylvie considered the way Lowen had spoken to her that morning. "I can't speak to him again. It doesn't matter how bad things were for him when we were kids, I can't go back after the way he spoke to me today."

"I really think you should. Don't leave things on a bad note."

Sylvie bit her lip. "I don't have any choice."

CHAPTER TWENTY-NINE

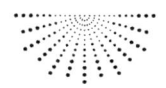

Lying on the bed, staring at the ceiling, Sylvie thought back to all those trips with her grandparents. They were cold, seemingly uncaring people – that wasn't a revelation – but Sylvie had always had her parents with her. When she considered how it must have been for Lowen, a painful lump lodged itself under her sternum.

An hour passed before she forced herself up and made her way downstairs. The house was quiet but she found Jago in the living room, scrolling on his phone.

"Hey," he said, his features radiating concern as he sat up straighter. "How are you?"

"Fine." She sat beside him.

"I wanted to come up but I thought you might want to be alone."

Sylvie nodded. "Where's your mum?"

"Gone to the shop."

Sylvie nodded again. "Good. I need to tell you something about Lowen."

"What?" His eyes narrowed.

"He lied to you," she told him, shifting on the couch to face him.

"How do you mean?"

"When you were kids, he told you he had a great time on all those holidays, but he didn't. He hated it."

"I don't think so," Jago muttered. "He was always showing off."

"It was all lies." Her stomach twisted at the thought of Lowen coming back and bragging about what a good time he'd had when she now realised how far from the truth that was. "Even the thing he told you about the clothes was wrong. Grandma didn't get the size wrong. Lowen purposely picked out clothes for you. It was always a nanny who took him shopping, and they didn't care if he slipped extra things in for you."

She waited but he didn't react, just stared at her as though not sure whether to believe her. "If we were there at the start of the holiday, Mum would volunteer to take him shopping. One time there was a very specific football shirt he wanted to buy for you, and we had to go into about ten shops until we found it in the right size."

"The England away strip," he said quietly. "I loved that shirt."

"I'm glad," she said, managing a smile. "Mum and I still curse you over that shopping trip."

"I remember him throwing it at me and complaining about how stupid his grandma was for getting the size wrong." He eyed her intently. "Why did he lie about it?"

"Maybe that was just his way of dealing with it." She stared down at her hands. "I knew my grandparents didn't treat Lowen very well, but I never considered just how hard it was for him. I suppose because I had my parents there. Mum tried to look out for Lowen, but we weren't there all the time, and even when we were it still must have been hard for him."

Pausing, Sylvie wiped tears as they fell from her lower lids. She told Jago about the time they'd arrived to find Lowen alone. Now that she'd spoken to her mum about it, it was as though her memories had been unlocked.

"How old was Lowen?" Jago asked eventually.

"Around eight or nine, I think." She chewed the inside of her lip. "I remember hearing Lowen crying for his mum. Dad ushered me out of the way and into bed, but I couldn't sleep. After a while I shouted for my mum and told her I needed to give Lowen a hug before I went to sleep. She took me to his bedroom and I climbed in and snuggled down next to him. Mum didn't bother to move me, so I slept like that." She smiled as she thought back. "I used to creep into his bed a lot after that."

Jago quirked an eyebrow. "*Really?*"

"We were kids! It was all very innocent. But it's part of why I always felt so close to him. Lying in bed, whispering in the dark night after night creates a special bond."

"Your grandparents must have felt terrible about him being left alone. They couldn't have known the babysitter would leave him."

"Grandma didn't think it was a big deal. She thought spending an evening alone would be character building."

"So that wasn't a one-off incident."

"I'd imagine it was one of the worst. After that we went away with them more. Mum wanted to be there to keep an eye on things. But she couldn't protect Lowen from everything. Grandma was always having a go at him for something. She hated his name and told him frequently. I guess even the clothes shopping wasn't fun for him, since it usually came after a lecture about what a state he looked and how his parents didn't know how to properly look after their kids and couldn't even provide them with clothes that didn't have stains and holes."

"What a bitch," Jago said.

"She was that." Sylvie reached for his hand. "I'm really angry with Lowen." Her chin wobbled. "I'm really hurt by the way he's treated me while I've been here, but I need you to know there's more to it."

"Will you speak to him again?"

"No." Her lower lip twitched and she caught it with her

teeth. "He doesn't want me in his life. He's made that very clear. Being around me apparently dredges up all these memories that he doesn't want to face. I can't keep forcing myself on him. I just don't want it to impact your relationship with him." She inhaled deeply. "And I don't know what this means for us."

He pulled her hand to his lips and kissed her palm. "I'll give Lowen time to cool off and then I'll talk to him. Everything will be okay. I'm just sorry your visit is ending on such a bad note."

"I'm thankful it hasn't all been bad." She slipped her arms around his waist and hugged him hard. "Thank you for everything." She didn't like to think about what the future held for her and Jago. Could they really be in a relationship with things the way they were with Lowen? She couldn't imagine Lowen would ever be okay with it.

"What do you want to do for the rest of today?" Jago asked as they pulled apart.

She really didn't feel like doing anything. "Curl up under the covers and hide from the world," she suggested.

"Can I tempt you to a chess rematch?"

"I'm not sure I can concentrate. My head is all over the place."

"That should give me a better chance at winning." With a mischievous grin, Jago moved to fetch the board. As they set up the pieces, Sylvie felt a rush of affection over the fact that he knew exactly what she needed.

"I have a confession to make," he said, holding her gaze after he moved his first pawn.

"What?"

"Mum wanted to cook something special tonight since it's your last night here." He twisted his lips. "I told her your favourite food is spaghetti and meatballs."

"I presume that's *your* favourite. Surely your mum was suspicious of my favourite food being the same as yours?"

"Lots of people must have the same favourite foods." He

wrinkled his nose. "Can you just go along with it? Don't make a liar of me."

She let out a short burst of laughter. "You made a liar of yourself when you lied!"

"Did I lie, though? Or did I just guess what your favourite food is?"

"You lied!" she said, then switched her focus to the chessboard.

Sylvie won the first game and was about to lose the second when Mirren put her head around the living room door.

"I'm making toad in the hole for dinner," she said. "That all right for you both?"

"Ooh," Sylvie replied. "That's my favourite."

"I know." Mirren scowled at Jago. "This one here tried to convince me otherwise. Since I wasn't born yesterday – as he apparently thinks – I gave your mum a call."

"I was only joking around!" Jago said, laughing.

"You lied," Mirren and Sylvie said at once, then grinned at each other.

"It'll be ready in about an hour," Mirren told them before leaving them alone again.

Sylvie shook her head as she looked at Jago. "I can't believe you lied to your mum."

"I can't believe I'm finally going to beat you at chess." With a cocky twitch of his eyebrow, he moved his queen and put her in check.

The rest of the afternoon went by surprisingly easily. A part of Sylvie expected Lowen to call or turn up. Presumably it was the part of her who still thought of him as the friendly kid she'd curled up in bed with so many times and whispered in the darkness with until they'd fallen asleep. The person who'd made all her childhood holidays fun and exciting.

As the evening drew on with no word from him, it became more and more apparent that the person in her head didn't exist any more. The adult version of him didn't want her in his life and wouldn't even acknowledge the bond they'd once shared.

Dinner with Mirren and Jago was pleasant – only strained by the thought that it was her last evening with them. Lowen had accused her of worming her way into the family and she knew that wasn't true. She was touched by the way they'd welcomed her. They'd enveloped her like a big group hug and treated her like family because that's the way they saw her.

Mirren shooed Sylvie away when she tried to help clear up the dinner things. Feeling emotionally exhausted, she took herself off for an early night.

In the comfort of the cosy guest room, she put her pyjamas on and snuggled under the covers, knowing there was no way she'd be able to switch her mind off for a while. Thoughts of Lowen swirled in her head and made every muscle in her body tense.

The heavy creak of floorboards on the landing alerted her to Jago's presence before the door eased open.

"Hey," he said, the light from the hallway illuminating him from behind. "Just checking you're all right."

"Not really," she managed through the lump in her throat. "Everything feels such a mess."

"Can I do anything?"

She lifted her head from the pillow. "I can't talk about it any more."

He stepped inside, closing the door softly. "We don't have to talk."

"My head is all over the place ..." And not even that, his mother was downstairs. It felt very inappropriate. "I'm not in the mood for ..."

"Get your mind out of the gutter," he said, his features flooding with amusement as he perched on the edge of the bed. "That's not what I meant. I just didn't want you to be alone when you're upset, but I'll go again if you'd rather."

She reached for his hand, slightly mortified for jumping to the wrong conclusion. "I don't want you to go."

He flashed her a smile, then lay on the bed beside her. With her head on his chest she could hear the steady thud of his heartbeat. It calmed her for a moment, as did the way he gently stroked her hair.

"I can't believe he hasn't called," she said, her words muffled by Jago's T-shirt. "He saw how upset I was and he just let me go without a word. Like he doesn't care at all." She felt the tightening of Jago's muscles beneath his T-shirt. "Sorry," she whispered. "He's your brother. I shouldn't complain about him to you."

"You can complain all you want. I'm already furious with him."

"I wish I was just angry with him," she said. "But mostly, I'm sad. It feels as though I lost something. Some*one*," she corrected. "I know that doesn't make a lot of sense."

"It does make sense," he said, continuing to stroke her hair.

Sylvie's thoughts shifted from Lowen to Jago, and how much she was going to miss him. As things stood, she didn't know what the future held for them. No matter what happened, she wasn't going to see him on a daily basis any more.

Her lungs tightened and she closed her eyes, as though she might be able to block the emotions out. When it didn't work she switched to focusing on his heartbeat and the fact that he was there with her now.

Tomorrow, she'd worry about saying goodbye.

CHAPTER THIRTY

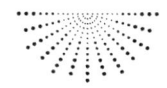

Jago couldn't bring himself to leave the airport until Sylvie's plane was in the air. They'd agreed they'd see each other when he was in London, but that was a week and a half away and felt like forever.

With a heavy heart he drove back to the house, where his mum was waiting in the kitchen.

"She's gone?" she asked sadly.

"She's gone," he repeated and sank into the chair adjacent to her.

"Do you want to tell me what the heck has gone on with Lowen?"

Jago rubbed at the space between his eyebrows. "What have you heard?"

"I didn't want to say anything in front of Sylvie, but Pippa called me this morning in a panic because she hadn't been able to get in touch with Lowen. I sent Trystan over first thing to check on him. Apparently he's upset about your relationship with Sylvie."

"That's part of it. He also told Sylvie he doesn't consider her family and doesn't want anything to do with her."

Mirren sighed heavily. "What a mess."

"What's wrong with him?" Jago snapped. "He treated Sylvie like crap the whole time she was here. Yesterday he really upset her."

"Things aren't as clear-cut as they seem when it comes to Lowen. I don't want to excuse his behaviour towards Sylvie, but he's had a lot to deal with. He's still dealing with a lot."

"I know," Jago said, his voice softening. "I know because of the snippets that Sylvie has told me. I'm just not sure why I never heard any of it from Lowen."

"He only recently opened up to me about it," she said. "I think burying it all was his way of coping for a long time."

"It doesn't mean it's okay that he treated Sylvie like crap."

"I agree." She twisted her wedding band on her finger. "You really like her, don't you?"

"Yes. I've no idea what's going to happen though. Lowen has made everything complicated."

"You'll be back in America soon anyway, but you can always keep in touch with her. And it would be nice if you talked to Lowen before you left."

He pulled his shoulders back. "I have every intention of talking to him," he said, his tone making it clear it wouldn't be a friendly chat.

His mum covered his hand with her own. "Try not to be too hard on him. You shouldn't leave on bad terms. It won't be good for either of you."

He shook his head, only then registering that she was still expecting him to return to America in a week. She probably also anticipated it being years before he got round to visiting again. Pulling his hands from hers, he rubbed at his temples, wishing he hadn't lied to her about his plans.

"I'm not going back." His voice was slightly muffled as he rubbed his hands down his face.

"Back where?"

"America." He winced at the surprise on his mum's features and the flicker of hope in her eyes. "My visa didn't get approved, so I have to leave the country." He screwed his face up and shook his head. "Not just because of the visa. I think I'd have left anyway. I've been thinking about a change for a while – the visa issue just gave me a push."

His mum opened and closed her mouth a few times. "When does your visa run out?"

"It already has. I am not going back."

"What about all your stuff?"

"I sold most of my worldly possessions. The rest is at a friend's place in London."

"What will you do? Where will you live?"

"In London, I think. I've been keeping an eye out for jobs but haven't found anything yet."

His mum blinked back tears. He had no idea whether she was happy about him moving so close to her or upset that he hadn't chosen to move back to Scilly and be closer still.

Finally, she pushed tears from her lower lids and smiled at him. "I'm very happy to hear that."

"Really?" He raised an eyebrow. "I was expecting you to try and convince me to move back here."

She lifted off her chair and kissed his temple. "I would love it If you moved back here. But most of all I want you to be happy. And London is much closer than New York."

His throat clenched with emotions. "I'll visit more often. I promise."

"That would be nice." She leaned in and gave him a side hug. "Now what the heck are you going to do for a week without Sylvie to keep you entertained?"

"That's a very good question." He ignored the knot in his stomach. "I guess I'll hang out with my mum."

Jago had planned on waiting a day or two before confronting Lowen, but it played on his mind. When his mum went out late in the afternoon he decided he'd rather get it over and done with. Given the calm weather, he got the boat out of the garage. It was easier than being reliant on the ferry.

This time, the ride over there wasn't so exhilarating. His mind was in chaos, jumping between thoughts of Sylvie and Lowen and trying to imagine how the whole mess would be resolved. He tied up at the jetty and marched across the island.

The sign on the door of the pottery studio was turned to closed but he tried the door regardless, then wandered inside.

"I wondered when you'd turn up," Lowen grumbled when Jago walked into the workshop at the back of the room.

"Sylvie left this morning," Jago told him, staying in the archway and trying not to let his anger run away with him.

Lowen didn't respond but wiped his hands on the towel resting on his thigh, then reached to stroke the cat which prowled around his legs.

"Are we going to have this out or what?" Jago snapped.

"I'm not sure what you're expecting me to say."

"Clearly you have a problem with me."

"I have a problem with you sleeping with my cousin."

"It's not as though I planned for things to work out like this. You also make it sound like it was some drunken hook-up or something …"

Lowen winced. "I don't want to hear about your relationship with Sylvie."

"But you're quite happy to be angry with me about it?" His shoulders tensed. "I don't even get it. You ignored her for most of the time she's been here. All she wanted was to spend time with you."

"And yet she actually spent all her time with you."

"Because you were giving her the cold shoulder," he spat out. "You treated her like crap. Do you even care about how upset she was when she left? Do you care about her at all?"

"Of course I care." The stool tipped over when Lowen stood, startling the cat so much that it hissed and scrambled up onto the sideboard and out through the open window. "She's my cousin. You have no idea of our history."

"You've got that right. I'm not sure I know anything about your childhood any more. Which is weird since I was there for it."

"What's that supposed to mean?"

"It means you always told me you had a great time with your grandparents, but Sylvie tells a different story. She was also under the impression that we were best buds growing up, which isn't how I remember our relationship."

"I see ... the two of you have been swapping stories about me."

Jago frowned. "It makes absolutely no difference what I say, does it? You won't discuss this properly and you're determined to be angry with me no matter what."

"Because you slept with my cousin," he said again.

"The cousin who you had zero interest in until you realised I was interested in her. And if you *do* care about her, you should probably be thanking me for looking out for her when she was upset."

"Looking out for her or taking advantage of the situation?"

For a moment, all Jago could do was stare incredulously. "You have no idea what you're talking about." He took a few steps to leave before pacing back again. "If that's really what you think of me, we don't need to have anything to do with each other. I wanted us to sort things out properly." He paused to catch his breath. "I'm not going back to America and I intended to talk to you about me seeing Sylvie again, but now I really don't give a damn what you think."

He left before Lowen could say any more. His brisk walk back across the island was fuelled by adrenaline while his mind replayed their conversation for the entire journey home.

He was still fuming when he arrived back at Old Town Bay.

After putting the boat away he stood on the lane, staring out to sea and taking deep breaths in a bid to compose himself before he went inside.

Knocking drew his attention, and he caught Trystan looking out at him from an upstairs window of his cottage. When he beckoned for Jago to come in, he didn't hesitate. He needed to let off steam, and venting to Trystan might just do the trick.

Thankfully, Beth and Ellie were out so Jago could pace the living room as he complained loudly about Lowen.

"Don't be too hard on him," Trystan finally said, sitting calmly in the armchair.

"Are you serious?" Jago threw his hands up. "He acts like a petulant child. You pandering to him and never challenging when he's being irrational probably doesn't help matters."

"You did sleep with his cousin. You're hardly blameless here."

"I don't even see why that's such a big deal."

Trystan folded his arms across his chest. "Really?"

"I mean … okay … I can see how it might be an issue, but he practically ignored her the whole time she was here. Pretty much the only time he paid her any attention was when he found out there was something going on between us."

Trystan's brow furrowed. "Does it ever occur to you that he's not our full sibling?"

"What?" Jago stared at him in confusion.

"He's only our half-brother. Do you ever think about that?"

"Of course I don't." Jago rested a hand on the mantelpiece. "He's my brother. End of."

"But you were born from different mothers. Biologically, he doesn't have the same relationship that you and I have."

"I hope you're trying to make a point," Jago said through gritted teeth.

"My point is that just because we don't think of him any differently doesn't mean he doesn't *feel* different."

"Mum always treated him the same as the rest of us. He doesn't remember having another mum. He was brought up the same as we were."

"Except for every school holiday when he was shipped off to his grandparents? Don't you think that might have been a small reminder that he was different to us?"

Jago puffed his cheeks out, not quite able to admit that Trystan might be right.

"From the snippets of what he's told me about his time with his grandparents," Trystan went on, "he didn't have anything like as much fun as he led us to believe."

"I know," Jago said.

"Did he talk to you about it?"

"No." He hung his head. "Sylvie told me a few things. It sounded pretty crap."

"There's no wonder his head's a mess," Trystan said. "Dad's death caused him a lot of issues too. Then Sylvie turned up. He doesn't know how to deal with any of it."

Jago moved to sit on the couch, sinking back into the cushions. "I really like her," he said wearily. "What am I supposed to do?"

"How do you mean?"

"I want to keep seeing her. But that's going to be complicated if Lowen continues to have an issue with it."

Trystan scratched his cheek. "It's also a bit difficult since you live on different continents."

"Oh." Jago grimaced. "I'm not going back to New York."

"Because of Sylvie?"

"No. My visa ran out." He was hit with another surge of guilt over keeping it from his family, but Trystan didn't seem too bothered by him not mentioning it before. He fired questions at him and appeared quite excited at the prospect of having Jago nearer again. He wasn't sure why he'd expected a different response.

"So do you think it's bad if I keep seeing Sylvie?" Jago finally asked.

"Depends," Trystan said calmly.

"On what?"

"On whether you ever want to have any sort of relationship with Lowen again."

CHAPTER THIRTY-ONE

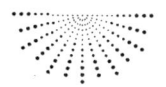

Over the next few days, Jago found a couple of jobs in London which he was more than qualified for. He had cover letters and his CV ready to send, but every time he went into his email account he couldn't bring himself to do it.

There was also the issue of where he would live. His friend Ryan had offered his spare room for the short term, but it wasn't a permanent solution.

Sitting in the living room on Monday morning with his laptop on his knees, he opened the property rental site and scrolled through the places he'd previously bookmarked. Compared to his apartment in New York, the options in his price range in London were really quite attractive. All he needed to do was make an appointment to look around them.

Yet again, he closed his laptop without taking any action. On Friday he'd be back in London and he'd have to stop procrastinating over making decisions. Plus when he'd spoken to Sylvie the previous evening, he'd told her definitively that he was going to send off the job applications.

As it often did now, his mind drifted to thoughts of opening his brewery. It had been a bad idea the first time, so it was ridiculous that he'd consider making the same mistake again.

On a surge of adrenaline he set his laptop on the coffee table and shot off the couch. Brewing his own beer wasn't a good idea, and if he could just get it out of his head he could start making realistic plans for his future.

Stepping outside, the frigid wind engulfed him and he cursed himself for not grabbing his coat. He wasn't going far though. Upping his pace, he arrived outside Noah's cottage in a matter of minutes.

Keira looked utterly confused when she answered the door.

"Noah's at work," she told him. "He's on a dayshift."

"I was actually hoping to talk to you, if you have a few minutes?" He had a rush of uncertainty about discussing things with Keira but blundered on nonetheless. "If you're busy, it doesn't matter. But it probably won't take long. I just wanted to pick your brains about something."

She opened the door wider and stepped aside. "Noah would no doubt say that picking my brains definitely wouldn't take long."

Jago smiled as he wiped his shoes on the mat.

"Do you want a coffee or anything?"

"Were you working?" he asked, eyeing her laptop on the coffee table with a notepad and pen beside it.

"Yes, but it's fine. I'm happy to take a break." She turned at the kitchen doorway. "Coffee?" she asked again.

"That would be great." He followed her and waited a moment while she set the machine running.

"What can I help you with then?" she asked with a smile.

"You work in advertising, right?"

"Yes, theoretically just part-time now, but the hours have been creeping up recently. Which is fine. Kit doesn't need me to help on the train in the winter, so I have more time on my hands." She rolled her eyes. "Sorry. That was a convoluted answer to a simple question. Yes, I work in advertising."

Smiling, he leaned against the counter. "So you run advertising campaigns for different products?"

"That's pretty much the gist of it."

He shifted his weight and tapped the countertop. "When you get a new project, do you tend to get a feeling for how easy or difficult it will be to market a product?"

"I guess so." She handed him his coffee. "Sometimes the client will have ideas about how to market their product. If they don't trust our judgement, it makes things more difficult. So often the ease of a campaign will be determined by how easy the clients are to work with."

He nodded along, regardless of the fact that she'd missed his point. "I was thinking specifically about the product. Some products must be easier to market than others."

"Yeah." She picked up her coffee and nodded towards the living room. "Definitely."

"Have you ever worked on campaigns for drinks?"

She tucked her legs under her on the armchair. "Yes. Lots of times."

"Is that a tough sell?"

"It depends." A flash of curiosity hit her features. "What type of drink are we talking about? Any kind of health drink is pretty easy to market these days."

He inhaled deeply. "What about alcohol?"

"Are we talking hypothetically? Because the more detail you can give me, the better the answer I can give you."

"It's hypothetical," he said slowly.

"But you have a specific product in mind?"

"Beer," he told her. "A local beer in a tourist hotspot."

The smile broke slowly over her face. "Would this conversation be easier if I promised not to mention it to anyone? Not even Noah."

He dragged his hands through his hair. "Okay," he said, starting over. "A friend and I went into business in the States, brewing our own beer. The business didn't work out, but I genuinely think the beer was good. We had a great product, but we were trying to sell it in a saturated market."

Keira dropped her feet to the floor and braced her elbows onto her knees. "You want to brew beer here? In the Scillies?"

He shrugged. "The idea has been niggling at me, but I think I'm probably deluded. I was confident we could make the business work in New York, but I was completely wrong."

"And now you don't trust your own judgement?" Keira asked.

He nodded. "Something like that."

"Is that what you used the money from Lowen's grandparents for? Noah mentioned something about you using it to pay off debts, but he didn't seem too sure."

"I used it to bail out the business before we got into debt," he told her. "Not all of it. I still have a decent amount left to play with. It just feels very risky after everything went wrong last time. I don't want to make the same mistake twice."

"I don't think any business idea is ever a sure thing."

"But some must have more potential than others. If I were to bring this project to you, what would you think?"

She leaned back in the chair. "I can definitely see how setting up an independent brewery in New York would be a hard sell."

"It seems obvious to me now too. Hindsight is great, isn't it?"

She chewed on her bottom lip. "I'd hate to get your hopes up and tell you that your new idea couldn't fail, but I'm struggling to think of a reason why it wouldn't work. You're local and have connections in every place that sells alcohol on the islands. I can't imagine why any of them wouldn't want to sell local beer. I bet they'd fall over each other for it." She tilted her head as though thinking about it more. "We could do some market research, but I really think it's a good idea."

"*We?*" he asked, raising an eyebrow.

"Yes, *we,*" she said emphatically. "If you're doing this, I want in. If you don't hire me as your marketing manager, I'm going to be very upset. My brain is already whirring with ideas."

Her eyebrows knitted together. "Wait, I thought you were going back to London this week?"

"I am. I think." He twisted his lips. "I really wanted you to tell me this was a terrible business idea so I could put it out of my head."

"Sorry," she said with a wry smile. "In my professional opinion it's a very good idea."

～

Leaving Jago ended up not being as hard as Sylvie expected. Mostly because he'd already messaged her by the time her plane landed in Exeter. Then he called her that evening and the next evening. Knowing she'd see him again soon helped too.

On Monday morning she was up early and caught her mum before she left for work.

"What are your plans for today?" Bess asked her across the kitchen table.

"I have no plans." She bit into a slice of toast, thinking that she should have stayed in bed longer. The day stretched out in front of her.

"I have an idea." Her mum focused on her coffee in a way that made Sylvie instantly suspicious.

"What?" she asked wearily.

"You need to find something to occupy you."

"I told you, it's a terrible time to look for a job."

"It would probably be easier if you were looking for something you actually want to do. You're in a very nice financial position. Why not take advantage of that?"

"How? I don't know what I'd do if I don't get a job in accounting. It's all I've ever done."

"No, it's not." Her mum let out an exasperated sigh. "You're a talented hairdresser. Why are you the only person who doesn't see that?"

"I don't want to spend the next few years training to be a hairdresser."

"You don't need to. You have so much experience. To most people that counts more than qualifications."

"I'd still need a qualification."

"Maybe." Her mum stood and put her mug in the dishwasher. "But you should do some research. Hairdressing courses don't necessarily take years. An intensive course would only be a few weeks out of your life."

"Really?"

Her mum nodded. "Look into it. You need to find something to fill your time."

She couldn't deny that. Hanging around the house was getting boring quickly. While her mum went to shower, Sylvie got her laptop out and started investigating. Quickly, she found her options were far wider than she'd expected. There were online courses and intensive courses which were actually pretty tempting.

"Oh, you actually took my advice," her mum remarked over her shoulder when she came back into the kitchen. "Find anything interesting?"

"Yes." She leaned back in the chair, the web page open on the course that appealed to her most. "This one sounds good. It's a four-week course which would get me the most basic qualification."

"When could you start?"

"January." She folded her arms across her chest. "It's expensive though. Plus it's in London. I'd have to get the train in every day."

"That's doable. It's only for four weeks. And the cost will be worth it." Her mum leaned closer to the screen. "What about this?" She pointed at the calendar of available courses. "That one starts next week and there's still availability for it."

"I can't just book on a course for next week."

"Why not? What else have you got on?"

She opened and closed her mouth a couple of times but didn't have a good answer.

"Do it!" Her mum gave her shoulder a nudge. "You can be a qualified hairdresser by Christmas."

"It seems a bit rushed. I need to think it through."

"Think about it this morning, then book it quick before all the spaces are taken." Her mum kissed the side of her head. "I need to get to work. See you later."

When she left, Sylvie remained staring at the computer screen. "I don't even know if I want to be a hairdresser," she mumbled to herself.

It played on her mind all day. She imagined how different her life would be if she could make her own schedule instead of sitting in a stuffy office all day. How lovely would it be if she had regular clients who she could chat to while doing their hair? She'd find out all about their lives and they'd become more like friends than clients.

With her mind on her hypothetical future as a hairdresser, it was the middle of the afternoon before she registered that she hadn't heard from Jago. It was unusual not to get a message or two from him throughout the day. When she found herself waiting to hear from him a couple of hours later, she chastised herself for being silly. Why was she waiting around for him when she could call him herself?

In the back of her mind she thought he'd probably be busy when she called him. That would explain why she hadn't heard from him. Except he answered on the third ring and said he was just hanging out at home.

"What have you been doing today?" she asked, and again waited for some explanation for not having heard from him.

"Not much. I had a coffee with Keira earlier …" He stopped abruptly as though he'd said something he shouldn't. Maybe he thought she'd be jealous. Which she was actually. She'd be jealous of anyone who got to spend time with Jago.

"How is she?" Sylvie asked.

"Fine. I just went and hung out for a bit since she works from home. I was bored."

"I know the feeling." Sylvie opened her mouth to mention the hairdressing course but stopped herself. She probably wouldn't do it anyway. "How's the job hunt going?" she asked instead.

"Erm …"

"That bad? Did you send off the applications at least?"

"No."

"Oh." The previous day he'd been adamant he was going to, so she was slightly surprised that he hadn't. "Are you going to?"

"I'm not sure. I started to think that maybe I should wait until the new year. Let myself enjoy the rest of the year off without worrying about finding a job."

"That's not a bad idea." She shuffled to the edge of the couch, feeling suddenly unsettled. "Will you still go back to London? Or stay longer on St Mary's?"

"I don't know."

Sylvie swallowed hard. She could tell from his voice that he *did* know really. He was going to stay on Scilly but was afraid of saying so because he knew it would upset her. Was he thinking of just staying there for the rest of the year, though, or permanently? She didn't dare ask and was sure he wouldn't be able to give her a straight answer anyway.

"I don't think I'll go back to London this week," he finally said. "If I'm not going to get stuck into job hunting, there doesn't seem to be much point." He fell silent and Sylvie could practically hear him wince. "I mean, I want to see you, obviously. But I might wait until the week after. I thought I could help Kit out with his house, and Mum has a few jobs for me in the rental cottages."

Sylvie forced brightness to her voice. "You shouldn't rush back to London if you have stuff to do with your family. I'm going to be busy here anyway," she added without thought.

"Yeah? What have you got on?"

"I'm going to do a hairdressing course," she said, reaching for her laptop as she said it. With so many aspects of her life feeling out of control, she had a sudden urge to take control where she could.

"Wow. That's great."

"It's an intensive, four-week course. Starts next week." Already, the thought of having something positive to focus on gave her a boost.

"I'm really pleased for you. Are you excited?"

"I think so. Nervous too." She switched the phone to speaker so she could enrol on the course while she chatted. "I think it will be really good though."

One thing was for certain: it would be a far better use of her time than sitting around her mum's house, wondering when she might see Jago again.

CHAPTER THIRTY-TWO

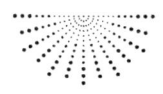

Enrolling in the hairdressing course turned out to be the saviour of Sylvie's sanity. It distracted her from thoughts of Jago, and the mess with Lowen. The long days were so tiring that by the time she arrived home in the evening all she could do was grab a bite to eat and collapse in bed.

With some routine in her life, she began to see things more clearly. She missed Jago and thought of him often, but realistically they'd only known each other a few weeks. Maybe it wasn't destined to be anything more than a fling. Given the way the contact between them had dwindled she was sure that he was also looking at things more realistically.

It was Thursday when he messaged to say he was heading back to London and asked if she had time to meet over the weekend. He offered to come to Cambridge, but she told him she could get the train into London. She was used to the trip after a week of commuting.

Her heart was galloping as the train pulled into the station on Saturday afternoon. She spotted Jago standing casually, wearing a dark shirt and with his hands tucked into the pockets of his jeans. She watched as he scanned her carriage, then felt as though her heart stopped dead when their eyes met. He moved along the platform as she walked through the carriage, only taking his eyes off her when he collided with a teenager wearing headphones.

Sylvie laughed so loudly that everyone around her turned to stare. Not that she cared, all she cared about was getting off the busy train and to Jago. It felt like an eternity as she waited for a family in front of her to wrangle their bags and children off the train.

Finally, she was standing in front of Jago, amid a bustle of people. All she wanted to do was throw her arms around him and kiss him, but nerves kicked in, and she found herself unsure of how to greet him.

"Hey," he said, looking slightly bashful before enveloping her in a bear hug. She sank against his chest, pushing her face into the warm skin of his neck and inhaling the scent of him while emotions swelled in her throat.

"I missed you," he said, his chin resting on top of her head. The words sent a surge of hope rushing through her. She'd told herself repeatedly that they were just friends meeting to catch up, but now he was in front of her it was clear that her feelings for him would never be just friendship.

"I missed you too." She lifted her face to look him in the eyes while she ran her hand down his cheek. "A lot."

He took her hand as someone jostled against his back. "Let's go and find somewhere we can talk."

The words sounded ominous, but Sylvie tried not to overthink it and instead focused on the firm grip of his hand as he led her through the throng on the platform, then out of the station and into the freezing air outside.

"Any preference for what you want to eat?" he asked.

With her stomach tied in knots, she didn't have any appetite at all. "I don't mind."

"I did a search for places nearby. There's an Italian around the corner with good reviews. Or a French bistro, or a steak place." His gaze shifted across the road. "Or that pub looks pretty nice," he said, pointing. "But if we go in there, my internet search was a complete waste of time. I haven't checked the reviews."

"The pub looks good," she said, bunching her shoulders up against the cold.

Five minutes later they were settled at a small table in a corner of the quiet pub. It didn't seem to be an overly popular spot, but it was clean and warm, with quaint wooden decor and a relaxed atmosphere.

Jago sipped his pint, then wiped the foam from his top lip. "So how's the hairdressing course going?"

"Good." She smiled. "It makes me feel old though. I think most of the people on the course are approximately half my age."

"Are you enjoying it?"

"Yes. It's interesting. And consuming enough that I barely have time to think of anything else."

"Like Lowen?" he asked sadly.

"Like Lowen," she confirmed, then shook her head. "I don't want to talk about him."

"Tell me about your course then. I want to hear all about it."

Sylvie took another sip of her drink, then settled in to telling him all about the interesting characters on her course, and what she was learning, and the teacher, and how fulfilling it felt to be doing something she was so enthusiastic about. She prattled away through two drinks, partly because she had so much to say, and partly because it felt like a safe topic of conversation.

"I don't know what will come of it," she said eventually. "Maybe I'll rent space in someone else's salon, or set myself up as a mobile hairdresser." She sat back in her seat as the barman arrived with the food, waiting until he left again before continuing. "Maybe I'll never do anything with it and find another job in accounting. But it's nice to do something different. It'll mean I always have the option for a career change if I feel like it."

"What about opening your own salon?"

"It would be difficult financially. It's not an easy business to be in these days given the price of rent and overheads. I wouldn't want to work for someone else though, so I'd either find salon space to rent, or do the mobile thing." She picked up her club sandwich but paused with it in front of her mouth. "Anyway, enough about me. What's going on with you? Have you had any luck on the job front?"

"Not really." He picked up his burger, then paused as though he was about to say something else but changed his mind and took a bite instead.

Sylvie's chest felt tight at the flicker of sadness in his eyes.

"Are you back in London for good?" she asked, knowing she might not like his answer but needing to know.

Idly, he dunked a chip into ketchup and avoided eye contact.

"Jago," she said, drawing his gaze. "Tell me what's going on, please?"

"I'm here for the weekend to collect the stuff I left at my friend's place."

"Then you're going back to St Mary's?"

He tossed his chip back onto the plate and nodded. "I should have said something on the phone, but I wanted to explain in person."

Sylvie's eyes dropped to her plate as she tried to hide her disappointment. Apparently telling herself repeatedly that nothing could happen between them and they were just meeting up as friends had done little to dampen her hope that there might be some kind of future for the two of them.

Under the table, Jago gave her foot a gentle kick. Their eyes locked for a moment when she forced her head up, and she at least had the feeling that it probably wasn't a decision he'd come to easily.

"Being back on Scilly just feels right for me at the moment," Jago told her hesitantly. "Aside from the issues with Lowen, being around my family feels comfortable. I never really imagined I could live there again, but I want to give it a try. It feels like the natural next step for me. I think you were right when you said the reason I couldn't find a job that appealed to me in London was because it wasn't where I wanted to be."

Sylvie picked up her sandwich again but realised there was no way she was getting anything past the lump in her throat.

Jago slipped his arm across the table and took her hand. "I'm sorry."

She shook her head and wiped a tear from the corner of her eye. "It's fine. It's not as though I thought ... I mean, we've only known each other for a matter of weeks. I loved hanging out with you but it's bad timing, not to mention the situation with Lowen."

"I thought maybe we could still see each other, but I'm not sure how realistic that is if you're in Cambridge and I'm on Scilly."

"It's not realistic at all," she said with a sad smile. "And it would be messy for us to keep seeing each other anyway. It'd no doubt cause all sorts of problems between you and Lowen. I don't want that."

"I'd like to say I don't care about that," he said, running his thumb over the back of her hand. "But I'm not sure it's true. Although currently we're not speaking, so I'm not sure things could get worse."

"You'll sort things out eventually though."

"Maybe. I hope he'll realise what an idiot he's been and make things right with you too."

"I don't think so." Sylvie's chin trembled and she swallowed her emotions. "He doesn't want anything to do with me."

"I honestly don't see how that could be true," Jago said.

Gently, she squeezed his hand and released it. "Anyway, I don't want to spend the evening being miserable and talking about what might have been." She took a few mouthfuls of her water, feeling self-conscious as Jago gazed at her intently.

"So ..." She forced her lips to a smile and blinked away the excess moisture from her eyes. "What are you going to do in

Scilly? Is there going to be a Scilly beer any time soon?" Her smile turned genuine. "You should totally call it Scilly beer."

"If I do, I'm afraid you won't be able to take any credit for it since Keira already has it on her list of potential names."

"So you're really doing it?"

"I'm not sure, but I'm starting to feel like I might not have any choice. Keira is probably going to bully me into submission soon. She may end up as my business partner at this rate."

"You've been talking to Keira about it?"

"She works in marketing, so I ran the idea by her to get her professional opinion on it."

"I take it, she thinks it's a good idea?"

He chewed slowly on his burger. "She's been pretty gung-ho about it since I first mentioned it. She went off and spoke to a few of the pub owners to see if they'd be interested."

Sylvie felt a stab of jealousy that Keira got to hang out with him. If he went ahead with his business idea, Keira would no doubt end up being his sounding board. She'd know every detail of it, while Sylvie might just get the odd update. That was if she and Jago kept in touch. Did she even want to keep in touch if they couldn't be together?

Lifting her head, she caught him looking at her. It made her stomach twist. "I hope you do it," she said quietly. "I really think you'd make it a success."

Maybe if he went ahead with his new business and she set up a hairdressing business it would give some meaning to their time together. They'd inspired each other to make changes in their lives.

"Thank you," Jago murmured.

A thought occurred to Sylvie, and she choked on a laugh.

"What's so funny?" Jago asked, his eyebrows twitching together.

"I just imagined the look on my grandmother's face if she knew one of Lowen's brothers was using her money to fund a brewery." She covered her mouth but snorted as her laughter increased.

It lightened the atmosphere considerably, and they chatted easily for another hour before Sylvie had to head back to the train.

"We'll keep in touch, right?" Jago asked her on the platform.

"Yes." A clean break was probably the sensible option, but she knew she wouldn't manage it. "Keep me updated on the brewery."

"I will." He wrapped his arms around her. "Let me know how the course goes."

She nodded but couldn't manage any more than that as she focused on the feel of his body against hers and the scent of him filling her nostrils. The train was waiting and she needed to get on it, but she also wanted to drag the moment out as long as possible.

He pulled away slightly to kiss her cheek and the gesture spurred her into action. Mirroring him, she kissed his cheek, then somehow managed to keep it together while she boarded the train.

She kept eyes on Jago while the train pulled away. When he disappeared from view, she pushed her head back into the seat and took steady breaths until the tension in her chest passed.

The feeling of loss was silly since they'd agreed to keep in touch. They'd still be friends and would most likely see each other again in the future. As she wiped a tear from her cheek, she reminded herself that they'd only known each other for a few weeks, so it really wasn't a huge loss.

It became her mantra for the train ride home.

Unfortunately, it seemed her heart didn't want to hear it and ached for what might have been.

CHAPTER THIRTY-THREE

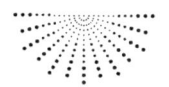

For the week after he saw Sylvie, Jago's instincts were at odds with each other. His overwhelming feeling was that he'd been an idiot to turn away from her. Especially when he'd tried to call her and she'd responded with a message saying she thought it better if they weren't in contact for a little while. She'd used the hairdressing course as an excuse, saying she needed to focus on that, but the implication had been clear: she wanted to move forward with her life and her future didn't involve him.

He couldn't blame her. If he had any sense he'd be focusing on the future too, but all he could think about was that he wanted to go back on his decision to stay on Scilly. He could get a job on the mainland and continue to see Sylvie – regardless of the consequences. If Lowen never spoke to either of them again, so be it. The only thing stopping him was the annoying, rational part of his brain which told him it wasn't the right thing to do.

Not only because of Lowen, but because living on Scilly really did feel right for him. The idea of the brewery niggled at him constantly. He was sure if he didn't give it a shot, he'd forever wonder what might have been. At the same time, he was terrified that it would all go wrong, like last time.

When his mum asked him about his plans that Wednesday morning, he gruffly told her that the end of the year was no time to be making decisions. He'd been focused on his career for almost twenty years and had earned a couple of months off. In January he'd figure out what he was going to do with his life.

Mirren agreed with him, which threw him slightly. He'd half expected she might want him out from under her feet, especially given how grumpy he'd been since Sylvie left.

In a fit of restlessness, he volunteered to tidy up the garage. It seemed like the perfect distraction for the first half an hour. Until he realised how big of a task it was and how it was the kind of job suited to spring and not November. Even with his thick coat the cold still seeped in quickly. At least it made him work fast.

When Mirren brought him a cuppa after a couple of hours he almost had everything straightened out.

"Does anyone ever take Dad's boat out?" he asked, warming his hands on the mug.

"Kit keeps her seaworthy and takes her out now and again."

"I should have guessed," Jago muttered.

Her mum propped her hands on her hips. "What was that?"

"Nothing."

"What's your problem with Kit?"

"I don't have a problem with Kit." He leaned against the bonnet of the car. Genuinely, he didn't have a problem with Kit. Except that his blood seemed to be simmering just below boiling point and everything annoyed him. "He really looks after you, doesn't he?" he asked in earnest. "Since Dad died he's just stepped in to take care of everything."

"He's been a big help," she said, searching his features. "You all have."

He choked out a laugh. "Liar!"

"I'm not lying. You all support me in different ways."

He felt like pointing out that from what he'd heard Lowen

had caused more problems for her than supported her, but it wasn't his issue. "Sorry I wasn't here for you," he said instead.

"It's not your job to be here for me," she told him. "You have your own life to live. But you also spent many hours patiently listening to me witter away over the phone."

He raised an eyebrow. "I wasn't always listening."

"I know!" She beamed. "But you pretended to. That was enough."

He inhaled deeply. "I thought I might take Dad's boat out."

"You can't sail."

"I think I can manage it. It's not as though I've never been in a sailing boat before."

"No."

Shocked by the firmness of her tone, Jago could only stare at her for a moment. "What do you mean *no?*"

"I mean you're not going out on her alone. Especially not at this time of year."

"The weather's fine today."

"Maybe, but the water's bloody freezing."

"I wasn't planning on getting in it." Heat seeped into his hands as he squeezed the mug too tightly. "You can't just ban me from going out on Dad's boat."

"Legally, it's my boat so I can."

"Why are you fine with Kit taking her out and not me?"

"Because Kit knows how to sail, and he's a stickler for water safety. He wouldn't do anything reckless."

"Neither would I."

"Apparently you would, since you want to go out on the boat alone in November when you don't know how to sail."

"I'd only go out in the bay. What exactly do you think is going to happen?" He wanted to take the words back as soon as they were out of his mouth. "Sorry," he said immediately.

"I don't want you going out on the sailboat when you don't know how to sail. Get Kit to take you out if you really want to go."

"I don't need Kit to take me out on the boat," he said petulantly.

"Then you're not going."

"Are you serious?"

"Very," she said before striding away.

Jago was absolutely fuming as he resumed clearing up. He was banging around, straightening up a few final things, when Noah appeared in the doorway.

"What did Mum bribe you with to organise all this?" he asked. "The garage has needed cleaning up for ages."

"I'm surprised Kit didn't do it," Jago grumbled.

"What?"

"Nothing." He closed the box with the sand toys and rubbed the back of his hand against his forehead.

"You okay?" Noah asked.

"Yeah." He walked out of the garage. "I wanted to take Dad's boat out but Mum's being weird about it."

Noah stared at him. "You can't sail."

"It's not as though it's a massive yacht. I sailed enough as a kid. I'd manage. Or I would if Mum hadn't banned me from going out on it."

"You can't really be surprised that Mum doesn't want you out on the boat."

"Kit goes out on it."

"Because he knows what he's doing. But he also doesn't go out very often, since he knows how much Mum worries when he does."

Jago wandered over to perch on the wall. "Why did she keep it?"

"Same reason you want to go out on it," Noah told him sadly.

"Because Dad loved it."

Noah moved to sit beside him. "Ask Kit to take you out on it."

"Maybe I will." He tipped his head back to look skywards.

"Can you check Mum's okay? I might have upset her."

"I was heading up there anyway." He gave Jago a friendly punch on the bicep before wandering off.

Reluctantly, Jago got his phone out. Kit answered after only one ring and the cheeriness of his voice gave Jago a stab of guilt for being annoyed with him for no reason.

"What's going on?" Kit asked.

"I've been clearing out the garage."

"That's good. I've been meaning to do it for ages but I kept putting it off. Was it a complete nightmare?"

"It wasn't exactly fun." At least it had kept his mind off Sylvie for a few hours. "I was wondering if you fancy taking Dad's boat out for a spin with me sometime?"

"I'd love to." Kit paused for a moment and Jago had the distinct feeling he was looking for an excuse not to. He'd probably say he was too busy with his house. "How about now?"

"*Now?*" Jago repeated.

"If you've got time? I've been working on the house but I can take a break. The weather's perfect for it."

"Now's great for me." After ending the call, Jago stayed on the wall and wallowed in guilt over his bitterness towards Kit and how grumpy he'd been with his mum. He didn't have long to wait before his little brother strolled along the lane.

"How's the house coming on?" Jago asked as they pulled the boat out. He'd fully intended to help him out with it, but so far it hadn't happened.

"Slowly," Kit said with his usual cheer. "I'd quite like to pay professionals and get everything done quickly, but Seren's insisting we do it ourselves."

"It'll be worth it in the end."

"That's what I keep telling myself."

Between them they pulled the boat out of the garage and Kit commented on how much easier it was with the place all neat and tidy.

"How are things between you and Lowen now?" he asked as they manoeuvred the boat trailer onto the sand.

Jago had lost track of which of his family members he'd had conversations with about it, but decided he hadn't really spoken to Kit about it at all so wasn't even sure what he knew.

"I argued with him about Sylvie," he said. "Then I tried calling him and messaging him last week but he ignored me completely." Seeing Sylvie had prompted him to try to contact his brother. Lowen being angry with him wasn't the worst thing in the world, but seeing how it upset Sylvie spurred him to at least try and sort things out. That seemed unlikely if Lowen wouldn't even speak to him.

"Sounds about right," Kit said.

"Do you think I should try speaking to him in person again?"

"You could," Kit replied noncommittally.

"What would you do?"

"Probably give him some space. He's crazy stubborn. I'd almost guarantee that trying to speak to him again now will only make things worse."

"That's what I thought."

"He'll come around eventually."

"You think so?"

They parked the trailer by the waterline while they removed their shoes and socks. "Don't repeat this to anyone," Kit said quietly, "but I don't think things are too good between Lowen and Pippa. At least that's what I heard from Mia."

"I can't say I'm surprised given how difficult Lowen is."

Kit slung his shoes and socks into the boat. "Pippa's only going to put up with his mood for so long. Eventually she'll tell him to sort himself out and I assume he'll listen to her. At least I hope he will."

"If that was all it took, surely she could have had a word with him earlier."

Kit shrugged and they fell silent as they worked together to get the boat in the water.

"Is this the first time you've been in a sailboat since the vomiting incident?" Kit asked, his features completely neutral as he took control of the boat to sail them out of the bay.

"No. I used to go out sometimes when I was a teenager." Jago thought back to his schooldays. "There was this girl I fancied, Lisa Morgan. Her dad had a really nice boat and used to let her take it out with friends. I could never say no when she invited me along."

"Did anything ever happen between you?"

"No." He smiled. "Probably because I turned green after five minutes on the boat and was too busy fighting off nausea to make conversation."

"Sounds awkward."

"It was."

"How are you feeling now?" Kit asked.

"Fine." He sucked in a lungful of sea air.

"It's beautiful out here, isn't it?"

"Yeah." Jago looked out at the endless blue sea. "I feel as though my life would have been completely different if I'd enjoyed being on the water as a kid."

"I can't imagine living anywhere that wasn't by the sea."

"It's all I dreamed of when I was a kid. I just wanted to get away."

"I guess things turn out as they're supposed to."

"You think so?"

Kit looked thoughtful for a moment. "Yeah, I do."

Just like that, Jago was back to thinking about Sylvie. He definitely didn't agree that things always turned out as they were supposed to.

"Do you always come this way when you take the boat out?" he asked Kit after a few minutes of silence.

"How do you mean?"

"East?"

Kit pursed his lips. "Yeah. I do. It's prettier."

"That's the way Dad always liked to go, right?"

"Yeah. Circling the Eastern Isles was his favourite route."

Jago nodded. "I did a boat trip over that way with Lowen and Pippa and Sylvie to look at the seals."

"Did you see many?"

"Yeah loads but ..." He trailed off when he couldn't find the right words.

"What?"

"I just ... it was ..." He swallowed hard and braced himself as the wind picked up, tilting the boat. "I found it hard," he said, without looking at Kit. "I kept thinking about Dad and wondering about ... I couldn't stop imagining ..." When he gave up on trying to find words, he looked to Kit and knew from the sympathetic rise of his eyebrows that he didn't need further explanation.

"I used to wonder too," Kit said. "I thought I didn't want to know any of the details about where exactly he was found, but my mind kept filling the blanks and inventing a bunch of images for me. Eventually, I got one of the guys from the coastguard who was one of the first on the scene to take me out there and talk me through it."

"Did it help?"

"It was pretty hard to hear, but yeah, it helped." His eyebrows drew together. "Want me to show you where they found him?"

Jago's chest tightened dramatically. "I don't know."

"I think it's easier than not knowing."

When Jago didn't answer, Kit took matters into his own hands. As they rounded the headland at Toll's Island, he pointed out where the boat had been found, deserted and drifting. Then he navigated out to the Eastern Isles with a strong tailwind that clearly excited him.

It meant Jago didn't have much time to think before Kit let out the sail and let the boat bob gently, parallel to a strip of pale sand.

"There." He pointed. "That's where they found him."

Jago clenched his jaw while Kit spoke softly about weather conditions and tides at the time their dad had gone missing.

"We were lucky really," he finally said, causing Jago to whip around to him, wide-eyed.

"How on earth were we lucky?"

Kit rested his elbow on the tiller. "That his body was found. It could easily have been washed away and swallowed up by the sea." He paused, gazing out at the beach. "I know we still don't know exactly what happened in his final moments, but can you imagine if he'd never been found?"

Jago felt as though a stone had lodged itself in the centre of his chest. "Mum would never have been able to move on," he murmured.

"I don't think any of us would," Kit said. "I'm fairly sure I'd still be out looking."

The lump that swelled in Jago's throat made it difficult to breathe, and the tears that filled his eyes refused to be held back. He lifted his chin as they slid silently down his cheeks.

"Do you want to sail back?" Kit asked after a moment.

Jago inhaled a shuddering breath and pushed his hands over his damp cheeks. "Yeah." He'd been avidly avoiding meeting his brother's gaze and only turned when Kit gave his leg a gentle nudge.

"I meant do *you* want to sail back?" He gestured at the tiller.

"Oh," he sniffed. "Yeah, okay."

The boat rocked as they swapped places.

"Need me to tell you what to do?" Kit asked.

He pursed his lips. "No. I think I'm good." The boom swung over when he shifted the tiller, then he pulled in the slack on the mainsheet and felt the wind fill the sail, pushing them effortlessly along.

"Can you do me a favour?" Jago asked Kit.

He gave a small shake of his head. "Don't worry, I'm not going to tell anyone you cried on the boat." A moment passed before the corners of Kit's lips hitched to a smirk. Grinning, Jago attempted to kick him but couldn't reach.

"I was going to ask if you can convince Mum to let me take the boat out on my own? She thinks I can't sail and I'm not safe out alone."

"Depends," Kit said. "Convince me you know what you're doing and I'll relay the information to Mum."

"Are you serious? Is this the boating version of a driving test?"

"Yeah." Kit sank down a little, making a show of getting comfy. "I guess it is."

"You're as bad as Mum," Jago grumbled.

Kit smiled. "When it comes to water safety I'm probably worse."

CHAPTER THIRTY-FOUR

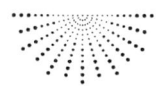

The weather held for the next few days and Jago got in a few sailing trips. Always with Kit. In part for the sake of Mirren's nerves and in part because he enjoyed the time with his youngest brother. When the calm days turned to rain and sleet, with winds that roused fierce waves in the Atlantic, Jago switched to hanging out with Kit at his place instead. The list of jobs that needed doing on the house was fairly endless, and the manual labour was a good way for Jago to work off his excess energy.

He contemplated getting in touch with Sylvie many times in the weeks leading up to Christmas. Once or twice he scrolled to her number, but always refrained from calling. It wouldn't be fair. He'd made his choice and now he had to live with it. However difficult that might be.

His path didn't cross with Lowen's at all. By all accounts his brother wasn't doing great. Their mum made mention of him going back to his old ways of hiding himself away. One day – after she'd met with Pippa – she'd spent the afternoon grumbling about how Lowen was probably about to lose the best thing that had ever happened to him.

Jago couldn't say he was overly concerned about Lowen's relationship with Pippa. In Jago's eyes, if they broke up that would be karma working as it should. Not that he particularly wished his brother ill. Just that he couldn't quite manage to dispel his anger at him.

His mum regularly asserted that spending time with Lowen might be helpful for the two of them to straighten things out, but Jago suspected the two of them in a room together would only end in another argument.

His theory wasn't tested until Christmas Day. Pippa had gone to Brighton to spend time with her family and Lowen was supposed to come over for lunch with them all. Eventually he messaged to say he was running late and would meet them in the pub for a drink. Apparently that was the tradition – to walk down to the pub in the afternoon.

It suited Jago, since the jovial crowd in the pub acted as the perfect buffer. He and Lowen exchanged a polite nod of acknowledgement and then ignored each other.

"You all right?" Noah asked him across the bar when he found a corner to lean against.

"Yeah."

"Did you speak to Lowen?"

"No." He felt his shoulders tense.

"Keira thinks Pippa broke up with him, but no one's sure what's going on with them. Her trip back to Brighton came out of the blue."

Jago shrugged, unsure what to say on the subject.

"Heard anything from Sylvie?" Noah asked while pouring a pint.

"No."

"Not even a 'happy Christmas'?"

"No."

Noah focused on serving the customer for a moment, then came back to Jago. "You should at least message and wish her a happy Christmas."

"Maybe," Jago said. He'd been thinking about it all day and had planned to wait until he was home and on his own, but on impulse he got his phone out and tapped out a quick message, then sent it before he could talk himself out of it.

She messaged back almost immediately, wishing him a merry Christmas. As the bustle of the pub seemed to fade around him, he concentrated on his phone, typing a message asking how she was.

Her reply was short, saying she was fine and that she'd finished her hairdressing course. While he congratulated her, she asked how his plans for the brewery were coming on.

Slowly, he replied, choosing not to mention the property Keira had found and taken him to look around the previous week. *Still no firm plans. What are your plans now that the course is finished?*

She told him she was going to enquire at a couple of local salons about renting space. Staring at the phone screen, Jago couldn't think of how to reply. All he could think was that nothing had changed since he last saw her. Including his feelings for her. He wanted to see her again so badly, but given the distance and their circumstances he couldn't figure out how that would work.

Maybe he'd call her. The desire to hear her voice was overwhelming and he made his way out of the pub with his phone in his hand. He was all set to hit dial when another message came through from her, telling him to enjoy the rest of his day and give her best wishes to the rest of the family.

The words seemed carefully intended to put an end to their exchange, and Jago's heart sank as he re-read the message a few times.

He tapped out three kisses and fired them off, all thoughts of calling whipped away with the wind.

On Boxing Day, Jago's melancholy over the situation with Sylvie intensified dramatically. For the sake of his sanity, he needed to stop thinking about her and get on with his life. With that in mind he took himself off for a walk across the island, ending up at the house he'd looked around the previous week. The cottage was quaint and cosy, but it was the large barn at the far end of the property that was the real draw. It would be ideal for his brewery.

He should go for it, he told himself, standing at the wooden gate and gazing across the deserted property. Forward momentum was what he needed in his life and starting a business would be just the thing. The wind ruffled his hair as he stood contemplating it. When he set off home half an hour later he was no closer to a decision. He'd have to make one soon though. Mooching about wasn't doing him any good.

Two days later he was still firmly in mooching mode when the door to his mum's place opened and Lowen wandered in, taking Jago by surprise. If he'd seen him coming he'd have made himself scarce.

"Mum's not here," Jago said by way of greeting.

"Okay." Lowen's gaze darted around the kitchen before he took a seat at the table opposite Jago. "I just picked Pippa up from the airport."

Jago stared at him, confused by the situation since, as far as he was concerned, he and his brother weren't on speaking terms. "Is she all right?" he asked to fill the silence.

He nodded slowly. "She broke up with me."

"When?" Jago asked, not bothering to try and sound surprised.

"She told me before Christmas she needed some space. That's why she went to her sister's place. We had a long chat on the phone on Boxing Day and she said she didn't see how things could continue with us." He tapped the table in front of him. "She doesn't want to be in a relationship with me any more."

Jago frowned. "I'll be honest, if you're looking for sympathy, you'd be better off picking any other member of the family to speak to."

A shadow of a smile played at Lowen's lips. "I'm not looking for sympathy."

"Why did you want to talk to me then?"

"Because I want to sort things out with Pippa, and I think the only chance I have at that is to fix things with you and with Sylvie."

Hearing Sylvie's name made Jago's heart rate increase.

"Pippa thinks I treated Sylvie badly when she was here," Lowen continued. "And you too. She also thinks I've been in a permanent bad mood since Sylvie showed up. Which I can't exactly argue with."

"So you thought if you came here grovelling it would magically make your problems with Pippa go away?"

"No." His gaze drifted out of the window. "I don't think there'll be anything magical about it. But I know that if I leave things as they are I definitely won't be able to sort things out with her."

Jago's eyebrows pulled together. "I'm not going to shake your hand and say we're cool just so you can patch things up with your girlfriend."

"I *am* sorry."

"But would you be here if it weren't for Pippa reading you the riot act?"

"Probably not."

Jago rubbed his temple. "As far as apologies go, this feels somewhat lacking."

"I just meant I wouldn't be here *yet*. I'd have come eventually."

"Why should I even forgive you? I still don't even know what your problem was."

"Having Sylvie here ..." He stopped talking and ran his fingers through his hair. "What did she tell you about me?"

"How do you mean?"

Lowen shifted in the chair then went to stand beside the sink. "She kept talking to me about our grandparents. There were moments when it was good to see her again, but then she'd bring something up from when we were kids." He gripped the edge of the sink. "It's not something I want to reminisce about."

Jago wasn't even sure he wanted to have this conversation with Lowen. Especially since he was only there to try to fix his relationship with Pippa. In the end, he couldn't stand the silence.

"Sylvie told me you didn't have a great time on those holidays," he remarked. "And that your grandparents didn't treat you very well."

"That's kind of an understatement," Lowen said bitterly.

Jago still couldn't get his head around the fact that his brother had lied to him for all those years. "You always bragged about what a great time you had."

"It was easier." His eyes darted, looking anywhere but at Jago. "Also it made you angry, which always felt pretty good."

"Thanks," Jago said sarcastically.

Lowen crossed the room and sat down again. "I was so jealous of you. You had everything I wanted, and a part of me hated you for it."

"What do you mean?"

"You got to stay at home for the school holidays. You weren't shipped off like some second-class family member."

"That's not how it was. Mum hated it when you were away."

"It's how it felt." Lowen's gaze fell to the table. "It felt like punishment."

Jago pondered his words, thinking of what Trystan had said about Lowen's time with his grandparents being a reminder that Lowen wasn't their full sibling. "Sylvie said you chose clothes for me," he said after a moment. "You always told me your grandma got the sizes wrong."

Lowen gave a small shake of the head. "I chose them," he confirmed.

"Why didn't you tell me that?" Jago suspected that if he'd known, it would have changed their entire relationship as teenagers. "Also, if you hated me why did you pick out clothes for me?"

"I said a *part of me* hated you. Another part missed you like crazy when I was away."

Jago rubbed his hands over his face, unsure what to say. "I still don't understand why you had such a problem with Sylvie. The whole time she was here it seemed as though you didn't want anything to do with her."

Lowen leaned back in his chair and stretched his neck. "Being around her brought back all this stuff from when we were kids. Memories that I don't want to think about, never mind talk about."

"Couldn't you just have told her that?"

"Maybe." He glanced at the door, and Jago had the feeling he might just bolt. "It wasn't just that I didn't want to talk about it," he said slowly. "It was the way she talked about our grandparents."

He paused, looking thoughtful, as though trying to figure out how to explain. "She laughs about our grandparents as though they're a funny anecdote. Them being mean didn't seem to affect her at all, which makes me question all my memories." He pressed his lips together. "How come she's so well adjusted while most of my life was consumed by hating my grandparents and being angry at Mum and Dad for sending me away with them?"

The hurt in Lowen's eyes made Jago's chest tighten. "I guess it was different for Sylvie since she had her parents there. She said one time your grandparents left you alone in some random house in France."

"They left me alone pretty often," Lowen said.

"She said there was a storm and a power cut."

"Oh yeah." Lowen's shoulders tensed. "That time was bad."

"Sylvie didn't experience any of that, so of course her memories are different."

Lowen gave a subtle nod. "It was easier when she and Bess were there, but they weren't always around."

"I can't believe you went through all that and came home and told us you had a great time."

"It always felt easier, since Mum and Dad forced me to go even when I told them I hated it."

"I don't think they realised how bad it was," he said with an edge of defensiveness.

"I know." Lowen blew out a breath. "It feels ridiculous to be hung up on it. It was so long ago. I'm a grown man, for goodness' sake."

The corners of Jago's lips twitched. "I still hate it when anyone mentions the time I vomited in the boat race."

"That was funny," Lowen said idly.

Jago stared at him. "Not for me. I still hate thinking about it. Whenever anyone brings it up, it's like I'm back there again, feeling all the same humiliation I did on the day."

"That's how I feel about my grandparents," Lowen said.

"So you can see how Sylvie can laugh at some of the incidents that you can't?"

"I guess." He leaned back in his seat, his eyes narrowing. "Are you still in touch with her?"

"I had dinner with her when I was in London, but we haven't had much contact since then. Just a couple of messages over Christmas."

"Will you see her again? I thought you wanted to keep seeing her."

"I wanted to, but …"

"But I messed things up?"

"Not just you." Jago rested his forearms on the table, focusing on the grooves in the wood. "After I decided to stay here, it got more complicated. She's doing the hairdressing, so we seem to be going in different directions."

"Mum said she's finished the hairdressing course."

Jago nodded. "She'll be looking for a job in Cambridge."

"Why not ask her to come over here? She can be a hairdresser anywhere."

Jago chuckled. "I've spent a grand total of three weeks with her. I can't ask her to move here. We hardly know each other." That felt wrong though; he might have only known her for a short time, but he felt as though he knew her as well as anyone in his life.

"I am sorry, you know? I should never have had a go at you about Sylvie."

Jago gave a one-shouldered shrug. As angry as he'd been with Lowen over the whole situation, it would be a massive relief to move past it. He wasn't about to hold a grudge and drag things out for the sake of it.

"She is your cousin," he said. "I totally think you overreacted, but I could probably have handled things better. I should have spoken to you about my feelings for her."

"I don't think that would have gone down well to be honest."

"No," Jago said lightly. "I don't suppose it would have."

"If I try and smooth things over with her will you get in touch with her again?"

"I told you, it wasn't just you that was the problem."

"The other problems are all easy to fix though, right?"

"I don't know." Jago also didn't know if he liked the spark of hope that ignited inside him.

"I tried calling her earlier," Lowen said. "She didn't answer. Neither did Bess."

"Try again later."

He twisted his lips. "I think I might need to go and speak to her in person."

"That's not a bad idea."

"I'm doing it." Lowen nodded slowly. "I'll speak to her and then you can talk to her. Then I'll fix things with Pippa. Everything will work out fine."

"It would be good if you sounded a bit more confident about all that."

"Everything will be great," he said forcefully.

Jago could only hope he was right.

CHAPTER THIRTY-FIVE

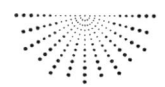

A quiet Christmas suited Sylvie perfectly. She'd seen her dad and had even been coaxed into an evening out with the girls from her hairdressing course, but apart from that it was a string of lazy days with her mum. She'd had a flurry of messages from various members of the Treneary family on Christmas Day, but it was the message from Jago that made her heart beat wildly ... until she realised that the situation hadn't changed and she remembered why she'd resisted contacting him. If she couldn't be with him, being in touch was too hard.

The last message she'd sent him intentionally hadn't invited further conversation, but over the next couple of days she found herself jumping every time a message came through on her phone, hoping it might be him.

Two days before New Year's Eve she was refining her list of hair salons that she intended to approach about renting a chair when her phone set off buzzing around the coffee table. She assumed it was her mum calling from the supermarket where she'd set off to half an hour ago.

Her breath caught in her throat when she plucked the phone from the table. Lowen's name flashing on the screen sent her heart rate crazy while the rest of her body froze. She still had the phone in her hand when the ringing stopped. She hadn't managed to answer it.

When her mum arrived home an hour later, Sylvie's mind was racing but she'd decided he'd probably called by accident. A pocket dial that he hadn't even noticed.

"Something weird happened while I was out," her mum said, dropping her bag of shopping at her feet when she perched on the arm of the couch. "Lowen called me."

Probably not a pocket dial then, Sylvie conceded. "Me too."

"What did he say?"

"I didn't answer. What did he say to you?"

"I didn't answer either. I had my hands full at the checkout." Bess pressed her lips together, looking decidedly sheepish. "I should probably tell you something … I've tried to call him a few times since you got back from visiting him."

"I'm not exactly surprised. Why didn't you tell me?"

"Because he didn't answer so there was nothing to tell, and you were already so upset about the whole thing. I knew you'd be more upset if you knew he was ignoring my calls."

"Not upset, *angry*. That's really rude."

"To be fair, I was intending on having a go at him and I guess he knew that."

"He should still have answered the phone. You're his aunt. You looked after him when he was a kid – cuddled him when he was upset and forced yourself to go on holidays with your awful in-laws just for his benefit. The least he could do is give you the respect of listening to you tell him off over the phone."

"I'm calling him back," her mum said, the phone at her ear before Sylvie could get another word in. Leaning closer, Sylvie forgot to breathe but there was only the sound of it ringing. "That's weird," her mum finally said. "Why would he call us and then not answer when we call back?"

"Maybe it was a pocket dial."

"To both of us?" Bess shook her head. "Not likely. You try calling him."

Sylvie bit the inside of her lip. "No."

"Why not?"

"Because I don't want to talk to him. He made it very clear that I mean nothing to him and never did."

Her mum looked at her sympathetically. "It doesn't make any sense. When the two of you were kids he doted on you."

"Not any more."

"It's so sad," her mum went on. "The Lowen I remember would never have done anything to upset you. In fact, there was one time your grandmother told you your hair looked stupid and Lowen snapped at her. He had a right go at her about it." She put a hand in front of her mouth as she suppressed a grin at the memory.

"Why is that so funny?" Sylvie asked, her mum's amusement infectious.

"I was thinking about your hair." She snorted a laugh. "It *did* look stupid. That might have been the only time I agreed with your grandmother about something."

"Mum!" Sylvie tried and failed to sound stern. Mostly because she remembered exactly the hairstyle she was referring to.

∽

By the following morning, Sylvie had convinced herself that Lowen's urge to speak to them – if that's what it was – had obviously passed. She couldn't exactly say she'd put it out of her head, but she was trying not to dwell on it. There were two days left of the year and she was determined she'd start the new year on a positive note. Admittedly, she was yet to figure out how, but the intention was there.

When her mum invited her to hit the sales with her, she declined and instead focused her unexpected burst of energy on a cleaning spree. She was mopping the floor when "Dancing Queen" came on the radio, taking her straight back to Beth's hen night. She stopped dead, thinking about how at home she'd felt with the entire Treneary family. She'd felt like one of them and now she wasn't sure if she'd even see them again.

The floor still had a sheen of water on the surface when the doorbell broke Sylvie from her melancholy. Propping the mop beside the door, she set off down the hall, pushing her hair from her face as she went. No doubt it would be a delivery of some sort. What had her mum ordered from the internet now? Or was it her? Had she ordered anything? She was wracking her brain as she opened the door, so it took her a moment to register it was Lowen on the doorstep.

"You're not the delivery guy," she said, staring at him.

"No." There was a hint of concern in his eyes and he seemed to be trying to figure out if she was drunk or had completely lost her marbles.

"I assumed it was a delivery. Mum's always ordering stuff she doesn't need." She shook her head. "What are you doing here? If you've come to apologise to Mum she's not here."

He squinted. "Why would I have come to apologise to Bess?"

"Because you didn't answer her calls. And after all she's ever done for you, I can't believe you wouldn't answer the phone to her."

"I tried to call her yesterday. I was actually trying to get hold of you."

"Mum tried calling you back and you didn't answer."

"Yeah." He shifted his weight from foot to foot. "I decided it would be better to speak to you in person. Can I come in?"

She folded her arms across her chest and stood squarely in the doorway. "You had plenty of opportunity to speak to me when I visited you. I practically begged you to talk to me and you didn't want to know. Give me one good reason why I shouldn't shut the door in your face."

"Because you're a better person than I am," he said wearily.

"You always were... you don't have the heart to close the door on anyone. Even me."

He was right; she was sorely tempted, but she couldn't bring herself to do it. Dropping her arms to her sides, she walked back into the house, leaving the door open for him.

"Thank you," he said, following her into the living room.

"What do you want?" she asked, lowering herself onto the couch.

"I want to explain..." He massaged the back of his neck and sank into the armchair.

"I'm listening," she said impatiently.

He rubbed his hands over his face. "You're not going to make this easy for me, are you?"

"Did you expect me to?"

"No." His jaw tightened and he inhaled slowly. "I never told my family what it was like with our grandparents."

"I kind of figured that out."

"I recently told them some of it," he went on. "Just the broad strokes."

Sylvie waited for him to continue.

"Mum had these old photos of you," he said. "I got thinking about you. Then Mum said she was going to get in touch with Bess and I had this urge to see you. I asked her to pass on my number."

"But you never answered the phone. I guess I should have taken that as a sign and left you alone."

"I didn't purposely ignore your calls. I actually wish I'd have answered."

"Why?"

"Because then you wouldn't just have turned up. I could have prepared myself ... or most likely I'd have realised by speaking to you on the phone that I couldn't face you."

Sylvie stared at her hands in her lap. "Thanks," she murmured sarcastically.

"It's not you," he said. "It was never about you."

"How can it *not* be about me?"

He closed his eyes briefly. "Seeing you brought back so many memories. Ones that I'd been trying hard to forget."

"We had a lot of good times too."

Methodically, he massaged the palm of his right hand, staring at it as though trying to process what she'd said. "I have no idea how I'd have coped without you and your mum. And I'm sorry I distanced myself from you, but I wanted to put that part of my life behind me. I might have some good memories of my time with you, but they're so wrapped up with painful memories that it's hard to separate them."

Sylvie kept quiet, unsure how to respond. Him suddenly opening up might be a case of too little too late as far as she was concerned.

"When you were on Scilly, I felt nervous the whole time," he told her.

She met his gaze. "Why?"

"Because I've spent so long trying to block out all those memories of the time with our grandparents. It was hard to do that when I had you as a reminder. Every time I saw you I wondered what you were going to say, which humiliating story you were going to bring up next." His eyes were fixed on the arm of the chair.

"I don't even think I know any humiliating stories."

He cocked his head. "The first time you met my family you told them how our grandmother thought me and my brothers all had stupid names, and that I'd almost got in a fight with her over it."

She cringed. "I was just joking around."

"That's the thing: I *can't* laugh about it. It wasn't funny for me." His eyes were so sorrowful that it made her chest ache. "It was different for you. Your parents were always there to protect you. Plus you had what our grandparents considered an appropriate education, and were always dressed presentably. They weren't embarrassed by you."

"I think they might have been a little embarrassed by me," she argued gently. "But I see your point."

He dragged his hands through his hair. "You felt so sorry for me that you used to come and sleep in my bed until you were a teenager."

"Not because I felt sorry for you," she replied, surprised by his take on it. "Because I hated being on my own. You were the closest thing I had to a sibling." She smiled sadly as a thought occurred to her. "Yesterday Mum was saying how you'd stood up to Grandma one time when she said something about my hair …"

Lowen nodded. "You were growing out your fringe and used to tie it on the top of your head. In fairness it did look ridiculous, but there was no need for Grandma to be mean about it."

"Mum said it looked stupid too. " Her mind drifted, thinking back to all those holidays and their grandmother's scathing tone. "I don't think the holidays were easier for me just because I had my parents there," she said eventually.

"How do you mean?"

"I mean it was easier for me because I had *you* looking out for me. Whenever Grandma was mean to me, you'd either have a go at her, or you'd take me off to do something fun and tell me not to listen to a crazy old woman who looked like a trout." Her lips spread to a smile. "Do you remember saying that?"

"It sounds about right."

"I'm sorry I didn't make things easier for you too," she told him, tears welling on her lower lids.

He leaned forwards in the chair. "You did."

"Clearly I didn't do such a good job."

"Do you remember the time in Italy when I annoyed Grandma and she made me spend extra time with the Italian tutor in that office with the big windows?"

Sylvie rolled her eyes. "I got you into more trouble. I kept pressing my face up against the window from outside."

"I laughed so much that the stuffy tutor told Grandma I was unteachable and left."

"He was a weird guy. He had that moustache that looked as though it was pulling his cheekbones up."

Lowen tilted his head. "I'd never have got through those holidays without you making me laugh."

They sat in silence for a moment.

"I wish you'd have told me how you felt sooner," Sylvie said eventually.

"After spending my life avoiding talking about it, I may have a few issues there." His gaze dropped to his hands. "I hate thinking about it. That's why being around you is so hard for me."

"But that's not fair."

"I realise that, and I'm sorry."

She sat up straighter. "I mean it's not fair *to you*. If you pretend none of it happened, you lose your good memories as well as the bad ones. And I promise you we have a lot of good memories."

"They're never the ones that come to mind."

"They're the ones *I* remember. That's why it hurt so much when you denied there was any kind of bond between us."

He scratched his eyebrow. "I only said that because I wanted to get rid of you. But I always felt that connection too. Even when I didn't see you for all those years I still felt it. I just didn't want to acknowledge it."

"I can understand why there's so much you don't want to think about," she said gently. "But some good came from those times too." Her lips curled to a small smile. "We did get a nice chunk of change out of them. That was pretty good."

"I gave mine away," he reminded her.

"Yeah, and Kit bought a train! How cool is that? Trystan and Noah have their houses. And if Jago goes ahead with the brewery that will really be the icing on the cake. I just wish I could tell Grandma about that one. Can you imagine her face?"

"I guess she'd have a few things to say about it."

"Is he doing it?" she asked, desperate for information.

"The brewery?"

"Yes."

"He's still considering it." He laced his fingers together causing a knuckle to crack. "I spoke to him yesterday. We chatted everything through. Sorted everything out."

"That's good," she said, her voice brittle as tears stung the back of her eyes. "I'm glad."

"I should never have commented about the two of you."

"I don't want to talk about Jago." The sound of her mum's keys clicking in the front door put a definitive end to the conversation. "Now you'll really have some explaining to do," she said with a playful grin.

CHAPTER THIRTY-SIX

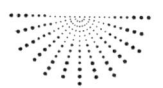

"You wouldn't believe the queues in the shops," Bess called from the hallway. "Absolutely heaving, it is. Wait until you see this gorgeous cardi I found though."

"Come and show me," Sylvie replied, giving Lowen what she hoped was a reassuring look.

"Hang on while I get my coat off. I swear my fingers are like blocks of ice."

She bustled around in the hall before wandering into the living room with a shopping bag in her hand. When her eyes landed on Lowen, she set the bag down and looked at him with a bemused smile that made Sylvie think she might not even recognise him.

"Hi, Aunt Bess," he said sheepishly.

Her eyes widened dramatically, confirming she hadn't known who it was. She stood open-mouthed, then swallowed hard. "You ignored my calls," she stated flatly.

"Yeah." He grimaced. "Sorry."

"You also upset Sylvie. Have you apologised to her?"

It was an effort for Sylvie not to laugh as her mother spoke to Lowen as though he was still a child and not a forty-year-old man. In response to the question he nodded and looked helplessly at Sylvie.

"We cleared some things up," she told her mum. "I think everything is good again." She looked to Lowen for confirmation. If she was honest, she wasn't sure if he wanted to rebuild their relationship or if he'd just come to smooth things over and soothe his conscience.

"It's really good to see you," he said to her mum, a nervous glint in his eyes that reminded Sylvie of his teenage self.

Bess flapped her hands in front of her. "Get over here for a hug right now," she demanded.

His features relaxed and he did as he was told.

"I missed you," Bess told him as she squeezed him tightly.

"I missed you too," he replied.

"Promise me you won't be a stranger from now on."

"I promise."

"Good. Because Mirren's invited me to stay, and I expect you to show me around when I visit."

"I will," he said then switched his gaze to Sylvie. "Will you come back too?"

"I'd like to, one day." It felt as though a weight had been lifted. Not only at the thought of having Lowen in her future but the rest of his family too. She didn't let herself think about Jago.

"Soon," Bess said. "Let's make it soon."

"I'm about to set up my own business," Sylvie said confidently. "So I probably can't make travel plans at the moment."

"I heard about that." Lowen sat back down, this time beside Sylvie. "You've done a hairdressing course, right?"

"Yes. I know it sounds ridiculous, changing career from accounting to hairdressing. There's a possibility it's a mid-life crisis."

"I don't think it's ridiculous," Lowen said.

Bess perched on the arm of the couch. "It's also not as though you just decided to become a hairdresser out of the blue. I'm fairly sure this idea's been brewing since you were about four, and I think Lowen was your first customer. Albeit an unwilling one."

"What are you talking about?" Sylvie asked.

Lowen flopped back on the couch, chuckling. "I'd forgotten about that."

"About what?" Sylvie demanded.

"You crept up behind me with a pair of scissors and cut chunks out of my hair."

"How come this is the first time I'm hearing that story?" Sylvie demanded.

"I'd forgotten all about it," Lowen said.

Her mum nodded, a faraway look in her eyes. "I bet I've got photos somewhere. We should get those boxes of old photos out of the attic and have a look through them."

After the conversation they'd just had, Sylvie was certain it was the last thing Lowen would want to do, but when she looked at him, she found him looking at her intently.

"It might be fun," he said with a gentle smile.

She nodded. "I think so."

"I'm going to stick the kettle on," Bess said and slipped out of the room. "Are you staying here tonight, Lowen?" she called behind her.

"If that's okay?" he replied, tilting his head towards the door.

"Of course it is. I'll make up the spare room. But you need to sleep in your own beds, no sneaking in for your midnight chats. You're too old for that now." They could hear her chuckling to herself in the kitchen.

Sylvie rolled her eyes at Lowen before her features turned serious. "We don't have to look through the photos. It's fine if you don't want to."

"It's okay. I think you were probably right. I spent so long focusing on the bad times that I forgot the good stuff. It might be helpful to be reminded."

"I hope so."

"We didn't finish our conversation," he said, raising his eyebrows. "We need to discuss things with Jago."

"Not now," she said. "Later."

"I'm also not sure that in all my waffling about the past that I actually apologised properly. I really am sorry. I hate that I hurt you. The way I spoke to you before you left was horrible."

"I just want you in my life again," she told him, shuffling over for a hug. "That's all I've wanted for a long time."

"Thank you," he whispered into her hair. "I don't know what I did to deserve you in my life."

"I don't know either." She pulled away and smirked. "I guess it must have been something really great."

~

The afternoon was spent sifting through old photos and recalling stories from long-ago holidays. Bess had been a stickler for noting places and dates on the back of the photos, which resulted in an entertaining game of them all guessing the destination before the picture was flipped over for a dramatic reveal. The list of places they'd visited was impressive, and Sylvie marvelled at what well-travelled children they'd been.

Throughout the afternoon, she kept a wary eye on Lowen, half expecting him to freak out at any moment and do a runner. The opposite turned out to be true: the more they chatted, the more he seemed to relax into the conversations – as though he realised no one was about to raise any of those memories he was so desperate to avoid.

For dinner, Lowen insisted on taking them out to a restaurant. They only ventured down the road to a cosy Italian with twinkling fairy lights and muted Christmas decorations.

To avoid the subject of Jago, Sylvie took herself off to bed once they got home, leaving her mum and Lowen to have another drink and continue chatting. Their laughter drifted up to her, causing warmth to bloom in her chest and giving her the overwhelming desire to call Jago. She valiantly ignored it.

There was no way she could avoid the topic completely, so when she walked into the kitchen the following morning to find Lowen already up and sipping coffee she realised her best option was to at least tackle it on her terms.

"I know you want to talk about Jago," she told him, sitting at the table opposite him. "But first I have stuff I need to talk to you about."

"Okay." He pursed his lips and set his mug down.

"First, I'd like to know what on earth has happened between you and Pippa."

He winced. "We've been having a rough patch."

"A rough patch?" She glared at him. "I messaged her this morning to say how good it was to have you here and she told me you've split up. What happened? And why didn't you say something yesterday?"

"I didn't want to spoil the mood."

Sylvie eyed him sadly. "What's happened?"

"It's a temporary glitch. At least I hope it's only a temporary thing. She definitely seems willing to talk things through if I sort myself out and stop being such an arse." He dragged his teeth along his lower lip. "I'm going to ask her to move in with me."

"Really? Shouldn't your relationship be solid before you take that kind of leap?"

"I think it is solid."

"That's weird considering Pippa doesn't even think you're currently together."

A muscle in his jaw twitched and he lowered his gaze. "I think we'll figure things out," he said softly.

"Sorry. I didn't mean to sound so harsh."

"It's okay." His fingers tapped the edge of his mug. "She'd dropped hints about moving into my place a while back. That's what spurred me into doing some work on it. But then everything went a bit wrong."

"When I arrived?"

"Yeah. Not that it was your fault. I didn't deal with it well."

"No, you didn't. Which brings me to the other thing I want to talk to you about."

He gave her a quizzical look, and she took a deep breath before continuing.

"Don't freak out and don't say no on impulse." She attempted to ready herself for a hostile response. "Just hear me out, okay?"

"I would if you'd get to your point."

"I think you should get some counselling. Talk to a therapist of some kind." She held a hand up even though he'd made no attempt to speak. "I really think it would be good for you to talk everything through. Clearly you have a lot of unresolved issues, and I know what you'll say – that yesterday you could talk about the past so therefore you're fine now. but I don't think that's how it works. I think this stuff is going to keep coming back to bite you."

Tears filled her eyes, blurring her vision so she couldn't even see Lowen properly. "The problem is, it's not only you who's affected by this. Whether you mean to or not, you're hurting the people around you and it's not fair. It's not fair on Pippa. And it's definitely not fair on you because the two of you make such a great couple ..." She sniffed loudly and stopped talking.

Lowen's hand covered hers on the table, squeezing gently.

"Sorry," she said, wiping at her eyes with her free hand. "Don't be angry with me again please."

"I'm not," he said softly. "You're right."

She managed a crooked smile. "I wasn't expecting you to think so."

"I've already been thinking about it. Pippa suggested I have counselling recently and I bit her head off, but I suspect it would be helpful."

"Can you please give it a try?"

"I'll look into it."

"And make an appointment? You can do it over videocalls these days so you've no excuse."

He gave a resigned sigh. "I'll make an appointment."

"Good." She pulled her hand from his and went to get herself a drink in order to dispel the tension.

"Can we talk about Jago now?" Lowen asked.

"I suppose so. Not that there's much to say. We got close when I was visiting, and I'm not going to deny I have feelings for him. But I'm just setting up my business here in Cambridge and he's staying in the Scillies."

"And that's the only reason there's nothing more between you?"

"*You* were a reason. Neither of us wanted to be together if it was going to be an issue for you."

"It was an issue for me," Lowen said. "But I was being completely irrational. It's not an issue for me any more."

"That's good to know," she said primly. "Not that it makes any difference."

Lowen's left eyebrow twitched. "He misses you."

To avoid looking at him, Sylvie busied herself making a cup of tea. "It was bad timing for us," she said.

"You're all done with your course though."

"So?"

"So you can work from anywhere. Why not have a working holiday on St Mary's and see where things go with you and Jago?"

"Do you have an ulterior motive here?"

"Kind of," he said. "Several actually. For a start I think having you around would help me smooth things over with Pippa. It'll also ease my conscience. I feel terrible about everything that happened when you were on St Mary's. I'd like a chance to make it up to you. And Jago."

Fighting the urge to ask if Jago had said anything about her, Sylvie focused instead on Lowen's relationship problems. "Are you okay?" she asked. "You seem very calm about the situation with Pippa."

"I keep telling myself we'll sort things out," he said, then paused. "I can't bring myself to think about the alternative. If we've actually broken up – for good – then I wouldn't be calm and I wouldn't be okay. But I'm not prepared to face that possibility yet."

"I saw how much she loves you," Sylvie told him, returning to the table. "I'm sure you can work things out."

She looked up as her mum walked in, wearing her fluffy dressing gown and slippers. Yawning, she said good morning then trained her gaze on Lowen.

"I have a question. Is January a good time of year to visit Scilly?"

He screwed his nose up. "I'd say it's probably the absolute worst time to visit. There's not much open and it's generally cold and dark."

"What about if it's not so much of a holiday as visiting family?"

"Then I don't think there's such a thing as a bad time to visit." He beamed at her. "What are you thinking?"

"I'm thinking it's about time I visited." She turned to Sylvie. "What do you say? Shall we go next week? I'm sure I can swing an extra few days off work."

"Next week?" Sylvie's heart thundered at the thought of seeing Jago again. And so soon. The prospect was terrifying but the fizz of anticipation deep in her belly thrilled her too.

"I'll get my laptop and we can check out flights," Bess said firmly, retreating from the kitchen.

Sylvie caught the twitch of Lowen's lips and shook her head. "I'm not sure about this."

"It'll be great," he said, his lips stretching to a proper smile. "Everyone will be happy to see you again."

A rush of nerves drowned out her previous burst of excitement at the thought of seeing Jago. "I've hardly spoken to Jago since I left. It might just be awkward."

Lowen's eyebrows twitched mischievously over the top of his coffee mug. "I'm sure it won't."

"I'll have to call him first," she said firmly. "I'm not making the mistake of surprising anyone again."

"You do that."

Reaching her foot out, Sylvie kicked him under the table. "Can you stop looking so amused?"

"Sorry." He grinned. "It's kind of funny to watch you squirm."

"You're really annoying," she told him, while making a poor attempt at looking stern. Having Lowen tease her felt comforting. It reminded her of when they were kids, and gave her hope that things might just work out after all.

CHAPTER THIRTY-SEVEN

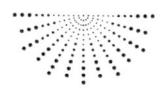

Knowing that Lowen was with Sylvie had Jago pacing the house for pretty much the entire day. In the evening he got a brief message from his brother saying that everything was going well and he'd fill him in when he got home. It did nothing to satisfy Jago's need for information, but since Lowen didn't answer his call there wasn't much he could do except wait.

He borrowed their mum's car the following afternoon to pick Lowen up from the airport.

"What happened?" he asked as soon as he clapped eyes on him.

"Nice to see you too." Lowen gave him a quick pat on the shoulder and glanced around the airport before heading straight for the door.

"Were you expecting someone else?" Jago asked, matching Lowen's stride.

"Not really. Pippa will be working."

Jago registered the worry lines across Lowen's brow but was currently more interested in hearing what had happened with Sylvie than counselling Lowen on his relationship problems.

"What happened with Sylvie?" he asked again as they exited the building into a fine mist of rain.

"It was good." Lowen cast him a sidelong glance. "We chatted everything through."

"How is she?"

"Good."

"You realise I'm going to shake you in a minute?" he snarled. "Did she say anything about me?"

"Haven't you heard from her?" Lowen asked, an annoying smirk brightening his features.

"No."

"She said she was going to call you."

"Well, she didn't."

"You'll talk to her soon anyway." They reached the car and he opened the passenger door. "She's coming to visit next week."

"Are you serious?" Jago slid into the car, not quite believing what he'd heard.

"Yes. Bess is desperate to meet Mum and see the islands."

"Sylvie's mum?"

"Yeah. They're both coming."

"Was it Sylvie's idea or her mum's?"

"Technically, her mum's but Sylvie seemed keen too. She's looking forward to seeing you."

"Did she say that?" He switched the engine on but turned in his seat, no intention of going anywhere until he had more information.

"Not in so many words. But it was pretty obvious."

"What exactly did she say about me?"

Lowen rolled his eyes. "She said that she had feelings for you and that it was partly me who'd come between you but also the whole situation with you staying on Scilly and her being in Cambridge."

"Did she say she *had* feelings for me or she *has?*"

"Bloody hell, I don't know. Why don't you drop me off, then you can call her and talk to her yourself?"

That was probably a good plan. "Where am I taking you?"

"The café," Lowen said flatly.

"How are things with Pippa?"

"We've only exchanged a few messages. I need to talk to her properly."

They fell into silence and arrived outside the café a few minutes later.

"Good luck with Pippa," Jago said, looking through the drizzle to the warm glow radiating from the windows of the café.

"Thanks. I assume I'll see you in the pub later?"

Jago looked at him questioningly.

"It's New Year's Eve. Everyone will be in the pub."

"Oh, yeah." He'd been so preoccupied wondering what was going on with Sylvie that he'd completely forgotten it was the last day of the year. "See you later."

Lowen thanked him for the lift and closed the door behind him. On the drive back to his mum's house all Jago could think about was seeing Sylvie again. He couldn't quite believe he'd see her again in a matter of days. As he parked the car he realised he didn't even know when exactly she was coming. He reached for the door handle but stopped and got his phone out instead.

After a moment's hesitation he hit dial on her number and pressed his head into the head rest while it rang.

"Hello, you," she said with such warmth to her tone that he immediately broke into a smile.

"Hi," he replied happily. "I heard you're coming back for a visit."

"You heard right. My mum's coming too. She's very excited."

He shifted, propping his elbow on the window. "And you?"

"I'm looking forward to it as well."

"When exactly do you arrive? Lowen just said next week."

"The third. Tuesday."

"Great. Not long to wait."

Her gentle laughter made him smile even wider. "You're not great at playing it cool, are you?"

"I could give it a go if you want?"

"No. That's okay."

"Good. Because I'm really looking forward to seeing you."

"I'm looking forward to seeing you too."

They chatted away for half an hour, until the car windows were fogged up and Jago's cheeks ached from smiling. When they finally ended the call, he still didn't move to get out of the car, but wiped at the window so he could look out over the bay where a collection of boats bobbed on gentle waves.

After spending weeks dithering over what to do with his life, one thing was suddenly very clear: he wanted Sylvie in his future.

And he was willing to do whatever it took to make it happen.

∼

As she ended the call with Jago, Sylvie leaned back on the couch and typed out a message to Pippa, telling her to let her know when she had time for a chat. The phone rang almost immediately.

"I didn't know if you'd be with Lowen," Sylvie said after a brief greeting.

"He's up in the flat. I'm taking my time cleaning up the cafe before I go and speak to him."

"That doesn't sound great."

"I realised that as I said it. I'm not avoiding him. It's more that Mia's up there and I thought the two of them could probably use some time together too."

"So you think you and Lowen will work things out?"

"I hope so. Things definitely need to change, but judging by his messages he seems to know that."

"He seemed genuinely remorseful about everything."

"I know. I want things to go back to how they were too." She sighed loudly. "Anyway, have you booked flights? Are you definitely coming to visit?"

Sylvie had messaged her about the trip that morning. "Yes," she said hesitantly. "Which is partly why I wanted to talk to you. I remembered the woman from the tourist office saying that you had a spare room you wanted to rent out ..."

"I've been thinking about it for a while." Her words were drawn out, as though she was trying to figure out why Sylvie was asking. "Did you want to stay at my place?"

"I wondered if it might be an option. I know Mirren would make space but I'm considering staying for longer."

An excited gasp came down the phone. "Seriously?" Pippa asked. "How long?"

"Lowen suggested I come for a working holiday and see how things go. I dismissed it to start with but it's been niggling at me. Plus, I just spoke to Jago."

"How was that?" Pippa asked.

"Really great."

"I bet he was happy about you coming back here."

"I only told him about coming for a visit. I hadn't really decided any more than that ... but speaking to him made the idea of staying for longer even more appealing."

"It's such a great idea. And I'd love for you to stay with me."

"Obviously, I'd pay rent. And you'd be entitled to free haircuts. I'm sure Mirren would offer for me to stay with her but ..."

"I totally get it," Pippa put in. "She probably wouldn't let you pay rent and you'd feel like a guest. I, on the other hand, will happily take your money."

Sylvie chuckled. "Thanks."

"The bedroom's pretty small, just to warn you. And Mia's here too, but she's off with Gareth or her friends a lot of the time."

Sylvie smiled widely. "You're making it all feel real now. I'm excited."

"Me too. It'll be fun being housemates."

"Can you do me a favour and not tell anyone for now? You can tell Lowen, of course, but I want to talk to Jago about it first. Make sure he's okay with it."

"I reckon he'll be more than okay with it."

Sylvie felt a buzz of excitement at the thought of sharing her plans with him. It was definitely a conversation she wanted to have in person.

"I should let you go and talk to Lowen," she said, remembering that the two of them still hadn't sorted things out properly. "Will you let me know how it goes?"

Pippa promised she would and they ended the call with excited chatter about seeing each other soon. It was a huge relief when a message came through late that evening saying that Pippa and Lowen were cautiously giving their relationship another chance.

It was the perfect news to end the year. Sylvie also received a flurry of messages from various members of the Treneary family that evening, all wishing her a happy new year and telling her they were excited to see her again. After sitting up with her mum until midnight she'd just crawled into bed when Jago called.

"You're really not good at playing it cool," she teased. "That's two phone calls in a day."

"It's a different day," he said cheerfully. "It's actually a whole different year."

"Funny how it only feels like a few hours," she said, smiling as she snuggled down under the duvet.

"I just wanted to say happy new year."

"Happy new year to you too."

"Got any big plans for the year?" he asked.

Briefly, she wondered if Pippa or Lowen had leaked her plan to spend more time on St Mary's before deciding that they wouldn't have. "I'm not sure yet," she told him. "How about you?"

"I have a few ideas. I'll tell you when I see you." There was noise in the background that faded again quickly.

"Where are you?"

"Outside the pub."

"It sounds lively."

"Yeah. It's been a fun evening." He paused for a moment and there was more noise in the background. "I should get back inside."

"Say hi to everyone for me. I'll see you in a few days."

"I can't wait."

After setting the phone on her bedside table, Sylvie sank back onto her pillows, filled with anticipation about seeing him again so soon.

CHAPTER THIRTY-EIGHT

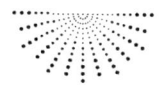

On a grey, drizzly day, the aerial view of the Devon coast and then the Scillies wasn't anywhere near as spectacular as when the sun was shining. With her mum peering out of the aeroplane window beside her, Sylvie tried to describe how fantastic the view was on a clear day. Thinking back to her first trip over there, she recalled how grumpy Jago had been and smiled to herself.

This trip felt so different. Seeing Lowen's smiling face at the airport made her heart swell. Even better, Jago was beside him. She gave Lowen a hasty squeeze and handed him her bag before turning her attention to Jago. He hugged her tightly, holding on for a fraction too long before releasing her to be introduced to Bess.

Sylvie desperately wanted time alone with Jago, but as she listened to Bess chat excitedly to Lowen on the short drive to Mirren's house she was aware that getting him alone might not be so easy. At the house she left Lowen pointing out who lived where to her mum and started up the path with Jago, her hand brushing against his as they walked.

"It's really good to see you," he told her.

"You too."

His easy smile wavered as he cast her a sidelong glance. "Are you sure you want to stay with Pippa? I tidied up the spare room so there's space for you here."

That had been her excuse when she'd told him she was staying at Pippa's place: the space issue. She hadn't mentioned the rest of it. "It's fine," she said. "Pippa offered her spare room and it felt easier."

"Not trying to avoid me or anything then?" The lightness in his voice barely covered the vulnerability behind his words.

"Definitely not." Gently, she swayed so her shoulder touched his. "I need to talk to you properly," she told him.

"I want to talk to you too." He winced at the sight of Mirren waving madly from the back door. "I'm not sure when we're going to get the chance though."

"We'll find time later," she said, then hurried to greet Mirren with a hug.

Sylvie had only just had time to introduce her mum to Mirren when Kit arrived. Ten minutes after that, Ellie came bounding into the kitchen closely followed by Trystan, Beth and Keira.

"You've got a proper bump now," Sylvie said excitedly as she embraced Beth. "You look amazing."

"Thank you. The morning sickness has passed and I feel human again."

"I'm glad."

Ellie appeared, holding out a transparent make-up bag which looked to be filled with hair accessories. "Can you make my hair look pretty?" she asked sweetly.

"It always looks pretty," Sylvie told her. "But hop up on a chair and I'll pop some of these sparkly things in for you."

While Sylvie styled Ellie's hair, Beth chatted to her about the pregnancy and how excited she was about her twenty-week scan which she was having later in the week, where they'd find out the sex of the baby.

At a break in the conversation, Sylvie glanced over at her

mum. Apparently undaunted by so many new faces, Bess seemed to be in her element as she chatted to Jago, asking him about his plans for the brewery, which instantly made Sylvie hone into the conversation. Keira handed Bess a glass of wine then rested a hand on Jago's shoulder.

"He's found the perfect premises," she said perkily. "We looked around the place a couple of weeks ago and it's gorgeous."

Jago's eyes darted nervously to Sylvie. "I don't know if I'll go ahead with it," he said to Bess. "It's just an idea."

"It sounds brilliant," Bess said. "And if you've found suitable premises it seems like fate."

"Maybe." He scratched at the back of his neck and shot Sylvie a crooked smile. "We'll see."

"Who's hungry?" Mirren said, pulling a lasagne from the oven.

Sylvie smiled and pulled out a chair at the table. "I have no idea how you can cook for so many people and make it look like no effort at all."

"Years of practice," Mirren said, elbowing Kit out of the way to put the dish down. "Besides, we're three people short this evening so it's quieter than it could be."

"Who's missing?" Bess asked.

"Seren and Noah are working in the pub," Mirren told her. "And Pippa is busy with the cafe. She's got a book club that's started meeting on Tuesday evenings. She has to keep them topped up with tea and biscuits."

"That sounds lovely," Bess said, taking a seat.

Mirren squeezed her shoulder. "I'll show you the cafe tomorrow. You'll love it."

As the two of them continued chatting about their plans for the next few days, Lowen appeared beside Sylvie. "It's kind of weird that our mums are only just meeting," he remarked.

"Yeah." She smiled up at him. "Are you okay?" she asked meaningfully.

"Yes." He nodded and pulled out the chair beside her, then chuckled and moved to the next seat when Jago glared at him.

When he sat beside her he was so close that his knee rested against hers under the table. Given the contact it was hard to focus on anything else, but she tried to keep up with Kit's update on the progress they'd made at the house and then a lively conversation about possible baby names. Trystan was keen to choose a Cornish name to follow family tradition.

By the time they'd all finished eating, Ellie was yawning madly and Beth and Trystan took her home to bed. Mirren and Bess were getting on like a house on fire and went off to the living room after topping up their wine glasses.

Sylvie pitched in with the others to tidy up the kitchen but hadn't got far when Jago tipped his chin towards the hallway. She followed him out there, feeling mischievous as he took her hand while they lingered at the foot of the stairs.

He opened his mouth to speak, then gave a subtle shake of the head and stepped closer to her. "It's really good to see you again."

"You too." She lay a hand at the side of his neck as she raised up on her toes to kiss him. It was only intended to be a peck but as her lips brushed over his she couldn't bring herself to pull away so leaned deeper instead.

His hand on the small of her back brought her hips flush against him and her knees felt as though they might give way as his tongue flicked into her mouth.

It felt like only the briefest moment before they were interrupted by Lowen, clearing his throat loudly.

Sylvie couldn't rouse any feelings of embarrassment and instead shot Lowen a look of contempt.

"Sorry," he said, looking thoroughly amused. "Pippa messaged to say she's finished with work. She wants to know whether to come up here or if we'll head down there soon?"

"We can go there," Sylvie said, her hands resting at Jago's waist. "I'll just be a minute." She waited until Lowen had gone back to the kitchen, then looked up at Jago. "We can talk properly tomorrow."

"I wanted to talk to you about what Keira was saying before. About the brewery."

"It's great that you found a place."

His brows pulled together. "It's not definite."

"Well, it should be. I want to hear all about it tomorrow." She ran a hand longingly down his torso. "For now I want to go and catch up with Pippa. Are things really fine between her and Lowen?" They'd both told her so over the phone, but she needed reassurance.

"Given the way they were all over each other on New Year's Eve I'd say so."

"That's good." She gave him a light kiss, then moved to say goodbye to everyone.

Lowen waited until they were settled in the car before he spoke. "I take it Jago was happy about your plans?"

"I haven't spoken to him yet." Given his reaction to seeing her again, she should have been sure that he'd welcome her news, but a part of her was still nervous about his reaction.

"I'm surprised he didn't guess by the size of your bag," Lowen remarked. "Though I suppose he only had eyes for you and didn't even register that your suitcase was slightly oversized for a long weekend."

"It all feels a bit surreal," she said, gazing out of the window at the light seeping from the houses as they approached her new home.

She let Lowen lug her case up to the flat and went ahead to give Pippa a big hug.

"Are you sure it's okay for me to stay here?" Sylvie asked.

"Yes! I'm excited. And it gave me the motivation to finally clear out all the junk from the spare room." Pippa led her along the hall and opened the door to a room with a double bed and a wardrobe. "How did it go with Jago, by the way? Was he excited to see you? I bet he's over the moon that you're staying."

"I haven't told him. I didn't even get two minutes to talk to him alone."

Lowen squeezed past them and deposited the case at the end of the bed. "That's not true. She just used her two minutes to stick her tongue down his throat rather than talk."

Glaring at him, Sylvie gave him a playful shove.

"Go and make drinks," Pippa instructed him gently. "The kettle's just boiled."

As the two women watched him walk along the hallway, Sylvie leaned in to whisper to Pippa. "Are things really okay with you two?"

"Yes." Pippa's affectionate smile was all the confirmation Sylvie needed. "Which is good news for you."

"How do you mean?"

"I'm going to move in with him," Pippa said, eyes sparkling.

Sylvie gasped and gripped Pippa's forearm. "That's brilliant." She beamed at Lowen, who stuck his head out of the kitchen door, clearly listening to the conversation. "I'm really happy for you both."

"I'm actually a bit sad that we won't get to be housemates," Pippa said to Sylvie. "I think it would have been fun. But it means you don't need to have the tiny bedroom. You can take my room once I've sorted my stuff out and properly moved. Obviously, you'll be living with Mia, but to be honest, for a teenager, she's pretty easy to live with."

She kept talking as they moved towards the kitchen. "I'll keep the small bedroom for myself in case there are days I can't get back to Bryher due to the weather, or if Lowen is driving me crazy." Pippa flashed him a mischievous smirk when they walked into the kitchen. In reply, he handed her a cup of tea and planted a tender kiss at her hairline.

"I really am so happy for you both," Sylvie said, taking a steaming mug from Lowen. "And for me, too. It seems as though the year is off to an exciting start for us all."

She felt utterly content as they moved to the comfort of the living room. While Pippa and Lowen sat together on the couch, Sylvie hovered by the window. It was too dark to see much, but knowing there was a beach and an endless stretch of water right outside gave her a thrill.

"I can't believe I'm actually going to live by the sea."

Pippa tilted her head to rest on Lowen's shoulder. "It's a nice feeling, isn't it?"

"It's a great feeling." Sylvie's phone buzzed in her pocket.

"Is that Jago?" Lowen asked while Sylvie read the message on the screen.

"It might be," she replied coyly.

Lowen raised an eyebrow. "Missing you already, is he?"

"Something like that." She couldn't stop grinning as she reread the message, which said exactly that.

CHAPTER THIRTY-NINE

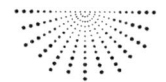

Sylvie unzipped her coat on the walk over to Old Town the following morning. The air was damp, giving a chill to the breeze, but the temperature was far milder than in Cambridge. She'd already messaged Jago to tell him she was on the way so wasn't entirely surprised to see him walking towards her on the lane leading to Mirren's house.

"Good morning," they said simultaneously, beaming at each other before Jago pressed a gentle kiss to her lips.

"I thought we could go for a walk," he said. "Get a bit of time to ourselves."

"Good idea." She slipped her hand into his as they turned back in the direction she'd come from. "How about you show me the site you found for the brewery?"

"I only really went to look because Keira insisted."

"But it's suitable for what you'd need?"

"Yeah." He bobbed his head ambiguously. "It could work."

"You don't sound enthusiastic."

"I'm just not sure it's the right thing for me."

"I want to see it anyway." She gave his arm a gentle squeeze, sure that his doubts were only due to his confidence being knocked after things hadn't worked out with the business in New York.

As they strolled through Old Town the only signs of life were the illuminated windows of the houses, and puffs of smoke rising from the chimneys. They stayed quiet on the steady incline towards the centre of the island. After passing the airport, they continued on until Jago stopped at a wooden gate which bridged the gap in the drystone wall beside the lane.

Turning in a circle, Sylvie took in the rolling hills around them. To the north they had a clear view of the sea and the Eastern Isles. Jago unlatched the gate and pushed it open. An uneven driveway led to a quaint stone cottage to their left. At the end of the long garden, if you could call it that – it was more of a field really – was a large barn.

"Are we allowed to be here?" Sylvie asked, stepping through the gate after Jago.

"Technically, we're trespassing, but the owners won't mind. The place is empty. I can't get into the house, but you can have a nosy through the windows if you want, and I can show you the barn, which is the most important part."

Sylvie felt suddenly choked up. "It really is perfect, isn't it?"

"It's a good location, I think." He didn't look at her as they walked towards the empty cottage. "The house is in pretty good nick. I could move straight in. The barn is structurally sound but would need a bit of work to repurpose it. I had an idea to produce five different variations of beer and name each of them after the main islands."

Nodding, Sylvie ducked her head to peer into the kitchen window, cupping her hands at the side of her face to see better. It also had the advantage of covering her expression from Jago. Her emotions were entirely mixed. On the one hand, she was happy for him and proud of what sounded like an amazing business venture. On the other hand, it made her realise that he'd been planning for a future that didn't include her.

"What do you think?" Jago asked hesitantly.

"It's gorgeous," she whispered.

"It's not definite," he said. "I haven't even put an offer on the place."

"Why not?" Finally she forced herself to look at him.

"I can't decide whether I should do it or not."

"You should," she said automatically. "It's a brilliant business idea. Don't let your stupid self-doubt hold you back."

Jago shifted his weight. "That's not really my issue."

"What then?"

"I haven't decided if I really want to stay here. On Scilly."

Sylvie's eyebrows drew together. "I thought that was definite. You love it here."

"I do," he said quietly. "But it turns out what I said to you before you left was true – I really love being here with *you*."

Sylvie opened her mouth but didn't quite manage to form any words.

"I know we've only really spent a short time together and this is probably crazy." His chest heaved as he drew in a long breath. "If my choice is between staying here and setting up my business or moving to London or Cambridge and finding any job and being with you … I choose you."

She closed her eyes momentarily, wondering if she was dreaming. "What?"

He pressed his lips together. "I haven't been able to stop thinking about you since you left. I want us to be together."

Sylvie stared at him. "And you would move to Cambridge to make that happen?"

"I've seen a couple of jobs in Cambridge. But if that feels like too much too soon, I could find something in London for now …"

She smiled when he trailed off. "I don't think anything could be too much too soon," she said. "But you need to be here. You need to open the brewery." She gazed around the property. "This is too good of an opportunity to pass up."

His eyes locked with hers. "I've thought about it. I feel as though it's all I've thought about since I left. The brewery isn't going to mean much to me if I don't have you in my life. And the jobs I've seen in Cambridge look pretty interesting."

"There's just one flaw to your plan." Stepping into his personal space, Sylvie draped her arms around his neck. "I'm not going to be in Cambridge. I decided it's about time I started ticking items off my bucket list."

His hands slid to her waist as his brow crinkled in confusion. "Wait ..." His eyes brightened. "You're going to live by the sea?"

"Yes!"

"*Here?* You're moving *here?*"

She nodded. "I'm going to move into Pippa's flat above the cafe. She's moving in with Lowen."

"That's why you're staying with her?"

"Yes. I thought it would be easier to get settled there straight away."

"Why didn't you tell me that before?"

"Because I was waiting to see how things were with you before I made a final decision. I wanted to speak to you about it in person."

"I don't even know what to say," he whispered, cupping her face as he dipped his head to softly brush his lips against hers. Sylvie's insides felt like mush and she closed the gap between them and deepened the kiss.

"I take it you like the idea?" she asked, forcing herself to break away from him.

"I love it. Are you still going to do your hairdressing?"

"Yes. From what I can gather there's a demand for a new hairdresser around here." She took his hand and ambled around the house, peeking in the windows as she went. "And you'll make an offer on this place?" she asked, beaming at him.

"Yes." He looked slightly stunned. "I guess so."

She squeezed his hand. "No time like the present."

He puffed out a breath which turned into a laugh, then pulled his phone from his pocket. Sylvie listened while he chatted with the estate agent.

"I didn't actually think you'd call right then," she said when he ended the call.

"Now I'm terrified." He draped his arm around her shoulders. "What if I don't get it? I already kind of love this place."

Sylvie rested her head against his shoulder. "I have a feeling they're going to accept your offer."

"That's the other terrifying prospect." He pressed a kiss to her forehead. "I can't believe I'm actually going to put myself through this again."

"This time it's going to work out."

"Promise?"

"I have full confidence in you. Now are you going to show me around the premises for your brewery or what?"

"Don't say things like that. You'll jinx it." He led her over to the barn. After a quick wander around the large open space, Jago switched from telling her about his vision for the brewery to kissing her instead.

Her head spun, partly from desire and partly from the speed at which her life was rocketing in a new direction.

They were about to set off back to Mirren's place when Jago's phone rang. With his eyes on the screen, he swore under his breath. "It's the estate agent," he told Sylvie.

"Answer it," she urged.

"Surely the owners won't have made a decision so quickly …"

"Answer it!" she said again.

He swiped the screen and put the phone to his ear, wandering away from Sylvie and back towards the house as he chatted to the estate agent.

It felt like an age before he slipped the phone back into his pocket and turned to look at Sylvie with the biggest smile on his face. "They accepted the offer! And they're keen to move forward fast."

"That's amazing." Sylvie rushed to him and hugged him tightly. "I'm so happy for you."

"I'm pretty scared," he said into her hair.

"Don't be. It's going to be brilliant."

He inhaled deeply. "It's kind of a shame that you're moving into hairdressing. I guess I'm going to need an accountant."

For a moment, she searched his features. "I could still be your accountant," she said hesitantly. "If you want me to?"

"I'd love it, but I thought you wanted to move away from that."

"I want to move away from working a stuffy corporate job, but this is completely different. I'd love to be involved with the brewery. If you don't think it would be weird to work together."

"I think it would be great."

"I'm going to set up as a mobile hairdresser too, but I'll have time for both." She looked around at the cottage and the barn and the gorgeous piece of land. "Now I'm even more excited for you." She beamed at him. "Let's go and tell your mum. She'll be over the moon. I think a celebratory drink is in order."

When she took a step, he tightened his grip on her hand and pulled her back.

"What?" she asked, chuckling as he snaked his arms around her waist and rubbed his nose against hers.

"This is one of my favourite days ever."

"Mine too," she said. "Now let's go and tell everyone that we're about to become Scilly's next big entrepreneurs."

CHAPTER FORTY

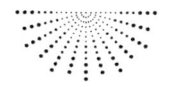

Warmth spread through every cell in Sylvie's body when she answered the door the following morning to find Jago on the doorstep.

"Good morning." His smile was smouldering as he stepped inside, slipping his arms around her waist and kissing her softly.

"I'm not even sure I should be letting you in." She pushed the door closed and draped her arms around his neck. "You're a wanted man, aren't you? Have you just come here to hide out?"

"I reckon this is the first place people would come looking if they wanted to find me." He rolled his eyes. "I don't even know how I won the bloody photo competition, considering I didn't enter it."

"The banter on your family's group chat this morning was very amusing anyway." Keira had added Sylvie to the group so she wouldn't miss out on the chatter about Jago winning the photography competition. "I was quite touched to be added to the group."

"Give it a few hours and you probably won't be so touched. They're non-stop."

Sylvie knew it would take far longer than that for the novelty to wear off. "Have you even spoken to Beth? Is she actually annoyed with you about the competition?"

"I haven't heard from her and she hasn't said anything on the group chat. Which I find more unnerving than if she had a go at me."

"She can't seriously be annoyed with you about it. You won fair and square. Apart from the fact that you didn't enter the competition, but that means she has even less reason to be angry."

"I'm sure it's fine. I'd just like to know which of my brothers stitched me up and entered my photo." Jago shook his head, signalling he was bored of talking about it. His lips grazed against hers, then he nudged her back against the wall, bringing his hands to her face as he kissed her deeply.

"Is Pippa at home?" he asked, slightly breathlessly when he drew back.

"No, she's in the café. But Mia is here."

He scrunched his face up in mock irritation. "For the first time since I got back here, I'm wishing I didn't live with my mum."

"Why's that then?" Sylvie asked with a smirk.

His hands slid down her back and pulled her hips flush against his. "Because I can't bring women back to my mum's house," he whispered in her ear.

"Have you got your eye on someone?"

He looked thoughtful. "No. I'm not fussy. Anyone would do."

Grinning, she gave him a friendly shove, then led the way up to the flat. Mia was in her room, and they didn't disturb her as Sylvie gave Jago a quick tour, which ended with her bedroom.

"I'll get the bigger room when Pippa moves out, but this is fine for now."

"It's nice." Jago sat on the bed, taking Sylvie's hand to pull her onto his lap. "It's just annoying that we're both living with other people. Maybe I should move into one of the cottages so I have my own space." He nuzzled her neck, making her smile widely.

"If you move out of your mum's place now, it's going to be quite obvious that you just want a place to have sex."

His eyes twinkled. "Do you have a problem with that?"

"It won't be long until you have your own house."

"Realistically, it's probably going to be two or three months before the sale goes through. Which feels like an eternity." He nibbled her ear lobe, and her stomach turned a somersault.

"Okay," she breathed. "Privacy would be nice."

"Sylvie!" Mia's voice reached them right before she appeared in the bedroom doorway. Sylvie attempted to remove herself from Jago's lap, but he clamped his arm around her, holding her in place.

"Oh, hi Jago," Mia said. "I didn't realise you were here. Congratulations on the photography competition. It's all over social media. You're like a celebrity."

"Thanks," he said unenthusiastically.

"Anyway, I'm off out. I'll probably be a while … a few hours at least." Her left eyebrow twitched. "I can message you when I'm on my way back, if you want." She flashed Jago a conspiratorial smile, then told them to have fun and waltzed away.

"I really like her," Jago said.

"I'm really embarrassed." Sylvie touched her cheek, sure she must be bright red.

"We seem to have the place to ourselves for a while, anyway." Jago kissed her in a way that made her stomach flutter, then shifted his weight and managed to manoeuvre them so they were lying on the bed without removing his lips from hers.

Longing for skin contact, Sylvie had just slipped her hands under his T-shirt when his phone began to vibrate in his pocket.

"Go away," he grumbled, pulling it from his pocket and aiming a finger at the screen as though he were about to reject the call. Instead, he swore lightly. "It's Beth. I should answer it, but hold that thought ..." He gave her a flirty smile as he pulled his arm from under her and sat up. After swiping his thumb over the screen, he held it in his hand beside him.

"You're on speaker and Sylvie is next to me so you're not allowed to shout at me ..."

"As if that would stop me."

"I didn't even enter the competition."

"I know that. I entered you into it."

Surprise flashed in his eyes. "Why?"

"Because I'd seen the other entries and knew my photo wasn't going to win, but yours could."

"I'm confused."

"I wanted the prize."

"What is it?"

"A two-night stay at the Sea Garden Resort on Tresco."

"Ooh, nice."

"You can't have it!"

"But I won."

"Only because I entered you. You have to give me the prize."

"What if I don't want to?"

"Then you'll make your pregnant sister-in-law very unhappy."

"I can probably live with that if I'm getting a luxury weekend away."

"Please." Beth's voice turned sickly sweet. "I was thinking Trystan and I could have a little honeymoon once the baby's born. Well, when he's big enough for us to leave him with your mum for a couple of nights."

"Urgh." Jago rolled his eyes. "This is starting to sound like emotional blackmail."

"Good," Beth said. "That's what I was aiming for."

"Wait!" Sylvie sat bolt upright. "Did you just say *he?* Are you having a boy?"

The smile was evident in Beth's voice. "Yes. I had my scan this morning. It's a boy."

"Wow. Is everything okay?" Sylvie asked.

"He looks perfect," Beth replied.

Jago beamed. "That's great."

"So, are you going to give me the prize or what?" Beth asked. "Don't make me get your mum involved."

Jago snorted a laugh.

"I can hang up and call her right now," Beth threatened.

"You can have the prize," Jago told her. "But you owe me one."

"Actually, it's you who owes me ... the ten-pound entrance fee for the competition."

Jago laughed again. "What exactly do I get out of this then?"

"You get all the glory," Beth said happily.

"I'll take it." He wrapped up the conversation and ended the call. Tossing the phone aside, he looked back at Sylvie. "What do you think about having a professional photographer for a boyfriend?"

"I think it sounds all right." She pursed her lips. "Where would I find one, though?"

"Hey!" Grinning, he slipped an arm around her waist and pulled her down to lie beside him again. "You're stuck with me I'm afraid."

She ran a hand down his cheek as she kissed him softly. "I like the sound of that too."

ALSO BY HANNAH ELLIS

The Isles of Scilly Series
The Weekend Getaway (Book 1)
A Change of Heart (Book 2)
The Summer Escape (Book 3)
The Potter's House (Book 4)
An Unexpected Guest (Book 5)

The Hope Cove Series
The Cottage at Hope Cove (Book 1)
Escape to Oakbrook Farm (Book 2)
Summer at The Old Boathouse (Book 3)
Whispers at the Bluebell Inn (Book 4)
The House on Lavender Lane (Book 5)
The Bookshop of Hopes and Dreams (Book 6)
Winter Wishes in Hope Cove (Book 7)
There's Something about Scarlett (Book 8)

The Loch Lannick Series
Coming Home to the Loch (Book 1)
The Castle by the Loch (Book 2)
Fireworks over the Loch (Book 3)
The Cafe at the Loch (Book 4)
Secrets at the Loch (Book 5)
Surprises at the Loch (Book 6)
Finding Hope at the Loch (Book 7)
Fragile Hearts by the Loch (Book 8)

New Arrivals at the Loch (Book 9)

<u>The Lucy Mitchell Series</u>
Beyond the Lens (Book 1)
Beneath These Stars (Book 2)

Always With You (Standalone novel)

<u>The Friends Like These Series</u>
Friends Like These (Book 1)
Christmas with Friends (Book 2)
My Kind of Perfect (Book 3)
A Friend in Need (Book 4)

Hannah has also written a series of children's books aimed at 5-9 year olds under the pen name, Hannah Sparks.

<u>The Land of Stars Series:</u>
Where Dragons Fly (Book 1)
Where Stars Fall (Book 2)
Where Penguins Party (Book 3)

Printed in Great Britain
by Amazon